NO PLACE FOR MONSTERS

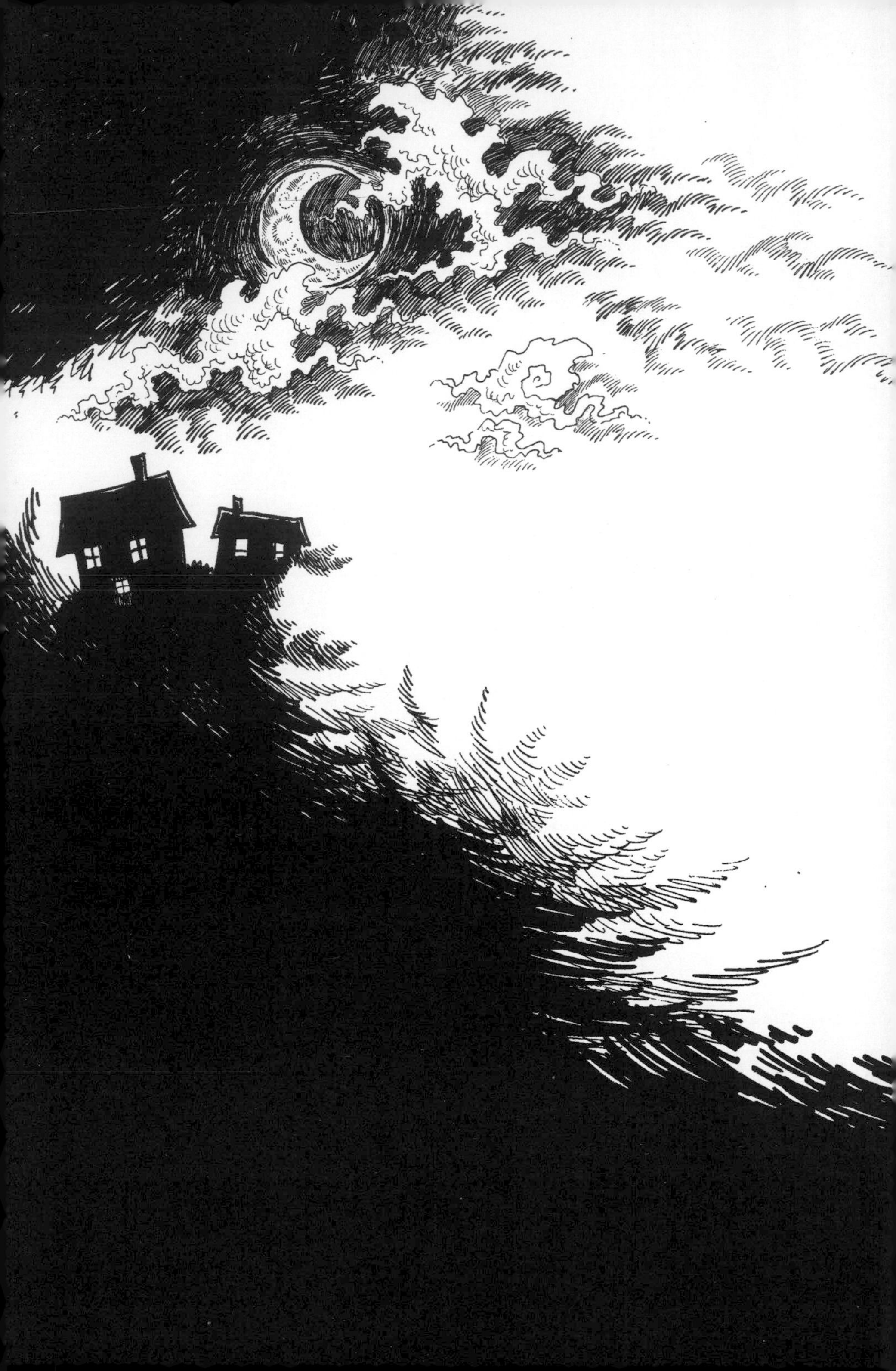

NO PLACE FOR MONSTERS

Written and Illustrated by
Kory Merritt

Houghton Mifflin Harcourt
Boston   New York

To my mother, Patti Pedersen Merritt, former public school teacher,
who read me many books and filled my childhood
with wonderful memories.

hmhbooks.com

The text was set in Charter ITC Std and Merritt Scary.
Hand-lettering by Kory Merritt
Cover and interior design by Celeste Knudsen

Library of Congress Cataloging-in-Publication Data is available.
ISBN 978-0-358-12853-3

Manufactured in China
SCP 10 9 8 7 6 5 4 3 2 1
4500799634

Sunset.

The sky dims from pink to purple.

Feel the chill of the night breeze.
Hear the whisper of dry grass,
the skitter of leaves down
empty sidewalks.

The shadows creep closer.

Once we feared those shadows.

Remember?

You've heard the stories.

Stories of Monsters.

Bogeys and boggarts and bugbears,
waiting to spring from the darkness.

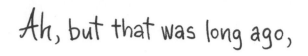

Ah, but that was long ago,

back when the woods were still wild
and the shadows untamed.

We are safe now.

There is no
place for
monsters
in
suburbia.

Chapter 1: Cindy Who?

On Monday Cindy Fogle woke her parents at 2 a.m. with a scream.

Mr. and Mrs. Fogle found Cindy sitting bolt upright in her bed, eyes wide and skin clammy. *Night terrors,* figured Mrs. Fogle. Cindy slept with her parents the rest of the night.

On Tuesday Cindy woke at 1:45 a.m. She was hysterical when her parents arrived to calm her.

She spent another restless night in her parents' room, babbling about *the Really Tall Man*.

On Wednesday Cindy's screams started shortly after midnight. She begged to spend the night in her parents' room again.

Her room was bad.

The closet was bad.

The curtains were bad.

Under the bed—***bad, bad, bad.***

Mr. Fogle even checked under the bed. See? No monsters. No "Really Tall Man." Just a plush rabbit that Mr. Fogle didn't remember buying.

At last her parents relented, and while Cindy snuggled between them, Mr. Fogle silently vowed this would be the final time his daughter slept in their bed.

On Thursday Mrs. Fogle was roused in the middle of the night by a faint shuffling noise. She held her breath and listened.

Silence.

Probably just the fridge or the water heater or one of many strange house noises she noticed only at night. She fell back into sleep.

In the morning Mr. and Mrs. Fogle woke and went about their business. They did not notice that Cindy was gone.

Her room was empty. The speckled wallpaper, the pony border, the Tinker Bell bed sheets, the toy chest, the clothes that should have been hanging in the closet: *gone.*

No, not gone. More like *never there to begin with.* It was just a spare room Mr. Fogle had been planning to fill with a pool table.

And the family portrait hanging in the hall? Oh, that was there. It showed Mr. and Mrs. Fogle holding hands and smiling. No Cindy between them. Why should there be a Cindy? The Fogles did not have a daughter.

And the school didn't call when Cindy failed to show. Why should they? There was no Cindy Fogle in their records.

Cindy?
Cindy who?

Chapter 2: Levi and Kat

Levi did not choose to be Kat Bombard's work buddy. No one in his right mind would want to work with Kat Bombard.

The decision was made by their homeroom teacher, Ms. Padilla, who, by the third week of school, had tried every trick in the district manual to keep Kat in line: special deals, calling home, taking away free time before lunch, taking away free time after lunch . . .

As a last resort, Ms. Padilla moved Kat's desk next to the desk of her quietest student.

For their first assignment, each student team had to research an invertebrate species. Levi and Kat were assigned the Portuguese man-of-war, a jellyfish-like ocean creature with a beautiful sail floating above the water and dangerous stinging tentacles below the surface.

Of course, Kat didn't exactly jump on the assignment . . .

Finally, when Kat broke out her Yoda impression, Levi lost his patience. "You going to help with this?"

"Help you I cannot," answered Yoda. "Learning too much can dangerous be."

"How can learning be dangerous?"

"In my case it can be," said Kat. "The more I know, the more danger I put the world in."

"Huh?"

"Listen: If the knowledge is in my brain, *they'll* be able to access it and use it against us."

"Who's *they?*"

Kat's voice dropped to a whisper. "*They* . . . are the extraterrestrial spies that visited my room last summer."

Levi snorted and turned back to his work.

"It happened on a hot, humid night," continued Kat. "I was chilling in my bedroom when suddenly I heard this strange humming outside . . .

"So I snuck out to the backyard, and soon every molecule in my body was vibrating. Even the nerves in my teeth were tingling . . .

"And then I looked *up* . . ."

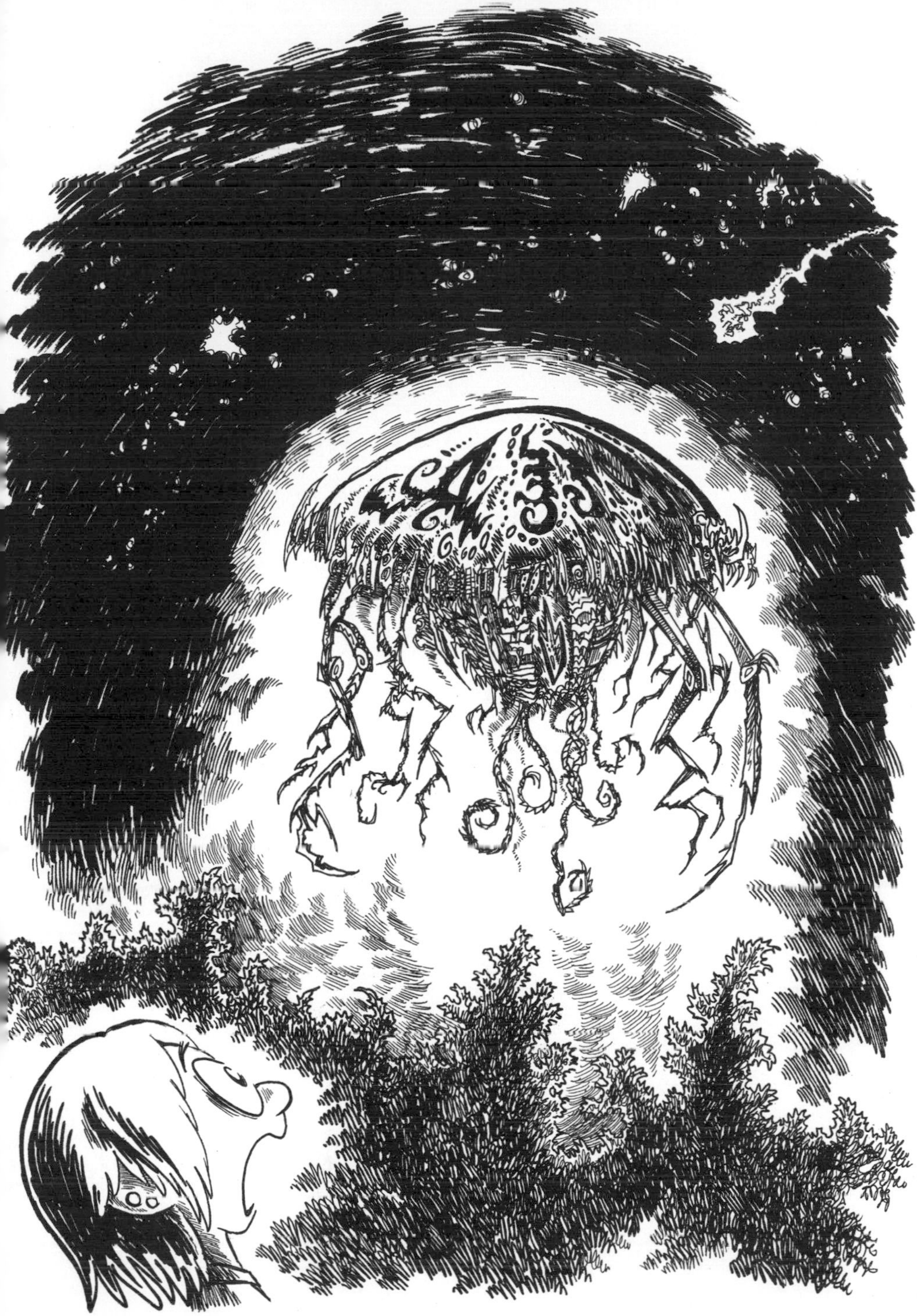

"A *spaceship?*"
said Levi. "Yeah,
right!"

"It's the
undiluted truth!"
insisted Kat. "I
swear!"

"Sure. How
stupid do you think
I am?" said Levi.

"So, uh . . .
What happened
next?"

"Okay, so . . . I tried to run, but they dragged me into their *Cross-Dimensional Laboratory of Horror!*

". . . So after they were done sifting through my mental archives, they erased my memory and returned me to my bed."

"Wait," said Levi, "but if they erased your memory, how were you able to tell me everything just now?"

Kat furrowed her brow. "Maybe the memory eraser malfunctioned. Or maybe my superior cerebrum resisted the beam."

Levi looked unconvinced.

"Well, anyway, that's the reason I can't help you with this stupid project! The more I know, the more dangerous I am."

"Doesn't matter anyway. The work's all done," said Levi. He wrote his name at the top of the packet, hesitated, and added Kat's name before turning it in.

Chapter 3: Alone

Last year Levi's family had moved to Cowslip Grove, and he'd never fully adjusted. It wasn't that his new classmates were mean to him. It was just . . .

Well, things had been different in the city.

In the city, Levi's world had been comfortable and familiar. His family's apartment had been small and busy. His mother had managed a warehouse by day and painted landscapes in the evening. His big sister, Regina, was all about music and sports. His father was always leaving on business trips overseas.

And then there was his little sister, Twila, who was his closest companion in the whole world.

"What are the pigeons' names again?"

"Bert and Bernice."

"Are they married?"

"Guess so. They got a nest with eggs."

"I can't wait to see the babies!"

But then last year the big changes had happened, and his *own little world* was shaken beyond repair.

First, after a bad month of fights with his mother, his father had taken yet another job overseas. That was the last Levi had seen of him.

Then his mother had decided the family needed a fresh start, so she'd accepted a job with the Slynderfell Ice Cream Factory in a safe suburban town called Cowslip Grove.

That was back in May. It was September now, and he still hadn't made friends at his new school. So Levi ate lunch alone each day.

And that was fine. He liked having a table all to himself. He liked savoring each bite of his mother's cheese-and-mustard sandwiches. He liked—

"Hi!"

Kat Bombard usually ate lunch alone too, exiled by the lunch ladies to the cafeteria's corner. But she had not yet been exiled on this particular day.

"What?" said Kat. "I can't sit here? It's a free country!"

Levi eyed the heap of plastic-wrapped food on Kat's tray. "Healthy lunch," he mumbled.

"Brain food!" said Kat. "Slynderfell's ice cream is good stuff!"

"My mom says it's all chemicals," said Levi. "And she would know—she works at the Slynderfell factory warehouse."

"Okay, sure, whatever. Let's move on to more important matters. You know, aliens and stuff."

Levi shrugged and took another bite of his sandwich.

"See," continued Kat between mouthfuls of ice cream, "now that I've told you about the intergalactic menace, I should make you my confidant, in case I disappear."

Shrug.

"Jeez, you shrug an awful lot. You got a shoulder spasm?"

Levi forced himself to be still.

"Just remember, this whole close-encounter thing has gotta stay our little secret for now. No sense in creating a premature panic. Hey, you done with that bag? Wanna see a cool trick?" She snatched Levi's lunch bag, exhaled into it, and

Levi and Kat ate their lunches alone after all.

Chapter 4: The Cryptid Research Station

"I don't get why people here mow their lawns so much," said Twila as she walked home from school with Levi. "It's like everyone in town is scared nature is going to rise up and attack them. When Ma said we were moving to the country—"

"Suburbs," corrected Levi, "not country."

"Whatever," said Twila. "I thought there'd be forests and animals and waterfalls and stuff. But turns out there's nothing but a bunch of boring lawns with short grass. Blah."

"When you grow up and own a lawn, you can do what you want with it."

"I'm gonna!" said Twila as she followed Levi into their house. "My lawn will be Neverland! You'll see, Brother-Man!"

Mrs. Galante was seated in the kitchen with her sketchpad.

"Ma!" Twila laughed. "Why am I a bird?"

"Your animal counterpart," said Mrs. Galante. "Always flitting about, twittering like a sparrow."

"And Regina's a giraffe!"

"Holds her head high and proud."

"And Levi's a turtle?"

"Yep. Safe in his shell."

"My friend Michaela wants to try painting," said Twila. "When she comes over, can you teach us?"

"No friends tonight. Mrs. Buckley called earlier. You've missed three homework assignments this month."

Twila's smile withered. "I'll catch up this weekend! Maaaa, please! If I have to do homework, it'll be too late for lacrosse!"

"Then I guess no lacrosse today."

Twila moaned and flopped into her beanbag chair.

"You and I could hang out after homework," said Levi as he fixed himself a plate of peanut butter crackers. "We could set up Levi's Café, like we used to. Remember?"

Twila clucked her tongue. "I'm not a little kid anymore."

Their conversation was cut short by a sharp knock on the front door. "That's probably Michaela now," said Twila. She jumped to her feet and skipped from the kitchen.

Levi sighed. Twila had made lots of new friends this year, and he secretly didn't care for any of them.

"Uh . . . yeah," said Twila from the other room. "Sure, he's in the kitchen."

Footsteps approached the kitchen. Two sets. One the soft padding of Twila's stockinged feet. The other the squeaking of eager sneakers. A familiar squeaking.

No. It couldn't be. It couldn't—

"Levi, Ol' Buddy-Bro-Dude-Boss-Man-Pal! How's we doin'?"

Kat spotted the plate of crackers. "Ah! Peanut butter!" She snagged a mitt-ful.

"Excuse me," said Mrs. Galante. "I didn't catch your name."

Kat flashed a peanut-buttery smile. "Name's Kat. *Agent* Kat to you, ma'am." She shot Levi an unsubtle wink. "Ready to go to Cowslip Park and continue our research?" She patted a worn book under her arm.

"The park?" sputtered Levi. "Uh, actually, I think I have to—"

"Sure he is!" said Twila, giving Levi a playful shove forward.

"But—"

"You'll be back by five thirty?" said Mrs. Galante.

"Aye, Captain!" said Kat.

"Have fun, Ol' Buddy-Bro-Dude-Boss-Man-Pal!" Twila called after them.

"Jeez, how can you stand having a little sister? I bet she drives you nuts."

"Yeah," Levi said after a moment. "Sure. Totally nuts."

It sounded like the right thing to say. Kids Levi's age weren't supposed to enjoy hanging with their little sisters. He turned it over in his mind, then added: "Back when we lived in the city, she never left me and all my friends alone."

"I feel bad for you, man," said Kat. "I don't have any sisters or brothers, and that's the way I like it."

Joey Downey and his snotty little brother, Edward, were playing wall ball when Levi and Kat walked by.

"Huh-oh!" called Joey. "Bombard got a boyfrieeeeend!"

"Shut up, Joey!" growled Kat.

"He's just messing with you," said Levi. "Ignore him."

"Katherine and Levi sittin' in a tree, K-I-S-S-E-N-G!"

This time it had been Snotty Edward.

Kat stood like an outlaw at a high-noon shootout. The moment seemed to pass in slow motion. Finally, she turned and stalked away. Levi released his breath and followed, ignoring the laughter behind them.

The tidy row of houses thinned and gave way to scrubgrass. Weeds twisted up from the cracks in the sidewalk.

"I thought we were going to the park," said Levi.

"Change of plans," said Kat.

They neared the last house on the street: the ivy-entangled Mushpit residence.

Mrs. Mushpit scrunched her face at the potential trespassers. Mr. Mushpit crossed his arms and glowered. Levi was glad when he and Kat turned a corner, though he could still feel the glares on the back of his neck.

Finally they crossed a field and reached the edge of the woods that bordered town.

"Now we get to work!" Kat pulled aside some brush to reveal a dilapidated car sprawled among the trees.

Levi's mouth fell open. "*This* is why you brought me here? We'll never get this piece of junk running!"

"Make it run? Levi, my ward, why would we want to make our research bunker run?"

"Bunker?"

"Right! A hideout, like the kind scientists use. We'll turn it into our Cryptid Research Station!"

Levi crossed his arms. "Not the aliens again."

"No, cryptids. Strange creatures unknown to mankind." She held up the book she'd been carrying. "It's all here in *Cryptopedia*." She flipped through the pages. "See?"

Levi snorted, but the illustrations had hooked his gaze.

"C'mon, Levi! You love science! You blew through that stupid jellyfish-thingy assignment before I even had a chance to contribute! And you always read that rainforest book during silent reading."

"I guess. But this isn't nature. This is . . . make-believe."
Kat shook her head. "It's all based on genuine reports.
Trust me!"

After some time, they turned their attention to the car. It was small and decrepit, but shave away some rust, rearrange the seats, fortify the windows . . . not a bad hideout.

And so they worked and schemed as the minutes slipped silently past, and the sky faded from pink to purple, and the shadows crept closer.

Chapter 5: The Stranger

"Wait . . . What time is it?"

"Dunno. Seven? Who cares?"

"It's getting dark. My mom wanted me home by five thirty!"

"*So?*"

"So I missed dinner. And she's gotta work tonight."

"Oh, jeez. Wow. Didn't know you were such a mama's boy."

"Gotta go. See ya."

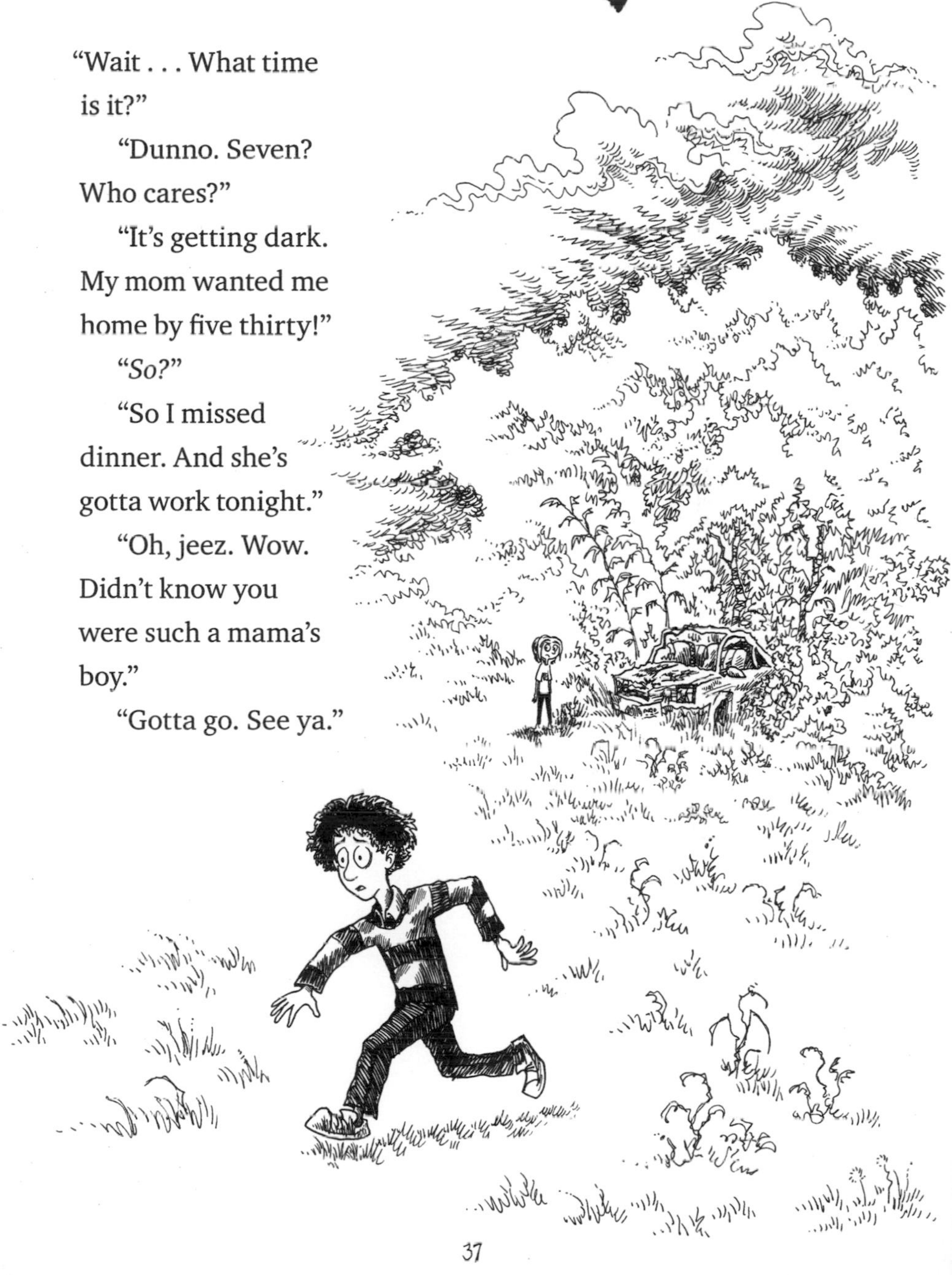

The neighborhood was silent.

The city had never been silent, not even at night. There had always been the drone of highways, the hum of traffic, the wail of sirens. The noise had been comforting.

But here in Cowslip Grove, his footsteps echoed down the empty street. Each step made him wince.

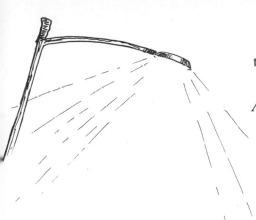

Something scurried across the road ahead of him.

Just an animal, he thought. *A cat or a dog.*

It didn't look like a cat or a dog. Its shoulders were hunched and its movements silky.

A wild animal from the woods, then. A fox or a raccoon.

The creature stopped just outside a streetlight's halo and looked at him. Its eyes flashed fluorescent green in the deepening shadows. Then it turned, slipped into the darkness, and was gone.

Just an animal.

He continued walking.

The shadows crept closer. The silence surrounded him. Swallowed him. His footsteps were thunderclaps.

Not much farther. You'll be fine. You'll—

Wait.

A sound? He stopped. Held his breath. His heartbeat thundered in his ears.

Behind him . . . Echoing out from the darkness . . . Someone whistling a happy tune.

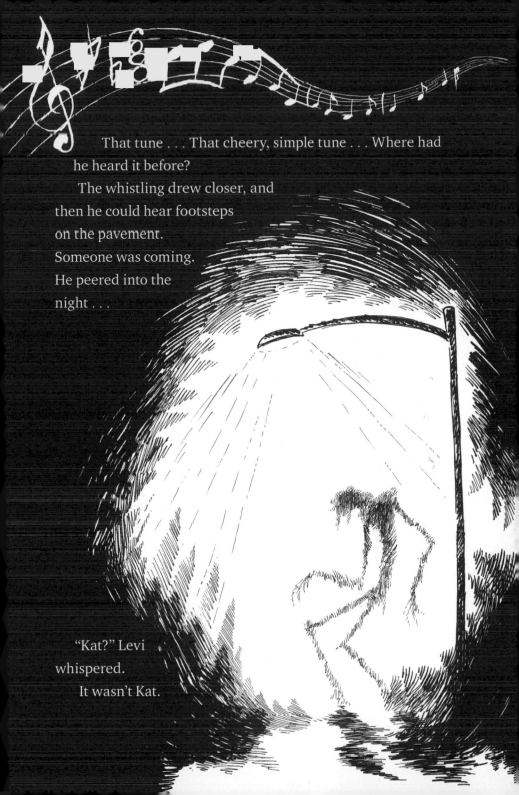

That tune . . . That cheery, simple tune . . . Where had
he heard it before?

The whistling drew closer, and
then he could hear footsteps
on the pavement.
Someone was coming.
He peered into the
night . . .

"Kat?" Levi
whispered.
It wasn't Kat.

The stranger stopped whistling . . . leaned against the lamppost . . . tipped its hat.

The world froze.

Levi turned away and continued walking on boneless legs.

Don't look back. It's just a neighbor out for a stroll.

Footsteps behind him.

Don't look back. Almost home.

The cheery whistling restarted.

Don't look back. Don't—

A rush of cold breath on his neck.

Levi ran.

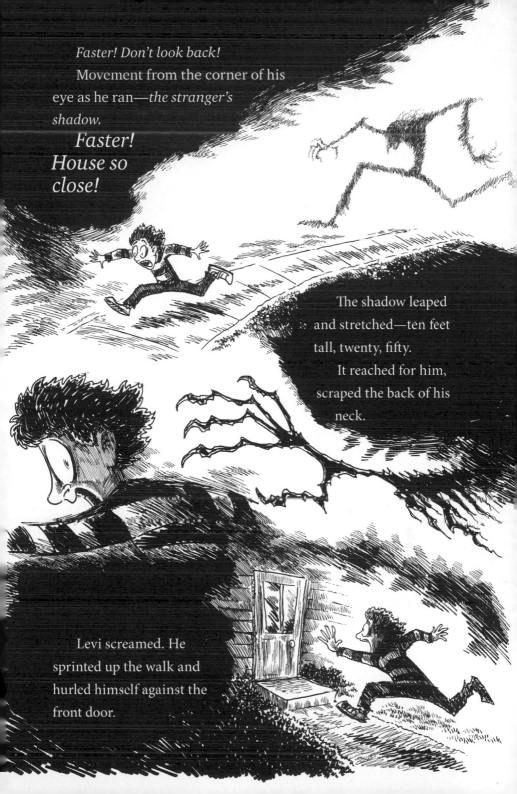

Faster! Don't look back!

Movement from the corner of his eye as he ran—*the stranger's shadow.*

Faster! House so close!

The shadow leaped and stretched—ten feet tall, twenty, fifty.

It reached for him, scraped the back of his neck.

Levi screamed. He sprinted up the walk and hurled himself against the front door.

"Levi!" said his mother. "Where have you—"

"There's a monster outside!" gasped Levi.

Regina snorted, but Mrs. Galante's face filled with concern.

"Don't!" said Levi. "It's out there! It's—"

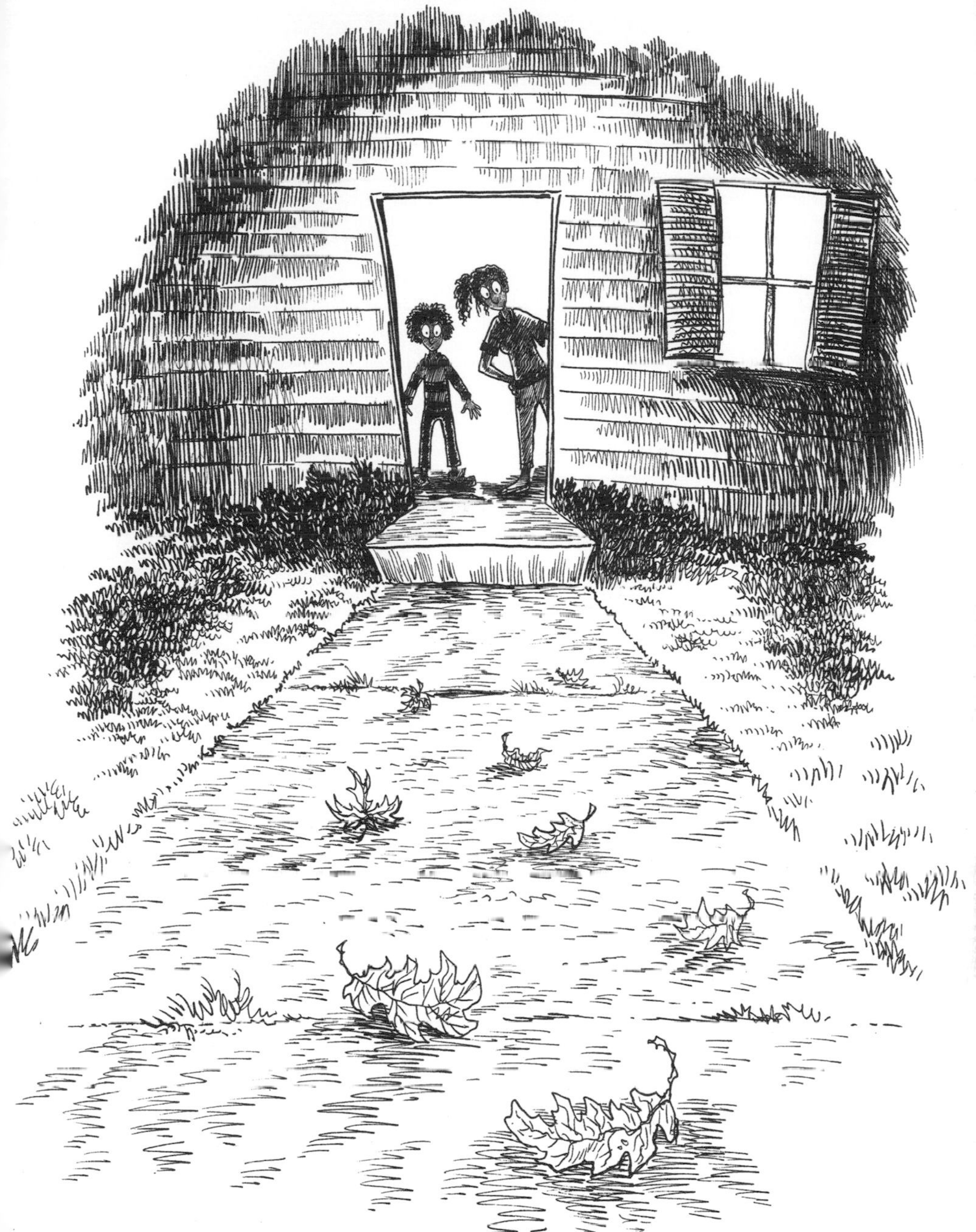

"Did this person say anything to you?" asked Mrs. Galante. "Hurt you?"

"N-no," said Levi.

"You said he chased you?"

"I . . . Well, his shadow looked weird." Levi lowered his eyes. His fear—the image of the shadowy stranger leaping across lawns and roofs, its limbs stretching to impossible lengths— was already starting to scramble in his mind.

Mrs. Galante sighed. "Did I not say home at five thirty? I should have you call the factory and tell them why I'm late."

Regina rolled her eyes. "Ma, I can't believe you're making me stay home to babysit this little freak."

"Quiet, Regina." Mrs. Galante tucked her purse under her arm and stormed out the front door. "Levi, your dinner is in the kitchen," she said over her shoulder.

"And if you want it reheated, don't ask me for help," muttered Regina. "You can't expect us to hold your hand forever."

"What did he look like?" Twila asked after their mother's car had disappeared down the road.

"What?" said Levi. "Who?"

"The scary man," said Twila. "Did he look like Freddy or Jason?"

"Shut up," said Levi as he spooned cold pasta onto his plate.

"Aw, c'mon," said Twila. "I'm just curious."

"I guess he was really tall," said Levi. "But I didn't get a good look. He was in the shadows." He took a bite of pasta and chewed thoughtfully. "Actually, it was probably just a creepy old neighbor out for a night walk."

47

"Maybe it's a vampire," said Twila. "That's why he wasn't there when Mom opened the door. 'Cause vampires can disappear into the night."

Levi made a face.

"Or he was the booooogeyman!" Twila grinned.

Levi shook his head. His imagination was twisted by too many hours of listening to Kat Bombard and her crazy alien-spaceship-Bigfoot conspiracies.

"Well, I think it's kinda cool," said Twila. "And creepy." She smiled—a warm, crooked smile that lit up her face. "This neighborhood could use a little excitement, don't you think?"

Chapter 6: The Cryptid Hunt

"No homework today!" said Twila the next afternoon as she bounced around the kitchen. "Going to the park to play lacrosse with Michaela! See ya!"

"Right now?" said Levi. "Maybe we could, I don't know, go out and investigate that weird dude I saw creeping around last night."

Twila smiled crookedly. "Vampires only come out after dark." She twirled her lacrosse stick and skipped out the door. "Bye, Ma. See ya, Brother-Man."

"Levi, I know change is hard for you," said his mom, "but this neighborhood has lots of kids your age. I wish you'd give it a chance."

"Are you working on your art?" asked Levi abruptly. He could see she wasn't, but he wanted her off his back.

She shuffled her paperwork awkwardly. "Not now. It's a busy time for the Slynderfell company."

A sharp knock interrupted them. The front door flew open.

"Have no fear! Agent Kat is here! Sorry to disturb teatime with your mom, Mr. Levi, but a cryptid is stalking the streets after dark, and you're the key witness!"

"But . . . I . . . Huh?" sputtered Levi.

"I ran into your little sis on the sidewalk, and she told me about your sinister encounter last night." She hoisted the camera strapped around her neck. "Come on! While the trail is fresh!"

Levi looked to his mother. "Home for dinner this time," she said, and went back to her forms.

A cheerful tinkling tune greeted them as they stepped into the brightness outside. Neighbors lined the sidewalk as the ice cream truck rolled down the street.

"Perfect timing!" said Kat as she flagged down the ice cream truck. "Top o' the afternoon, old bean! I'll have two cones: one Rocky Road to Perdition, and one Chubby Checker with a Lemon Twist."

The ice cream man gave a friendly smile as he prepared the cones. "Fueling up for an adventure, Kat?"

"You bet!" said Kat. "Me and Levi are on a secret mission!"

The ice cream man chuckled. "I can't imagine. The most exciting thing that's happened *here* in the last ten years is someone violating the noise ordinance with soft rock after sunset."

Kat chewed her lip, then leaned forward and whispered, "We're investigating something my pal Levi saw last night."

The ice cream man smiled at Levi. "Howdy-ho. You're new to town, right?"

Levi nodded and quickly looked down at his feet. The ice cream man was a bit too cheerful for his comfort.

"Well, welcome to Cowslip Grove." The ice cream man handed Kat the cones. "There you are, Kat."

"That's *Agent* Kat, Mr. Ice Cream Guy."

"Agent Kat." The ice cream man nodded. "Keeping the streets safe. Good to know."

"Thanks!"

CHOMP!
Mmph!
SLURP!
NUM!

"For what?"

"Um . . . nothing."

"Now," said Kat through a mouthful of ice cream, "about that monster you saw last night."

"It wasn't a monster. It was just some weird skinny dude."

"Levi, old sport, when you've been studying the supernatural as long as I have, you learn to trust your instincts. And my instincts say it's time to hunt."

They retraced Levi's course from the previous night, scanning the sidewalks and street gutters for clues.

"Hello, Katherine," said a neighbor who was hacking her hedges into perfect cubes. "What are you kids doing?"

"Hunting a cryptid, Mrs. Palmer," said Kat. "See anything strange lately?"

"Cryptid?" Mrs. Palmer shook her head. "Katherine, this is not appropriate behavior for a girl your age."

A man across the street stopped spraying his lawn with weed killer and joined the conversation. "Katherine Bombard! As Acting Vice President of the Cowslip Grove Neighborhood Watch, I must warn you that you are in violation of Ordinance 217: Conspiracy to Commit Peace Disruption and Loitering."

"Well, Mr. Lowe," said Kat, *"you're* in violation of Ordinance 23-Whatever: Conspiracy to Commit Being a Dorkenstein."

"I think your father needs to hear about your attitude, Katherine," said a shocked Mrs. Palmer.

Levi winced. Fortunately, the argument was cut short.

"Great merciful heavens!" shrieked Mrs. Palmer.

"Jumbo mamba!" trilled Kat.

"Kill it!" screeched Mrs. Palmer. "It's poisonous!"

"That's a mauve-banded king snake," said Levi. He'd seen pictures in one of his wildlife books. "It's not venomous. It squeezes its prey."

"I'll get my weed whacker!" bellowed Mr. Lowe. "Shred it to bits!"

Before his brain could fully register what he was doing, Levi was dashing across Mrs. Palmer's lawn and scooping the thrashing snake into his arms.

"Drop that creature immediately!" barked Mr. Lowe. "You are in violation of Ordinance 307: Harboring Dangerous Wildlife!"

Kat grabbed Levi's shoulder. "C'mon, let's get it out of here before they break out the torches and pitchforks!"

They raced down the street until they reached the edge
of town. Levi crossed the field and lowered the snake to the
ground.

"Don't let it go!" said Kat. "I got an empty terrarium at
home!"

Levi looked down at the reptile and marveled at its
beautiful markings, its flickering tongue, its bright glassy eyes.
"No. We can't take it away from its home." He watched the
snake slide from his hands and disappear into the tall grass.

"Fine," huffed Kat. "Let's
get back to the hunt." She
stepped through the
brambles, past the old car,
and into the forest.

"We can't go in there!" said Levi. "It's wild! It's—"
"The perfect place for a monster to hide," said Kat.

They listened . . . heard the drone of insects . . . the whisper of the breeze . . . and then—yes! The rustle of undergrowth as something moved closer . . . closer . . . *stopped.*

"It's over there," said Kat in a low voice. "Behind the reeds."
She crept to the rustling vegetation. Levi reluctantly followed.

"Three . . . two . . . one."

Kat raised her camera and pulled a clump of reeds aside.
Something darted from the undergrowth and disappeared
into the forest.

"Shoot!" hissed Kat. "I missed it!" She turned to Levi. "Did
you see what it was?"

Levi's mouth was open wide. His eyes were even wider.

"Well?" said Kat. "What did you see?"

What should he tell her? *Fluorescent green eyes? Hideous hunched back with sharp sinister spines?* It had moved so quickly. His mind was playing tricks again.

"A squirrel," he blurted.

"That's it?"

"Uh, yep."

They continued through the forest, Kat with her camera poised for action, and Levi silently convincing himself that in the right light, even a squirrel can look like a monster.

Chapter 7: The Mushpits

The sky had faded from blue to purple by the time Levi and Kat reemerged from the woods.

"What a waste," muttered Kat. "No monsters. No extradimensional abominations. My day is ruined."

"At least we got to see a big snake," said Levi.

"*Pfft!* Laaaaame." And then her eyes fixed on the ivy-strangled house across the street. "You know, there's always been something strange about the Mushpits."

Levi nodded. "But I kinda like their garden. It has its own personality."

"My dad says they're a menace to the neighborhood," continued Kat. "They don't mow their lawn. They let crazy plants grow wild and ruin their yard."

"Whatever," said Levi. He noticed the long shadows stretching across the sidewalk. "I gotta get home."

Kat caught his arm. "Hold on, Sundance. Our monster hunt ain't over yet." She nodded to the Mushpits' fence. "Sneak over and see what they're hiding back there."

"No way! That's trespassing!"

"If you don't go, I'll tell everyone in school that you're a mama's boy."

"Am not!"

"You're the mama's boy poster child. And unless you want everyone at school to know, you'd better get over there."

Levi sighed. "I'll just peek over the fence, okay?"

He crossed the street and inched up to the flaky picket fence.

"Okay, I'm looking. Nothing but plants."

"Stop wimping out and get closer!"

Levi leaned over the fence. "Nope. Just a bunch of—"

"Well done, Private," said Kat, stepping through the new gap in the fence. "It was high time you did something useful."

Levi felt the anger rising inside him. He started to sit up, opening his mouth to tell Kat he understood why no one liked her at school . . .

But he never had the chance.

"What the—?" screamed Kat. *"Get 'em off me!"*

Vines had twisted up her legs. Creepers had sprung from the ground and seized her arms. Levi felt the ivy coiling around his own limbs. Flowers snapped their petals like jaws. Pods burst, engulfing them in a cloud of spores. They flailed and shouted and sneezed, but the garden refused to let them go.

And then came a quavering voice behind them.

"Heavens to rutabaga! What have you done to my garden?"

Mrs. Mushpit.

"Please!" gasped Levi. "The garden!"

But then he looked down and saw the garden was just a garden. No thrashing vines. No snapping flowers. No exploding pods. A cloud of disturbed pollen still hovered in the air, and he was indeed tangled in some particularly thorny shrubs, but that was it.

"Yes, yes, my garden," spat Mrs. Mushpit as she stumped down the walkway. "You've certainly made a mess of it, haven't you?" She raised a bony finger. "You! Yes, you! Don't take another step!"

Kat had torn herself free from the tangle and was backing toward the sidewalk.

"Don't pretend you don't hear me, you muckraking gahoonigan! March your carcass over here this instant!"

Kat froze in place so suddenly that Levi wondered if Mrs. Mushpit had cast a magic spell and transformed her into a kid-shaped lawn ornament. But after a moment, Kat snapped back to life, shook a creeper from her leg, and bolted down the sidewalk.

Mrs. Mushpit scowled. "I'll deal with that weasel later." She seized Levi by the collar and hauled him to his feet. "You come with me!"

". . . Complete shambles! Wood splintered,
paint powdered . . .

And then the damage to the garden itself!

A fence is just a fence, but the plants are priceless!

Eh? What's that? *Help?*

No, no, Rebecca, dear. I don't want any more
children poking around my property.

You just keep a short leash on your
son. The world isn't as safe as you've
come to believe.

Oh . . . And should young
Levi experience any . . .
reactions . . . well, I simply
won't be held accountable.

There's a reason
we keep a fence
around our garden."

Chapter 8: ELEPHANTS for LUNCH

"Psst! Levi!"

This, of course, was not part of the story Ms. Padilla was reading to the class. Levi sat perfectly still, refusing to acknowledge the most unsubtle whisper in the history of unsubtle whispers.

"*Psst!* Levi! Over here!"

Levi clenched his teeth. *Don't turn around,* he told himself.

"*PSST!* Levi! I know you can hear me!"

"Shhh!" said Lydia Schnell. "Be quiet!"

"*You* be quiet!" snapped Kat.

Ms. Padilla cleared her throat. "Problem, Miss Bombard?"

Kat's face reddened. "Levi won't answer me!"

"Maybe Levi knows it's rude to talk when your teacher is reading a story," said Ms. Padilla.

"But he . . . But I . . . I . . ." Kat's flustered voice trailed off. She slumped back into her seat. "This story stinks," she mumbled.

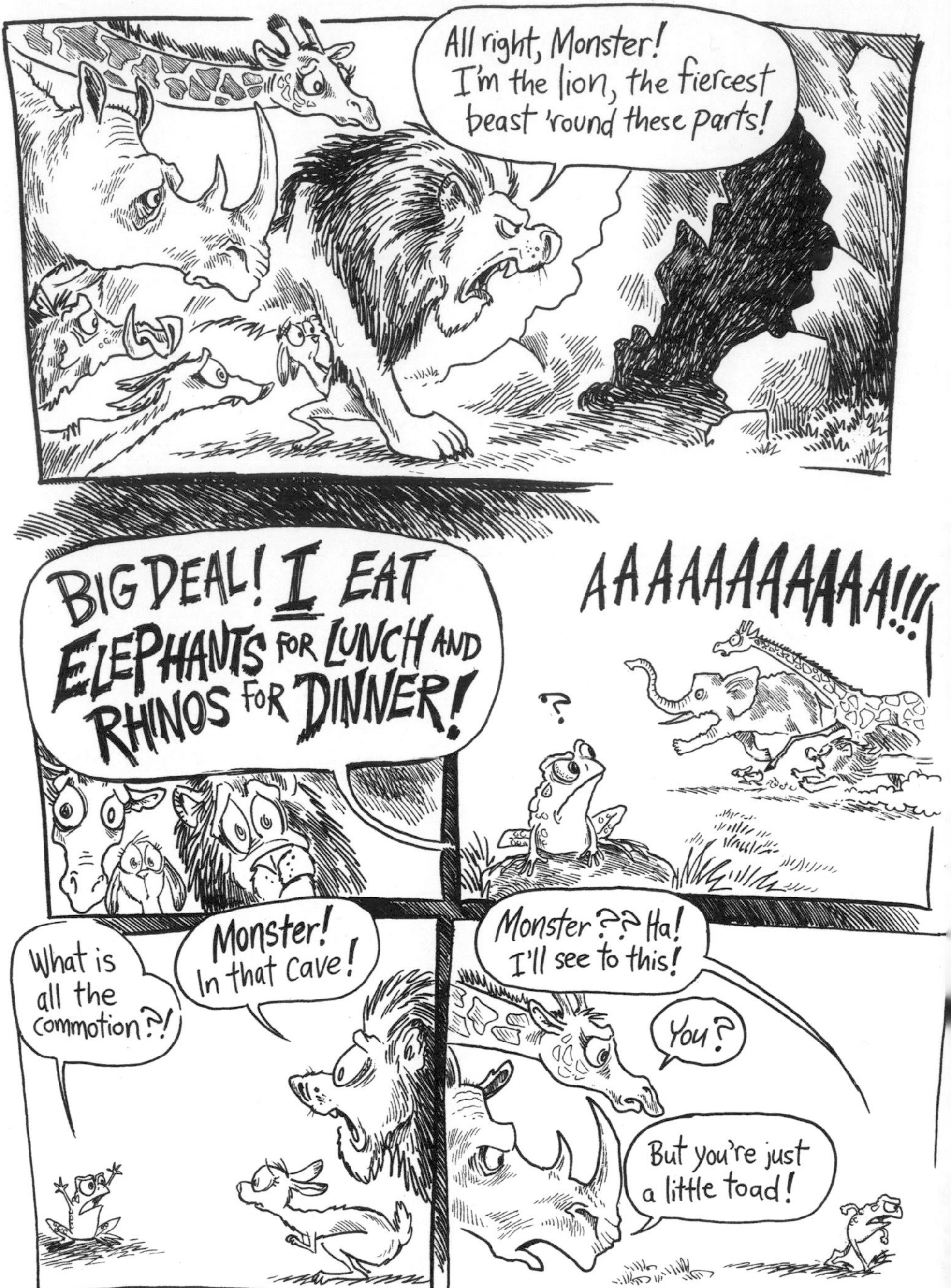
All right, Monster! I'm the lion, the fiercest beast 'round these parts!
BIG DEAL! I EAT ELEPHANTS FOR LUNCH AND RHINOS FOR DINNER!
AAAAAAAAAAA!!!
?
What is all the commotion?!
Monster! In that cave!
Monster?? Ha! I'll see to this!
You?
But you're just a little toad!

Ms. Padilla closed the book and explained that what she'd just read was based on a Maasai folktale, and that many folktales used animal characters to illustrate life lessons, and—

BRR-R-R-R-I-I-I-I-HINNG!

Class dismissed.

Chapter 9: Snotty Who?

"Levi! Levi, over here!"

Levi marched past Kat, surveyed the lack of empty tables, and headed for the primary school area.

It was taboo for middle school students to eat with the primary kids, but Levi was desperate. He found Twila sitting at a big table with a gaggle of third-graders.

"Can I join you?" he asked.

The girls broke into giggles. "Aren't you a little old to be eating lunch with third-graders, Gramps?" Twila grinned.

"So? Can I eat with you or not?"

"Depends," said Twila.

"Depends on what?"

"Depends on if you brought your Depends, Gramps!"

Levi's face burned. He trudged back to the middle school tables and plunked himself down beside Kat.

"So!" said Kat. "You done with this little silent-treatment drama show? I hope so, 'cause we got lots to discuss, starting with that insane garden."

"It wasn't insane," said Levi. "There weren't any monsters or cryptoid-dimensional whatevers. It was just a garden. And you ditched me there."

Kat opened her mouth to object, but she was cut off by a familiar voice:

"*BOOOOMBaaaard!*"

"Shut up, Joey! Or I'll shove that lunch tray down your ugly gullet!"

"Watch out, Levi!" shouted Joey. "If she kisses you, she'll give you brain-eating worms!"

"You'll be sorry!" barked Kat. "You and your snotty little brother!"

"Brother?" Joey guffawed. "I don't have a brother!"

"Yes you *do,* you . . . you . . . you oaf! Snotty Edward!"

"It's finally happened!" Joey announced to the lunchroom. "Bombard's finally gone completely bonkers!"

Kat's face twisted into a Picasso painting.

"Take it easy," said Levi. "Count to ten."

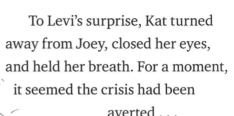

To Levi's surprise, Kat turned away from Joey, closed her eyes, and held her breath. For a moment, it seemed the crisis had been averted . . .

And then an apple bounced off Kat's head.

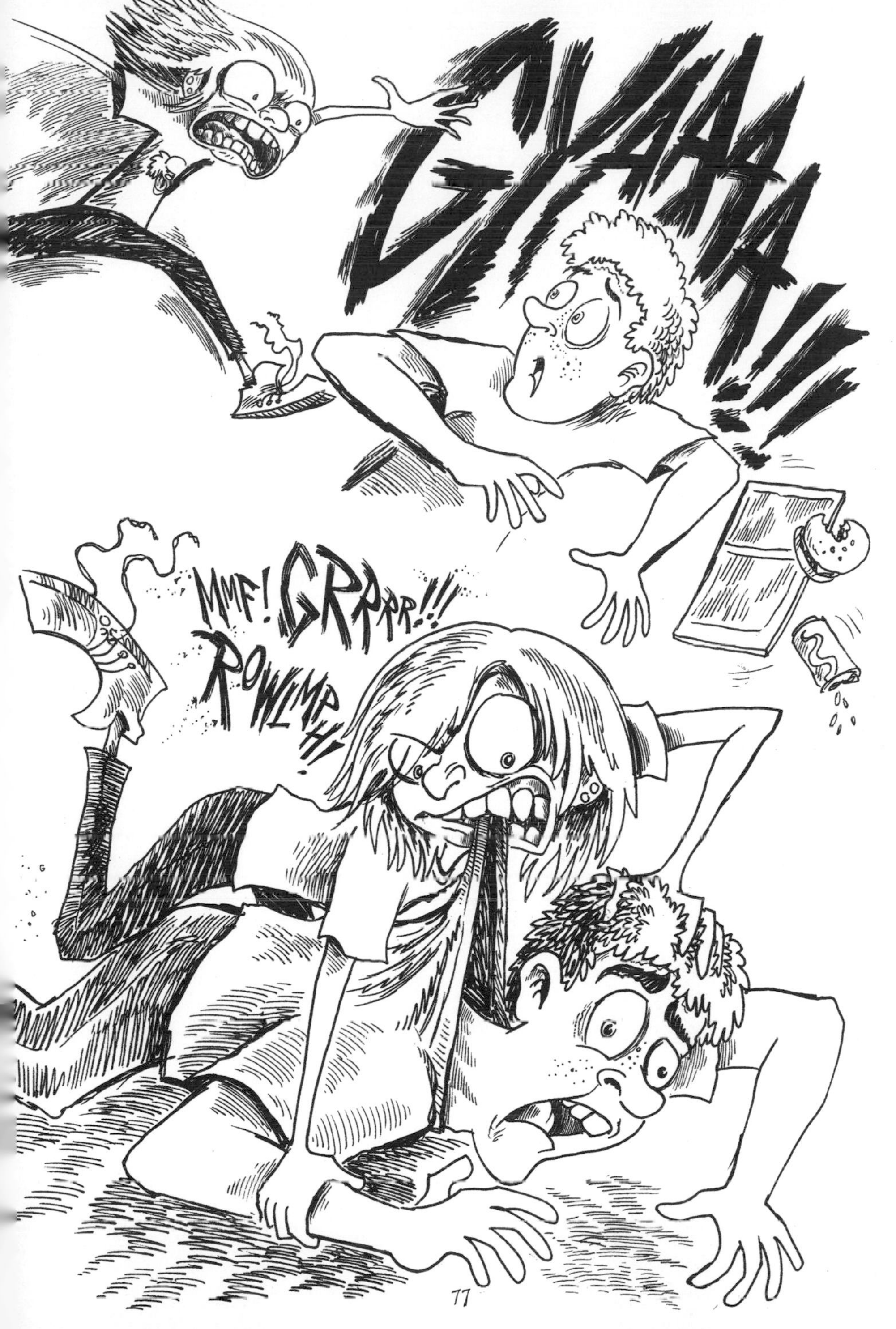
GYAAAA!!
MMF! GRRrrr!!!
ROWLMPH!!

Kat was not seen for the rest of the school day.

Chapter 10: Not Quite Right

The knock on the Galantes' front door was timid.

"Hey."

"Hey."

Kat's eyes were red and swollen.

"Did you get detention?"

"No. I got suspended. Three days. But I don't care. It'll be a vacation." The tremble in her voice didn't sound happy.

"So wanna go work on the Research Bunker?"

"Levi," interrupted Mrs. Galante, "may I speak with you a moment?" She ushered Levi back inside and closed the door.

"Levi, I want you to ask yourself if this is a friendship worth keeping."

"I thought you wanted me to make more friends."

"I do. Ever since the move, you've shut yourself off from everyone but Twila." She took a deliberate breath. "But I want you to think about Kat. Her behavior at school, what happened with the Mushpits." She saw Levi shifting uneasily and patted his shoulder. "Whatever you decide, I want you back before dark. I've got enough to worry about with Twila."

"What's wrong with Twila?"

"Oh, she's coming down with something. She barely slept last night. You didn't hear her moaning?"

He hadn't. He was a sound sleeper.

"Home before dark," repeated Mrs. Galante. "Better go now. The days are getting shorter."

"Something's wrong," said Kat as she paced back and forth like a wind-up toy. "It just doesn't add up."

"I told you to ignore Joey," said Levi.

"No, no. *His brother.* He says he doesn't have a brother. And then the principal also says he doesn't. And his parents. None of them remember Snotty Little Edward."

"So he doesn't have a brother."

"He *does* have a brother! Remember? You saw him yourself that day I first brought you to this car!"

Levi searched his memory, and for a moment there was a glimmer of recognition. Joey *had* been with someone that day. Not just anyone . . . It had been Snotty Little . . . No. No, Kat was twisting his mind again.

Kat stopped pacing and buried her face in her hands. "You think I'm making this up? Well, I'm not! Something's wrong. Very wrong."

"Does it have anything to do with those mind-snatching aliens?"

"No, that wasn't . . . They weren't really . . . No."

"What about your cryptid book? Bigfoot?"

Kat flopped down in the grass. "I don't know what's happening. But you've got to believe me: something *is* wrong. Can't you feel it? Even the air seems different."

Levi sighed and leaned back on the car's hood. Kat continued to rant and ramble, but Levi wasn't listening. He was thinking about what his mother had said.

The sun was sinking below the western horizon when Levi arrived home. Twila was sitting on the front steps.

"How ya feeling?"

"Blah," she said. "Having trouble sleeping."

"What kind of soup is that?"

"Noodle."

"Hmm. Well, I bet you'd be feeling a lot better if that soup was from Levi's Café."

Back when the Galante family lived in the city, before Twila was in school, she'd suffered chronic ear infections. To take her mind off the pain, Levi would turn a laundry basket upside down, spread a bed sheet over the top, and pretend it was a table in a ritzy restaurant. Twila loved the idea and ate all her meals on the makeshift table. "Levi's Café," she'd called it.

Twila looked up at Levi with big glassy eyes, and for a moment he worried she had forgotten Levi's Café. Then she smiled. It was a warm smile—not the smirk she wore when trying to impress her friends. It was *her* smile.

"I haven't been to Levi's Café in years!"

"Then we should go. Tomorrow after school?"

"Cool, Big Brother-Man. What's on the menu?"

Levi shrugged. "Something good. You've got Chef Levi's personal guarantee."

The air was crisp, the night breeze cool and comforting as it sighed through the open window. Levi felt the day's events fading from his mind . . .

Kat Bombard and her paranoid delusions, his mother's warning, Twila and her new friends at lunch . . .

It all seemed distant now.

Now?

Now his pillow was so soft,
the neighborhood so quiet,
and outside, the sky faded from
pink to purple, and the stars glittered . . .

and the night breeze whispered.

Chapter 11: Twila

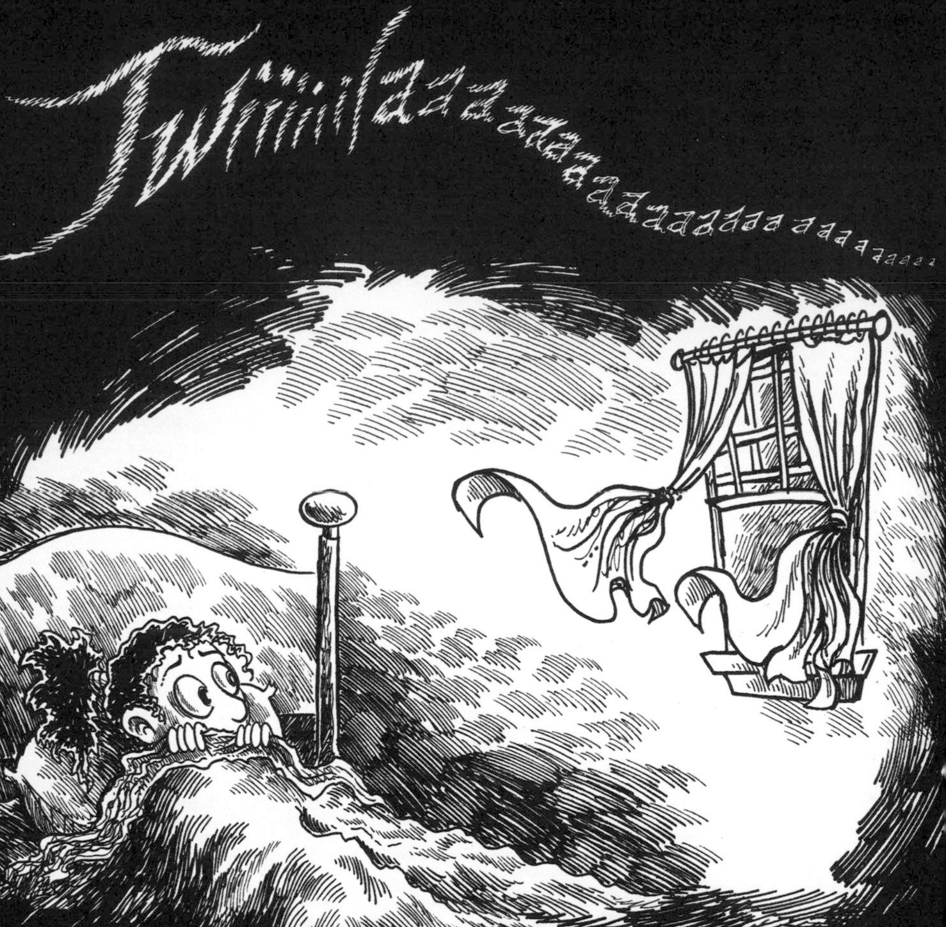
Twiiiiilaaaaaaaaaaaaaaaaaaaaaaaaaaaaa

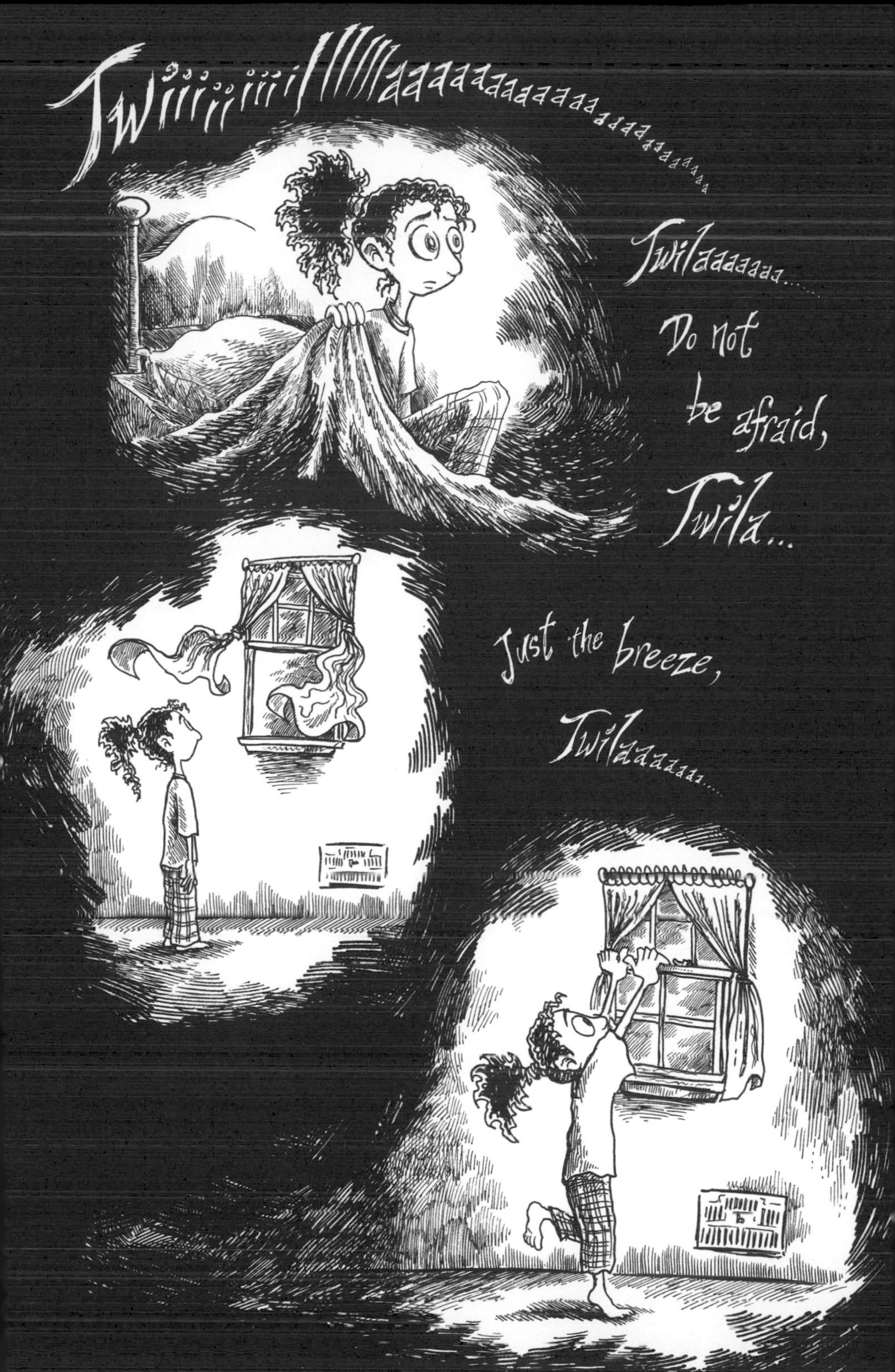
Twiiiiiiiiiiilllllllaaaaaaaaaaaaaaaaaaaaaaa
Twilaaaaaaa...
Do not be afraid, Twila...
Just the breeze, Twilaaaaaaa...

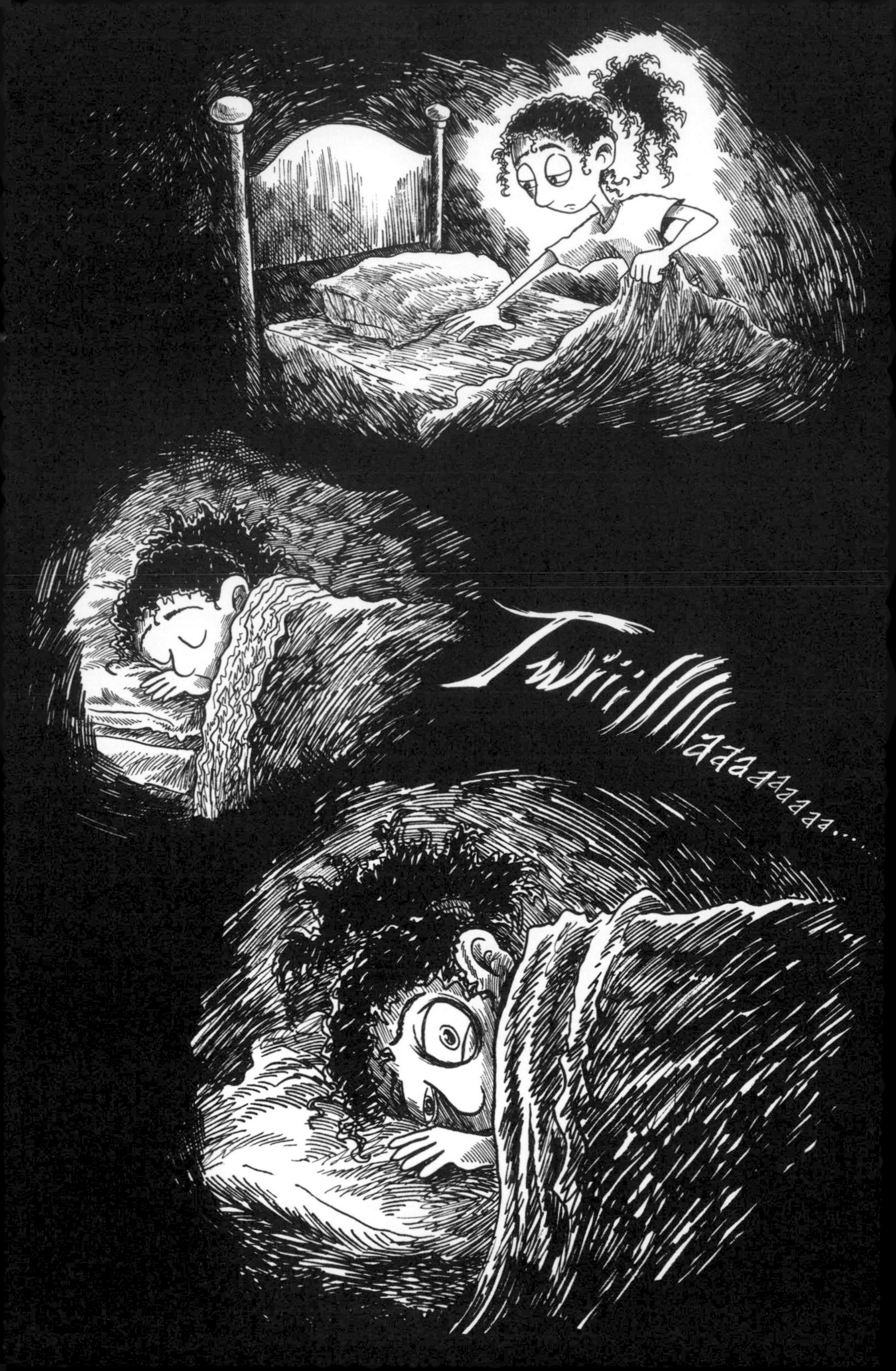
Twiiilllaaaaaaaaa...

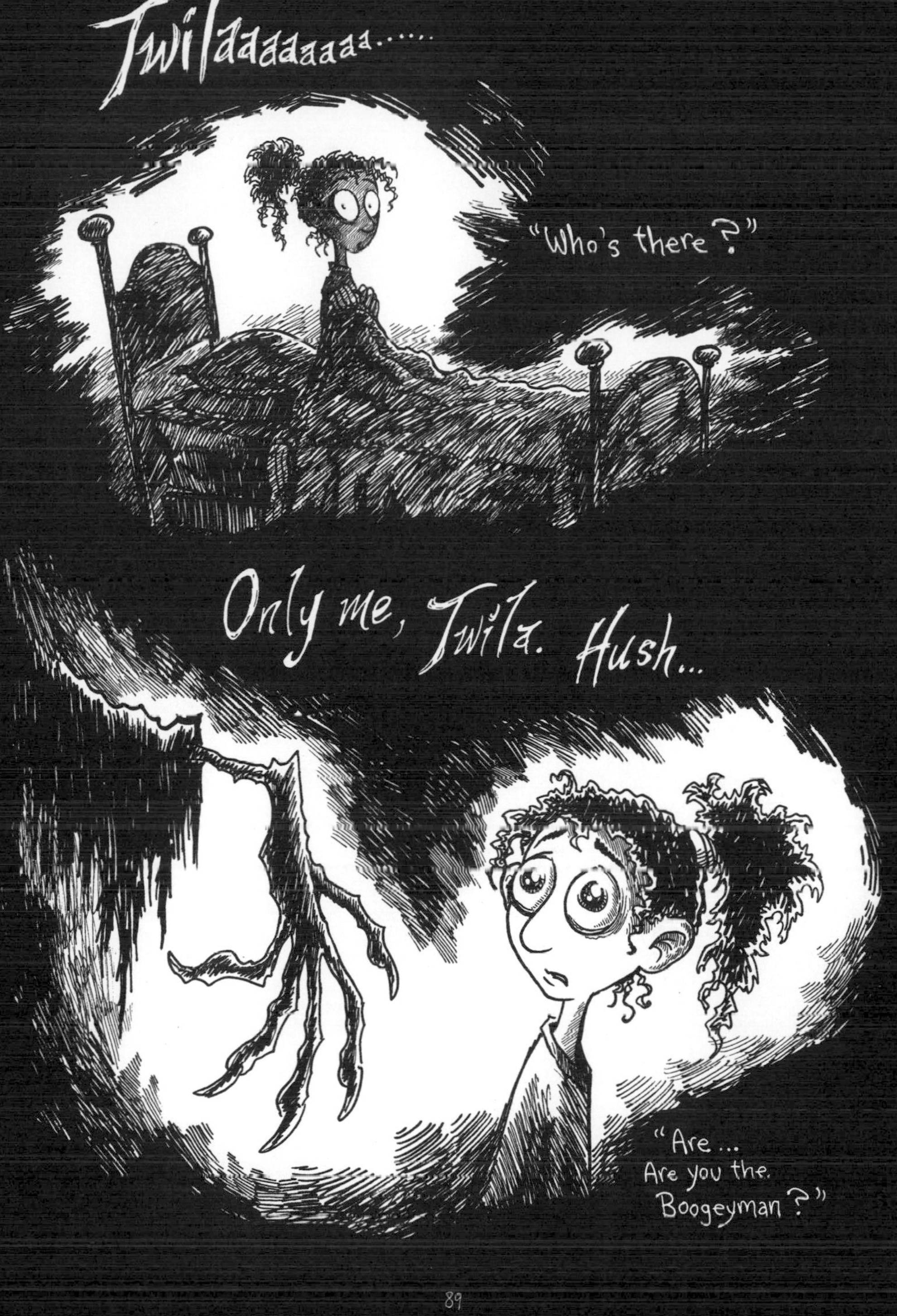
Twilaaaaaaaa.....
"Who's there?"
Only me, Twila. Hush...
"Are...
Are you the
Boogeyman?"

Not quite.

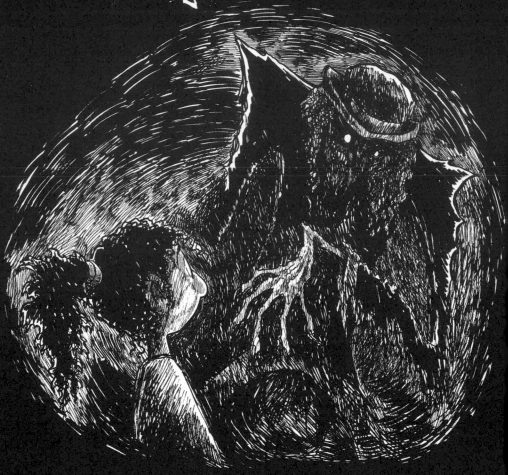

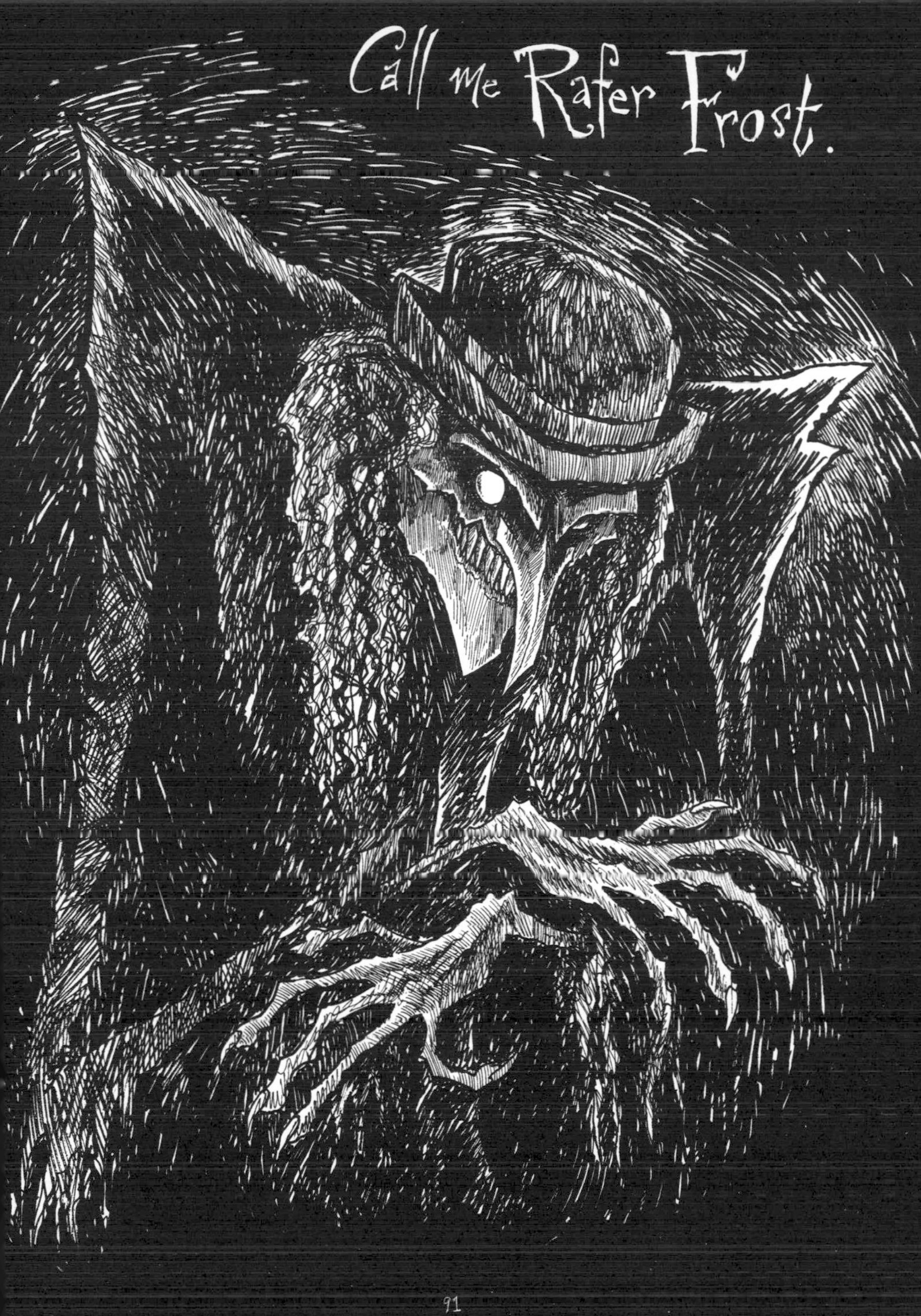
Call me Rafer Frost.

Chapter 12: Morning

Levi woke at 7:15, a half-hour later than usual.

He sat up in bed. Stretched his arms.

Trudged to the kitchen.

"Morning, Levi," said his mother. "We'll have to move quickly. I overslept too."

He downed a hasty breakfast, threw on clothes, grabbed his backpack, and followed Regina out the door. The morning sun shook them from their daze as they marched down the sidewalk.

But after a minute, Levi felt a sinking sensation in his stomach. He was forgetting something. Homework? No. Lunch?

"If you don't keep up, I'm leaving you behind!" snapped Regina.

Levi hitched up his backpack and scooted to Regina's side.

The feeling persisted. His mind ran through his schedule, trying to pinpoint what he'd forgotten.

. . . Morning activity at 8:15, then math . . . No, nothing with school. Did he have plans with Kat? No, Kat was acting weird, even weirder than usual, and his mother didn't want Kat around, and he'd already made a reservation at good ol' Levi's Café so he could spend the evening with Twi—*TWILA!*

"Hey!" he shouted. "We forgot Twila!"

Regina pulled out an earbud. "What are you squawkin' about?"

"Is she still sick?" asked Levi. "Is she staying home today?"

"Who's sick?"

"*Twila!*"

Regina crossed her arms. *"Who?"*

The question stung Levi. "Um. Twila. Our *sister*."

"I'm your sister, dum-dum."

Was she
messing with
him? There was
no humor in
Regina's
face.

He turned and ran back to the house.

"I'm not waiting for you!" shouted Regina. He ignored her.

"Ma?" he called. No answer.
"Ma? Where's Twila?"

He heard
the shower
running. His
mother was getting
ready for work.

He crept down the hall.

Knocked on Twila's door.

"Twila?"
No answer.
"Are you still
in bed?"

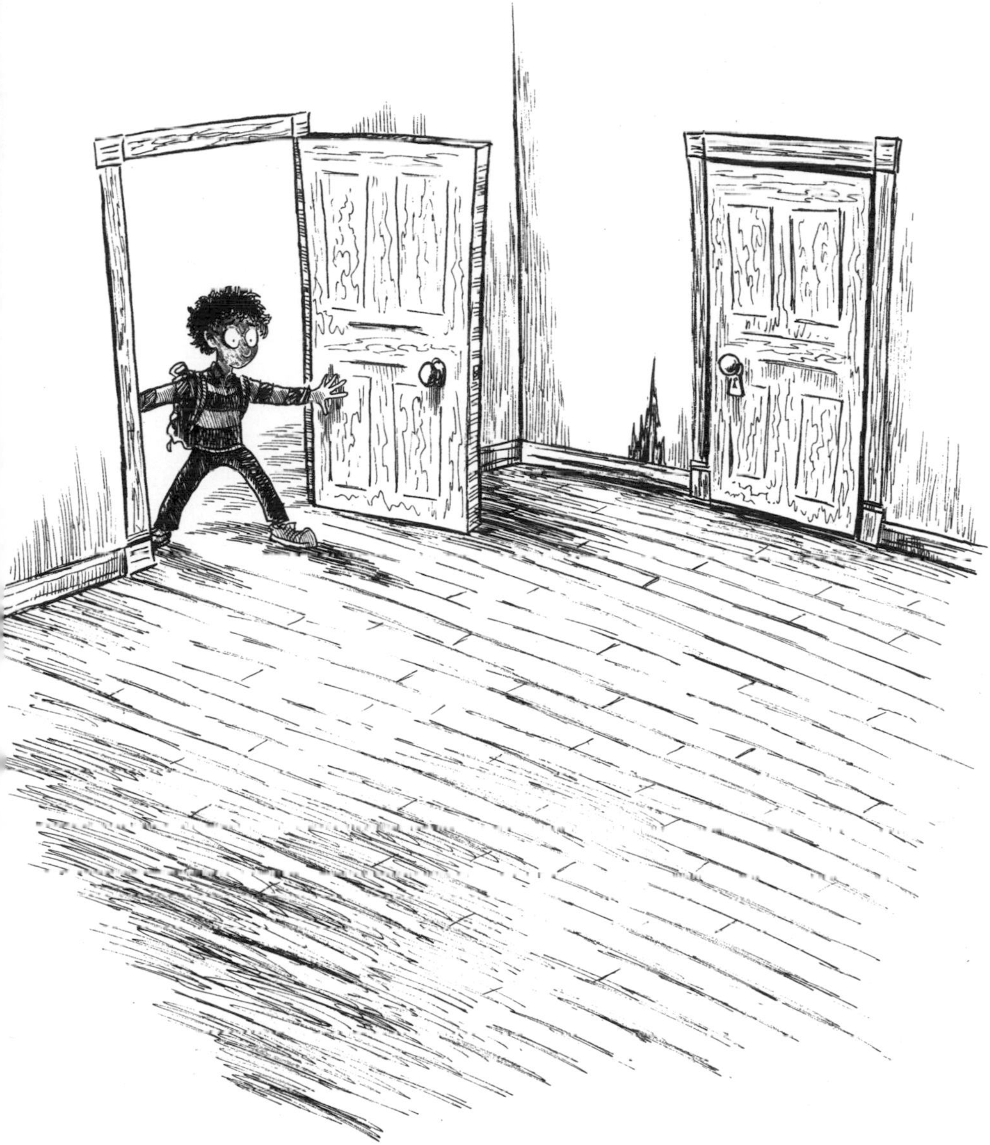

"MOM!"

"Levi, what are you still doing here? You'll be late for school!"

"Where's Twila? What happened to her room?"

"Levi, honey, I have no idea what you're talking ab—"

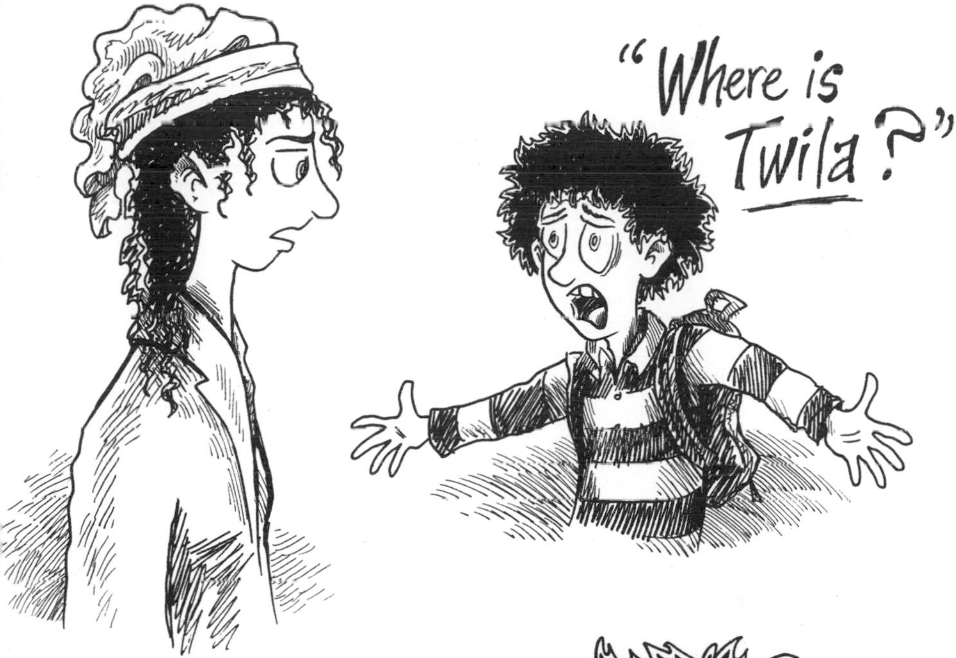
"Where is Twila?"

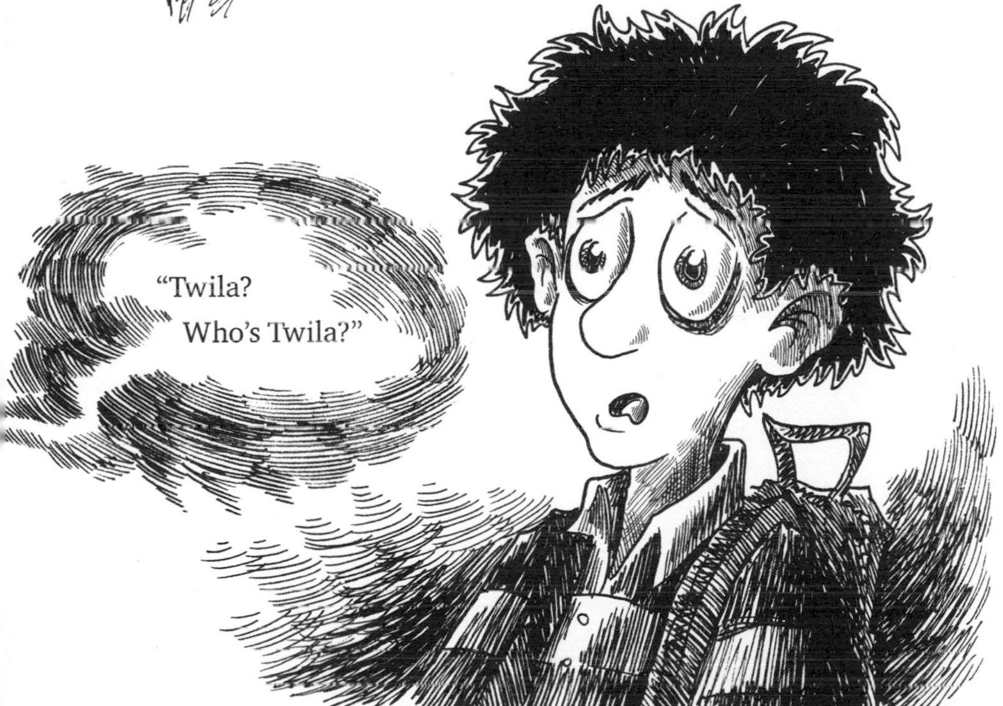
"Twila?
Who's Twila?"

Chapter 13: The Loose Pieces

"Levi? Are you feeling all right?"

Levi looked up from his desk and gave a weak smile.

"Do you need a drink of water?"

Levi shook his head.

Ms. Padilla patted his shoulder. "Let me know if you need anything."

Levi slouched in his seat and reopened his silent-reading book. Of course he wasn't really *reading*—concentration was out of the question—but what else could he do? How could he explain the impossible?

Gee, Ms. Padilla, no, I am not all right. My little sister seems to have disappeared from the face of the planet, except maybe she hasn't, 'cause everyone, even my own family, has no idea there ever was a little sister to begin with.

And there's nothing that proves she was here just yesterday except an empty room, but my mom says it should be empty, 'cause it's being converted into an office or something. So maybe I am crazy after all, especially since my own memory seems to be getting fuzzier the longer this miserable day slogs on.

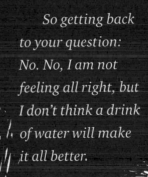

So getting back to your question: No. No, I am not feeling all right, but I don't think a drink of water will make it all better.

No, he couldn't say that to Ms. Padilla.

When the last bell finally rang, Levi gathered his books, stepped out into the afternoon sun, and lingered by the street curb, hoping—just *hoping*—that maybe this whole nightmare was a big mix-up, and Twila would join him, and they would walk home together like they had since her first day of kindergarten. But of course Twila didn't show, so Levi started for home alone.

And then a familiar voice.

"Hey! Levi! Levi, buddy, over here!"

Kat Bombard scuttled across the street. "So how was school? I tell ya, getting suspended ain't so bad. I've been living life to the fullest!"

Levi was silent.

"Jeez, what's wrong with you?"

Levi opened his mouth to speak, but no words came out—just a strangled sob.

"You okay, buddy?"

Levi didn't want to cry in front of Kat, but at this point nothing mattered. Big sloppy tears tumbled down his cheeks.

"What happened, Levi?" For once Kat actually sounded concerned.

"T-Twila," he squeaked.

"Your sister? What about her?"

Levi stopped sobbing and stared at Kat in astonishment. *"You remember her?"*

Kat looked confused. "Why wouldn't I?"

"Because," said Levi as his voice choked again, "n-no one else does!"

"What are you talking about?"

Levi scrubbed away the tears, took a deep breath, and told Kat everything.

"It's the same thing that happened to Edward Downey," Kat said when he'd finished.

"Huh?"

"Snotty Little Edward Downey. No one remembers him, not even his brother. He's gone, and it's like he was never here to begin with."

Levi felt lightheaded. He had the need to sit down or continue walking. He chose to walk.

Kat shuffled beside him. "Something's happening, Levi. First Edward Downey, and now Twila."

"But *what's* happened to Twila?"

"Dunno. But maybe we can figure it out. How many people have you mentioned this to?"

"Uh . . . my mom . . . Regina . . . Twila's teacher, Mrs. Buckley . . . Principal Rounds . . . But they don't believe me. They think I'm freaking out because I miss the city."

"Okay. Well, don't mention it to anyone else. It's a good thing you didn't flip out in front of your mom."

"I sorta did. But since you remember Twila too, maybe we can go to the police and convince them we're right."

"No, Levi. If you go to the authorities, there's only two things that could happen: One, they won't believe you, and you'll be taken away by the Men in White Coats, or two, they *will* believe you, and you'll be taken away by the Men in Black Suits."

"What is that supposed to m—"

"I'm saying either they'll think you're crazy, or they'll think you know too much."

"Too much?"

"Right. They'll think you're a threat to the peace. Look at me—I mention one missing kid, and I get suspended."

"You got suspended for beating up Joey Downey."

"Believe me, Levi. The authorities can't do anything. There's no record of Twila anywhere. No one at school remembers her; you say even the photos in your house have changed. Your own family has forgotten her. There's no evidence she ever existed."

Levi's chest tightened. "Then what do we do?"

"Do? What else *can* we do? We gotta fight back!"

"You mean . . . just *us?*" Levi licked his lips. "But we don't even know what we're fighting!"

"True," said Kat. "But we know some things. We know it comes at night. And it comes quietly."

Levi caught Kat by the arm. "Those aliens you were talking about—the ones I didn't believe existed . . . Do you think—was that a true story?"

Kat answered with a sheepish look.

"Well," continued Levi, "even if that didn't actually happen, maybe the aliens are real this time."

"Maybe," said Kat. "Or maybe it's something else. Guess we'll find out tonight. It'll be back, so it's important to stick together. My parents won't be home till late, so I'll go to your house."

They reached the end of the sidewalk, and Levi realized they had walked right past his home. Ahead was the overgrown field, and beyond that, the edge of the forest, its trees dark and skeletal against the pale autumn sky.

"How do you know it will be back tonight?" asked Levi.

"Because," said Kat, "we remembered."

Levi looked puzzled.

"Don't you get it? *We* are the loose pieces! And if this thing can erase a thousand memories or even change reality itself in a single evening, then it's smart enough to know we somehow resisted its power . . .

"And you can bet it's not happy about that."

Chapter 14: Plans

"Trust me, Rebecca, it's completely, totally, one hundred per-cent safe. I can call you Rebecca, right?"

"I'd prefer 'Mrs. Galante,' Kat," said Mrs. Galante. "So show me how all this works. It's for science class?"

"The science fair, to be precise. And with this bottle-rocket launcher, me and Levi will knock the judges' socks off. Maybe literally! Right, Levi?"

"Uh, right."

"Okay, so this wooden stand is the launch pad . . .

"And this two-liter soda bottle is the rocket. See, I've added plastic fins and a nose cone to make it more aerodynamic. It'll cut through the air like a flying mako shark!

"The rocket fits onto the launch tube; then I place this metal clip into the two slits on the stand. This holds the rocket in place . . .

"This electric air pump hooks in under the launch tube. Plug it in and turn it on . . ."

"Um . . ."

"Never fear, Mrs. Galante! It's noisy, but totally safe! Just air!

"To launch it, I'll stamp on this foot pedal.

"The foot pedal is tied to the metal clip. The clip pulls loose and lets all the air out the bottle's bottom, and

VOOOOOSH!

The rocket flies into the stratosphere!"

"Very . . . intriguing, Kat. I'm excited to see it in action. Outside, of course. Not in Levi's bedroom."

"Oh, of course, Mrs. Galante. I'd never dream of launching a rocket inside!"

"Good. All right, it's getting late. Do you need a ride home?"

"Naw. I live only one street over. I'll walk. But it's okay if I leave the launcher and stuff with Levi? It's a lot to lug."

"Well . . . It's all unplugged? Yes, then that's fine. Good night, Kat."

"Good night, Mrs. G. See ya, Levi."

Five minutes later, Levi heard a tap on his window. "Is the coast clear?"

Kat tossed a duffel bag through the open window and hauled herself over the windowsill. "I still think this sneaking around is stupid. I totally charmed your mom tonight. She'd let me stay over."

"Uh, I don't think so." He watched as Kat emptied the duffel bag's contents. "How is all this stuff going to help us fight . . . whatever took Twila?"

"Not sure," said Kat, "but it never hurts to be prepared." She pawed through the equipment. "Superduper bright flashlight, in case the monster's light sensitive . . . basic blunt defense weapons . . . and my trusty camera, for documentation." She nodded to the loaded rocket launcher. "And we've got our secret weapon."

"I don't know," said Levi. "A soda bottle isn't going to scare anyone."

"It's a *rocket!* That nose cone is weighted with three hundred grams of metal washers! It's lethal!"

"You told my mom it was safe."

"Holy schnikes, Levi! Priorities! We've got a dangerous night ahead, and I'm not going to let your Eeyore attitude foil my brilliant plan!"

"Shhh," hissed Levi. "My mom!"

As if in response, there was a knock on the door. "Levi? Are you all right?"

Levi and Kat exchanged panicked looks.

Kat disappeared under Levi's bed just as the door opened.

"I thought I heard a voice," said Mrs. Galante.

"Uh, sorry," said Levi. "I was talking to myself."

Mrs. Galante was quiet for a moment. "I called Dr. Aharon's office, but they couldn't squeeze you in until Monday."

"Um, thanks," said Levi. "Sorry about the freak-out this morning. I'm fine, I swear. My mind was just foggy today."

Mrs. Galante gave a sympathetic smile and started to close the door.

"Mom," said Levi.

"Yes?"

"You really don't remember her?"

There was a long pause. The lines in Mrs. Galante's brow knitted.

Levi forced a smile. "I mean, um . . . nothing." He swallowed. His throat clicked. "Good night, Ma."

Chapter 15: BUMP in the Night

"*Psst!*" hissed Kat. "Wake up!"

"I *am* awake."

"I thought I saw your eyes close."

"They didn't. Why are you watching my eyes?"

"Just checking."

They were crouched against the wall opposite the bed with Kat's rocket launcher propped between them and aimed at the window. The bed was stuffed with pillows, and in the darkness, it made a passable decoy.

It was after midnight. Regina had come home from her team victory party a while ago, and his mother had been asleep for hours.

Kat had been right—his eyes *had* closed for a moment. But he wasn't asleep. No, he could never sleep at a time like this. It was just the stress of the longest day ever. His body was tired, true, but his mind was sharp.

He was ready . . .

Ready for . . .

For . . .

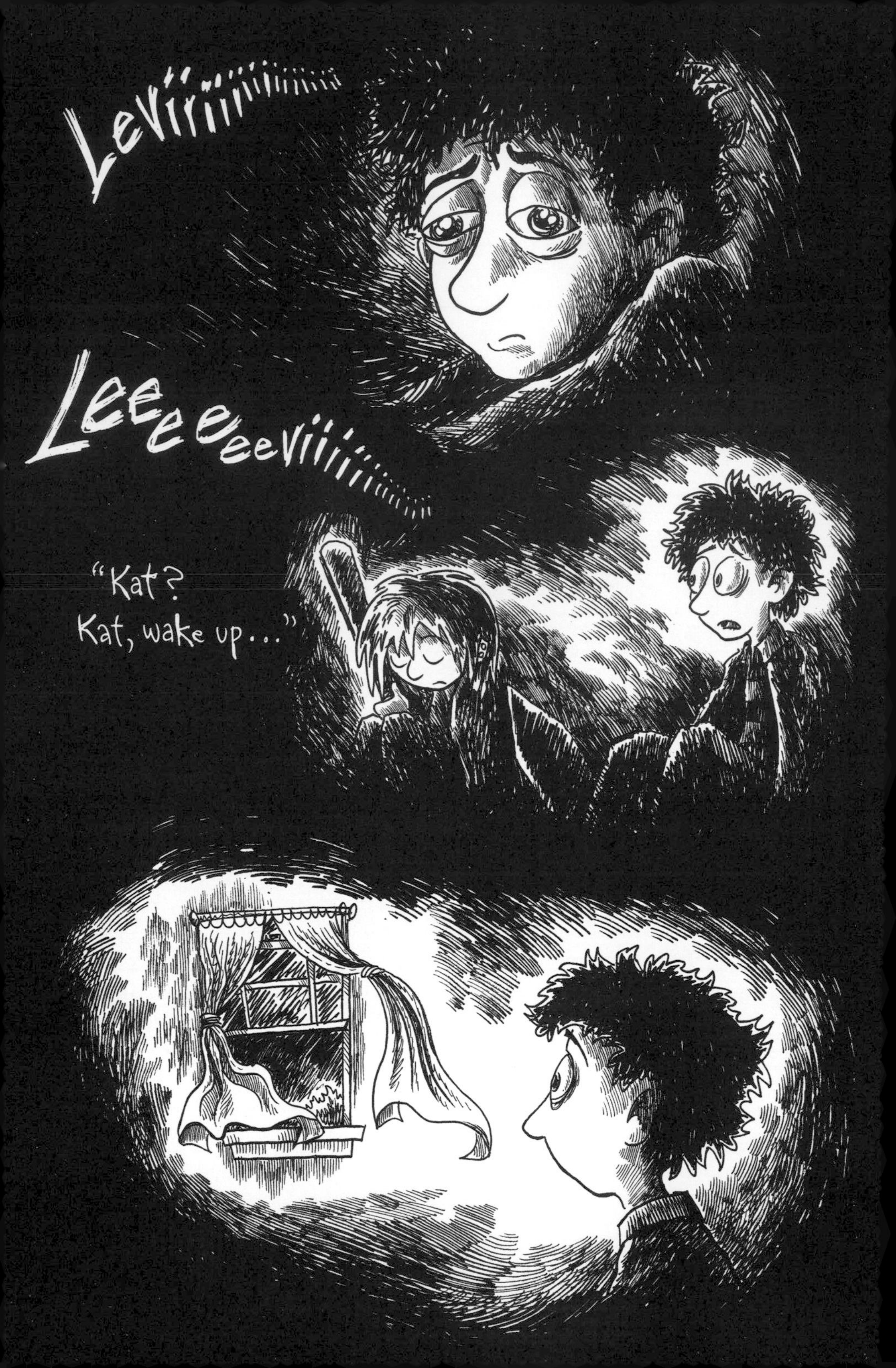
Leviiiiiiiiiiii
Leeeeeeeviiiiiiiiii
"Kat?
Kat, wake up..."

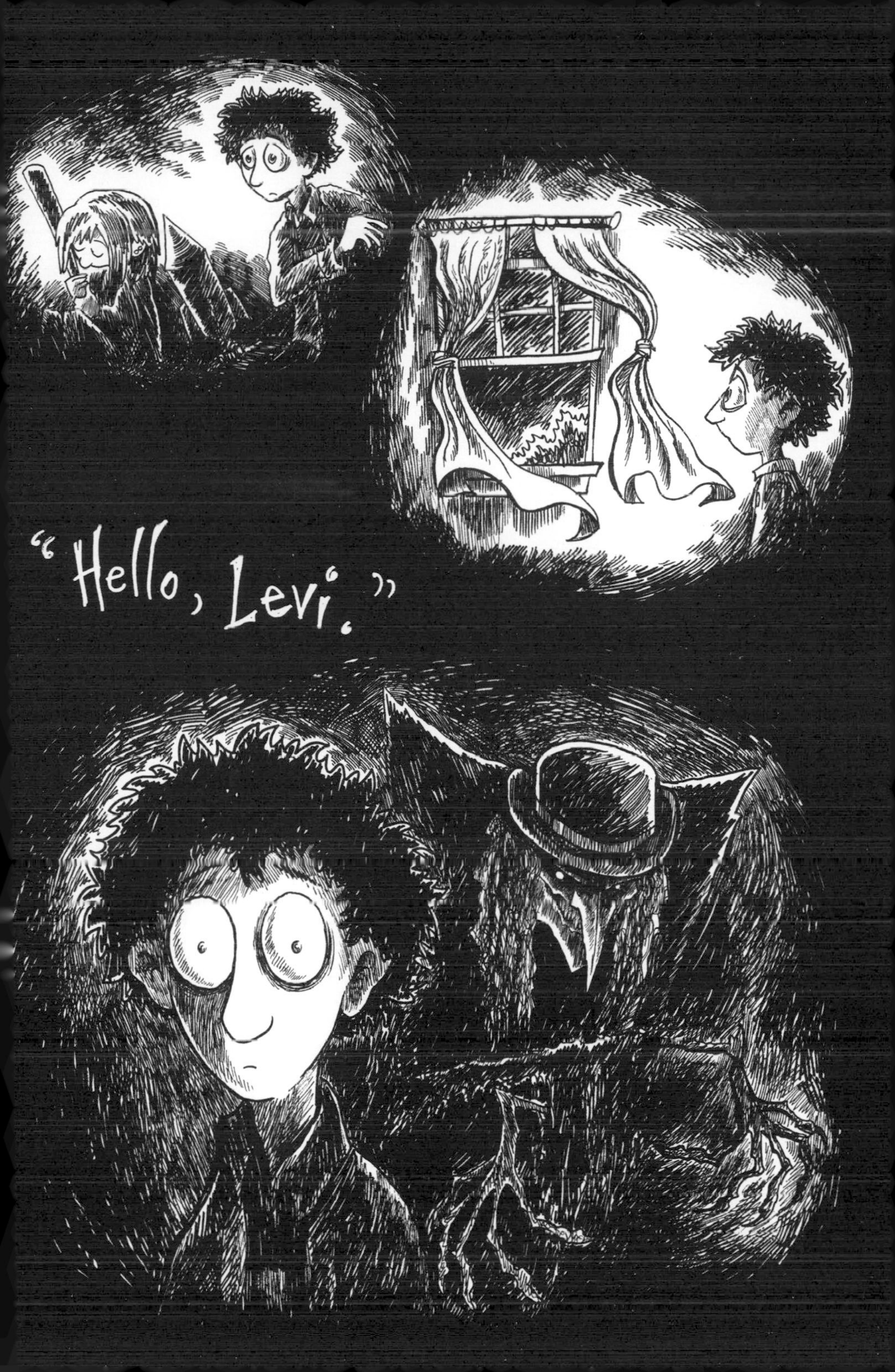
"Hello, Levi."

"Mmph!"
Hush.
Sleeeeeeeep...
"Poor Levi.
You miss your lovely little
sister, yes?"

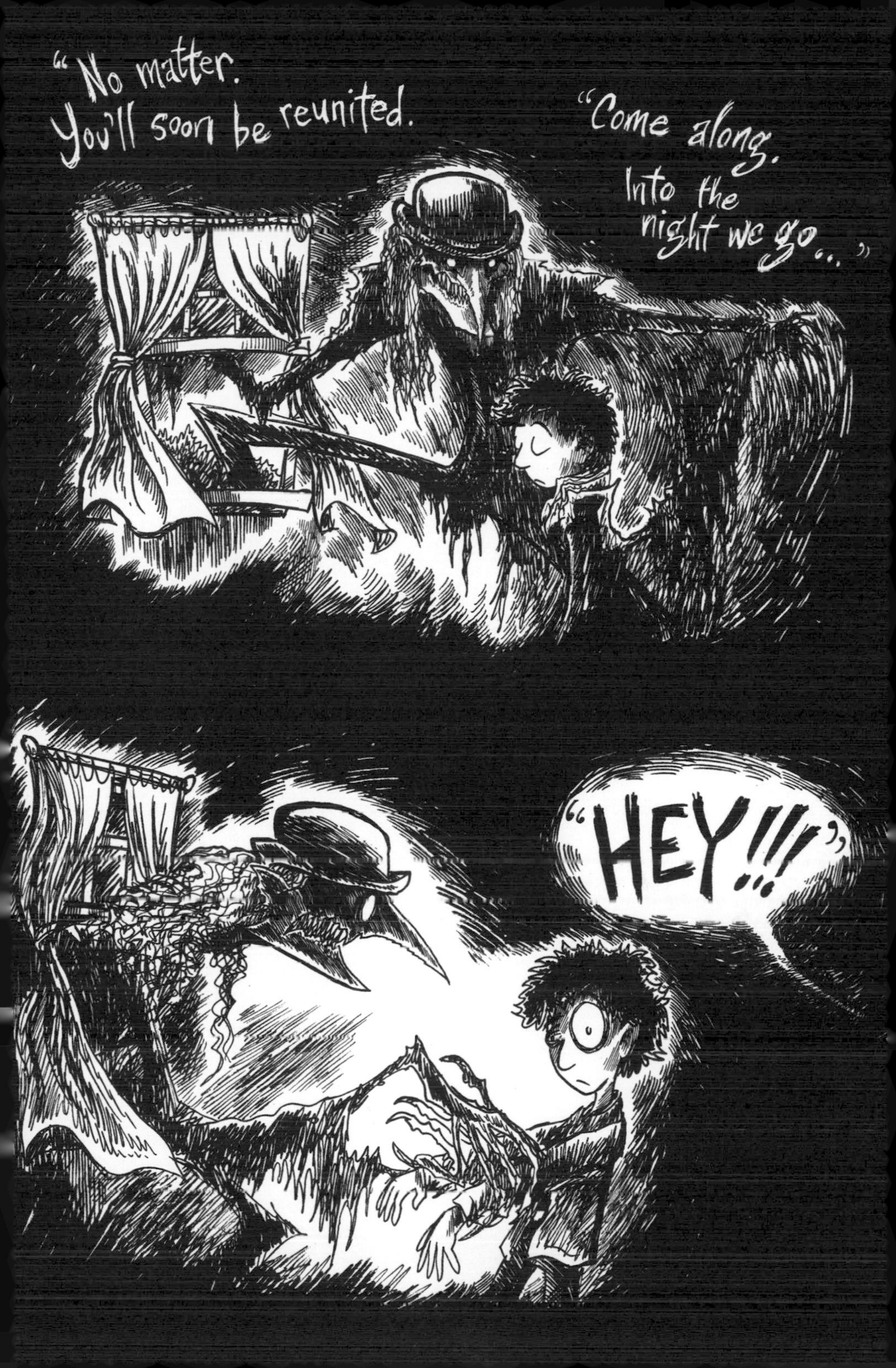
"No matter. You'll soon be reunited.
"Come along. Into the night we go..."
"HEY!!!"

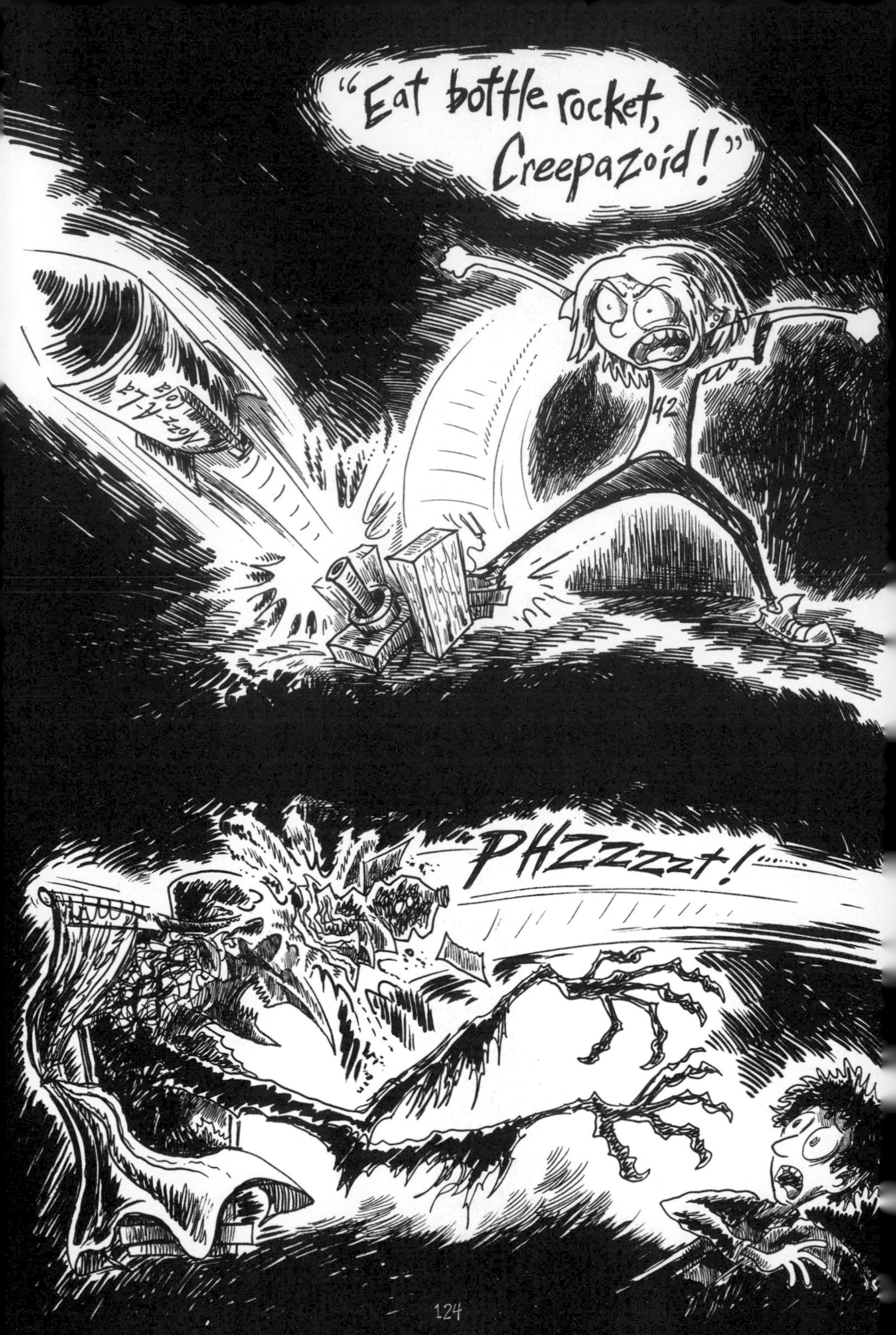
"Eat bottle rocket, Creepazoid!"
Nozz-A-La Cola
42
PHZZzzzt!

"Levi! Levi, you okay?"

"Wha... What happened?"

"Levi! C'mon, man, wake up!"

"L-Levi... please..."

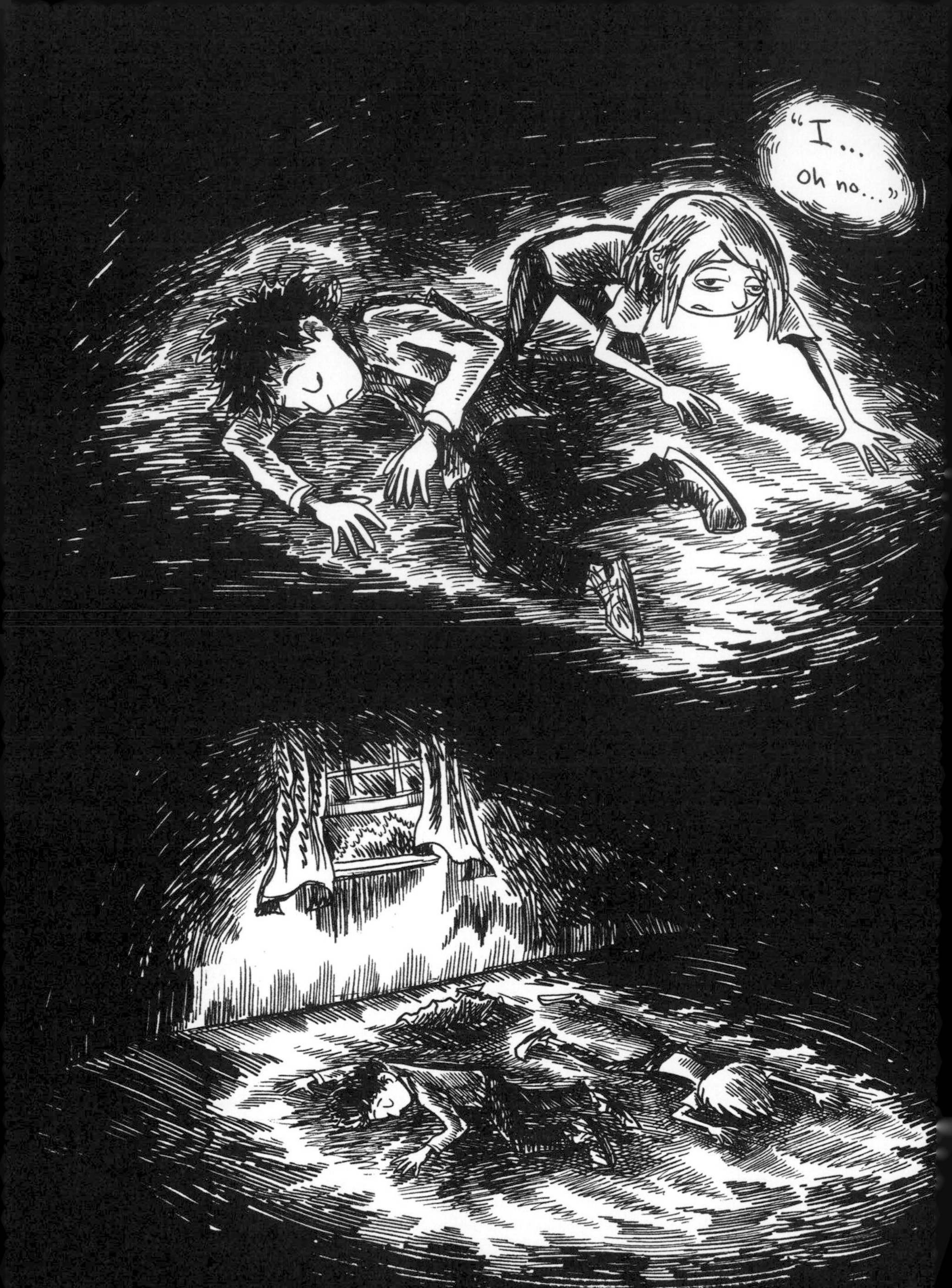
"I...
oh no..."

Chapter 16: Strangers in a Strange Land

Levi? Levi...

Levi's eyes fluttered open. The ground was hard. Cold. A floor.

"Levi, c'mon!" Kat Bombard's voice. *Kat?*

And then the memories came flooding back. "The monster!" he gasped. "The stranger who followed me home! It was here!"

"It's okay! It's gone!" said Kat. "But, uh . . . see for yourself . . ."

"It almost got you, man! It had you in some sort of trance and was dragging you out the window. That's when I shot that sucker square in the face with the rocket!" Kat's voice buzzed with nervous energy. "But then—I don't know. I couldn't keep my eyes open, like I was hit with a sleeping spell, and I guess we both blacked out and . . ."

Levi said nothing.

"It took my stuff, too!" continued Kat. "My bag, my camera, even my rocket launcher! It must've come back for those things, but then there's the mystery of why it left us lying unconscious on the floor. Unless maybe our stuff just vanished into thin air."

Noises came from the kitchen—dishes clinking, cupboards slamming. Levi and Kat exchanged anxious looks.

"It's just Regina fixing breakfast," said Levi after a moment. He could tell from the pale light streaming through the window that it was morning.

Kat followed him down the hall. "Be careful what you tell them," she warned.

But Levi's mind was set—he wouldn't be hysterical this time. He'd just show his mom and Regina the empty room, and then they'd finally see he was right all a—

"Jeez, Regina!" said Levi. "Calm down! It's only us."

Regina's face was a mask of shock and fury. "How did you get in here?"

"Chill! This is Kat. She's my friend."

"Stay back! You little creeps are soooo busted!"

"Relax! I know she wasn't supposed to stay over, but it was an emergenc—"

"Mom! It's a break-in! Call the Police!"

"Regina! Stop it! She's just my friend from school." But now he saw Regina wasn't looking at Kat. His stomach fluttered.

Hurried footsteps sounded behind them, and Rebecca Galante appeared in the doorway.

"Ma, it's okay," Levi said in a trembling voice. "It's just me and Kat."

"Don't listen to them, Mom!" screeched Regina. "They're robbing us!"

"Quiet, Regina," said Mrs. Galante. "They're just kids."

"Ma," continued Levi. Panic was creeping into his voice. "Please, Ma!" He looked into his mother's eyes, and his stomach dropped. He saw no anger—what he saw was much worse.

"Ma," he whispered. "Please. It's me. It's Levi."

Her brow creased. "I think there's been a mistake. You have the wrong house," she said at last. "But we'll sort this out. I'll call the police and we'll get you home."

Levi felt the world swimming away from him.

A hand grabbed his sleeve. "We gotta get out of here," hissed Kat. She turned to run, pulling him along with her, and then they were racing out of the kitchen.

Out the front door . . .

Down the sidewalk . . .

Past the rows of houses and the manicured lawns . . .

Until they reached the overgrown field
at the edge of the woods.

Levi collapsed in the wet morning grass.

"The memories!" said Kat as she paced in frantic little circles around the old car. "I shoulda known!"

"We've got to go back!" sobbed Levi. "We'll explain the whole thing! My mom will believe us!"

"Don't be stupid!" snapped Kat. "They were calling the cops. You're a stranger to them now! Same thing as Twila." She paused. "No. Not the same as Twila. It stole your stuff and it stole your family's memories of you, but, thanks to me, it didn't get *you*."

"Wish it had. Might've taken me to Twila."

Kat stopped pacing and turned on him. "That's crazy talk! We want to fight this thing, not bow down to its will!" She chewed her lip. "We need a new plan."

"Where are you going?"

"To my house. It got my camera and rocket, but I have more weapons. The war is just beginning."

Levi lingered in the field for a moment, his mind still spinning. Then he took a deep breath, shook himself, and started after Kat.

Chapter 17: BOMBARDed

"This is your house?"

"Yeah."

"It's big."

"I guess. So?"

"Nothing." Levi realized he had never been to Kat's house before.

"Wait out here," said Kat. "My parents don't know you. I'll tell them you're coming over to work on a project." She saw the worried look on his face. "Just stay by the street and try not to draw attention."

She ran up the walkway, fished a key from under a flowerpot, and disappeared into the big house. A minute of quiet passed, and then a storm of screams and shouts erupted from within. The front door burst open and Kat sprinted across the lawn like a squirrel with its tail ablaze. A woman and a very angry man appeared in the doorway.

Kat reached the sidewalk and gave the dumbfounded Levi a shove. *"RUN!"* she screamed.

The houses blurred past them, and the man's furious threats grew distant. They rounded a corner and ducked behind Archer's Mini-Mart. For a minute, the only sound was their breath.

"Who was that guy?" gasped Levi.

Kat's eyes were huge in her pale face. "My dad," she said in a faint voice. "It happened to me, too."

"What?"

"My parents don't know me. They thought I was a home invader. And my room was empty. All my stuff is gone."

Kat sank to the ground. She suddenly looked very small and very afraid. Levi sat next to her. He thought about putting his arm around her shoulder, comforting her, but that didn't feel right.

"They seemed really . . . mad," said Levi.

Kat gave him a sideways look. "Of course they were mad. They thought they were being robbed."

"Oh," said Levi. He wiped sweat from his brow. "Your dad looked like he was going to murder us."

"He's not normally like that!"

"Okay."

"This is worse than I thought," said Kat. "That thing knew I was helping you. That's why it stole my life too. We need to figure this out. Fast."

Levi nodded.

They sat for a long time and watched the morning shadows ooze across the mini-mart's back parking lot.

"I feel sick," said Kat at last.

"Me too," said Levi.

"No, seriously, if I don't eat something, I'm going to pass out. And I can't think on an empty stomach." She stood and started for the mini-mart's entrance. "I'm getting some brain food. Want anything?"

Levi shook his head. His appetite had disappeared with Twila.

He leaned against the brick wall and watched as the day warmed and the neighborhood filled with the sounds of cars and lawnmowers and playing children. A familiar tinkling approached, and children and adults alike poured from their homes as the ice cream truck rounded a corner.

He stared longingly at the people lining the streets as they chatted and laughed and savored their frozen treats. Last weekend his life had been just as sweet and simple, though he hadn't been aware of it at the time. The thought made his stomach clench.

Kat reemerged from the mini-mart with a granola bar, a Slynderfell-brand ice cream-sicle, some beef jerky strips, and a newspaper. Levi accepted the granola bar. He wondered briefly how Kat had acquired the food—she didn't seem to be carrying any money—but decided that was one mystery he didn't care to have answered.

"Aaaand I got more than just munchies," said Kat as she flourished the newspaper and pointed to an article. "Ta-da! A clue!"

The Cowslip Grove Examiner

FIRST COPY FREE, ADDITIONAL 25¢

VOL. XCI

Garman Farm Sheep Killed by Unidentified Predator

C. KOLCHAK
STAFF WRITER

Three sheep have been found dead over the course of a week at Garman Farm. The bodies were examined by livestock specialist Andrew McElfresh, who reported distinct bite marks on the jugular veins. Further examination by Brockleport University's biology department confirmed that the sheep had been drained of at least 50 percent of their blood.

McElfresh compared the killings to similar reports in southern states, attacks attributed to the "Chupacabra," an animal commonly considered a modern legend.

Ralph Garman had this to say: "If I catch any person or beast snooping around my property, I'll shoot them in the badonga [sic]."

"First kids disappear; then sheep die mysteriously at night. Don't you think that's a strange coincidence? Especially in Cowslip Grove?"

"But people remember the sheep. No memories were changed. It was probably just coyotes."

"Coyotes? Levi, their blood was drained!" Kat's voice had recovered its usual zest. "Look, it's our only lead. Garman Farm is less than a mile from here. I say we investigate. We'll go after sunset, when the farmer won't see us. We'll just have to keep a low profile in town until then."

Levi nodded and forced a smile. The wait until sunset was going to be an eternity. He couldn't decide if that was a good thing or a bad thing.

Chapter 18: Goatsucker

"Do you think we should move closer?"

"Heck, no! Stealth is our motto tonight! Don't want to get spotted by farmers. Or monsters."

They were crouched on the edge of a brambly copse overlooking the Garman Farm pasture. Above them, a toenail of moon struggled to break free from the clouds.

With them was a cache of equipment—a loaded tranquilizer-dart launcher, a flashlight, a harness, a muzzle, a leash, and a carrier cage. They'd stolen—*borrowed*—all this from Mr. Jess's shed. Mr. Jess, who lived near Kat's street, worked for Animal Control.

Levi had been reluctant—the nocturnal stranger would hardly be intimidated by muzzles and animal carriers. But Kat had insisted it was better to take it all and be overly prepared.

And now they
waited. The shadows
were dark and the
breeze had a bite,
and every now and
then, a branch groaned
and they'd whip their heads
around, expecting to see a looming
figure stepping out from the trees.

Levi shivered and tucked his hands
into his jacket. He wondered if the stranger was
searching for them, stalking the empty streets on spidery legs.
He wondered if it was safe to be sitting next to Kat Bombard
while she held a loaded tranq-dart launcher.

He wondered about Twila and where she was right now.
Was she alone? Did she know he was looking for her?

He wondered about his mother. Did some part of her sense
her life was wrong, even if she had no memory of her missing
children?

He shook himself and watched the flock in the paddock below. The sheep were restless. The flock spasmed as sheep on the edges fought their way inward. A flicker of movement pulled Levi's eyes away from the sheep.

There—

On the far side of the pasture, sliding noiselessly through the tall grass toward the herd . . .

It's just an animal, he thought. *A fox or—*

The thing lunged at the flock.

The sheep erupted in a wave of confusion and terror, and a runt on the fringe was torn from the mass.

The attacker was small but wrestled its prey to the ground with ease and wrapped itself around the neck.

Stay calm! Levi warned himself. *Remember what Kat said! Gotta be stealthy! Whatever you do, don't—*

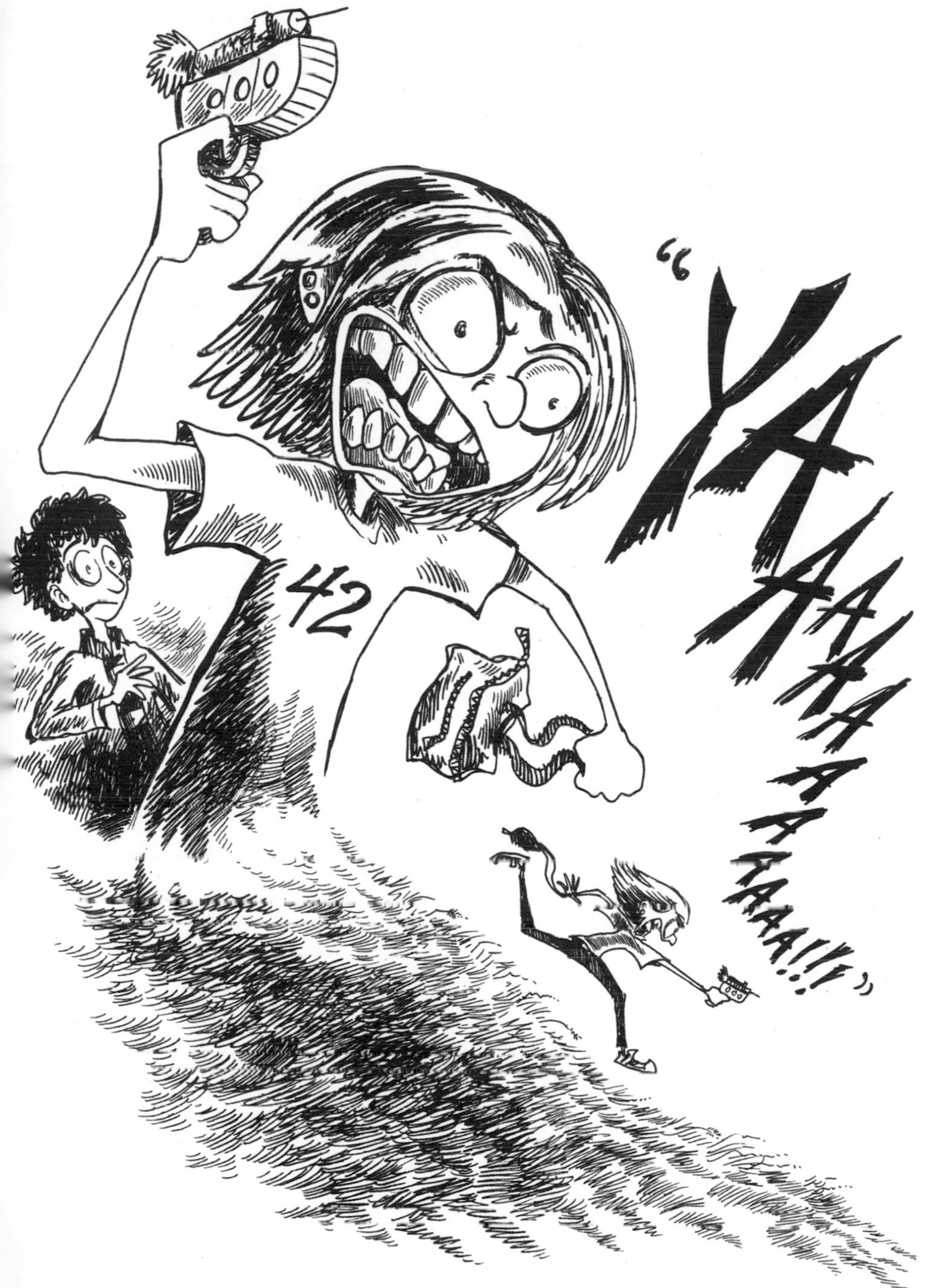
42
"YAAAAAAAAAAA!!!"

The creature released the sheep and
bolted back across the paddock.

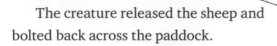

Kat fired the first
tranquilizer dart. It
zinged overhead and
stuck in a fence post.
She cursed and loaded
the second—and
final—dart.

The creature scrambled under
the fence, gained speed, and—

THUNK!

It staggered,

stumbled . . .   twitched . . .

stopped.

Kat approached the still form like a cat approaching a cucumber. "Levi!" she called. "Bring the flashlight and gloves!"

Levi raced to Kat's side and switched on the flashlight. They gasped.

"What is it?"

"A very strange cryptid, that's what!"

"Maybe it's a coyote?"

"It doesn't have fur! Look at its scaly skin! And the spines along its back!"

"A mangy, malnourished freak coyote?"

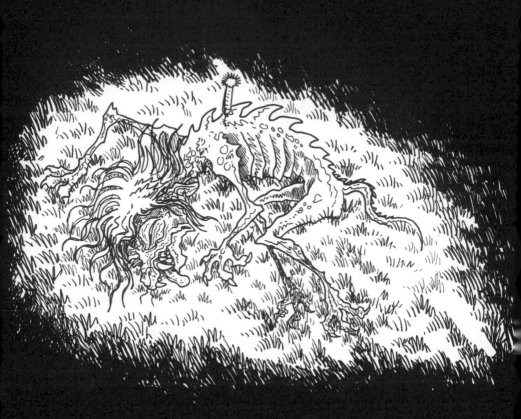

"Oh, shoot! A light just turned on in the farmhouse!"

"They probably heard you screaming! I thought we were supposed to be stealthy!"

"I know, I just . . . Well, I made the shot, didn't I? That was a one-in-a-million shot!"

"What do we do?"

"Pass me the gloves. We're getting this thing to the carrier cage, and then we're splittin' the scene before the farmer takes a shot at us. You can bet he won't be firing tranquilizer darts."

Chapter 19 : Good Cop, Bad Cop

"It's waking up! See? It's twitching!"

There was a flash of green fluorescence as the creature's eyes flickered open. It raised its head.

. . . And threw itself against the metal grille of the cage.

Levi and Kat leaped back as it snapped its jaws, gnashed its fangs, clawed and hissed and spat.

"So!" said Kat, prodding the cage with a stick. "The tranq wearing off? Good, 'cause we want answers!"

The creature curled its lip and snarled.

"Hissy-fit all you want," said Kat. "Won't do ya any good."

"It can't talk," said Levi softly. "It's just an animal."

"The heck it is! It's a sentient cryptid for sure!" She rapped on the cage again. "Talk already, you nasty little rotter!"

"Kat, c'mon, go easy. We can't expect this thing to—"

Levi and Kat nearly did a synchronized backward somersault.

"Let me out, or I will break out and chew your soft, squishy toes off! I will break out and bite off your head-melons and feast on the pink inside-head jelly!"

The creature stopped and panted heavily. Kat gingerly probed the cage with her stick. "You done?"

"I will break out and use your skins as sleeping burrow nests! I will pluck out your stubby finger-claws with my teeth! I will feed on your big fleshy rumplebuffins!"

Kat kicked the cage's grille, and the creature yipped and shrank into a corner. "That's better!" said Kat.

"What *is* it?" squeaked Levi.

"A chupacabra, I think," said Kat. "The legendary goatsucker. Not the cryptid we want, but it may have answers." She clacked her stick against the bars. "Tell us all you know about the missing kids!"

"Kiddies?"

"Right! If you want to keep your creepy skin, you'll tell us everything!"

"Willow eats sheep. Never kiddies! The human-folk would kill poor Willow with fire and traps and doggos!"

"So you know nothing about a certain acquaintance of ours? Tall fellow? Dark clothes? Sneaks through bedroom windows at night?"

"Noooo."

"Liar!" Kat rattled the cage. "We're done playing games!"

Levi looked into the creature's frightened fluorescent eyes, and for a moment all he felt was pity. "Let me try something," he said to Kat. He knelt beside the cage. "Hello," he said in a soft voice. "You can stop shivering. We're not going to hurt you."

"*Might* not hurt you," said Kat. "If you cooperate."

Levi continued: "It's just that my sister has been taken. You don't know anything about that?"

The creature eyed Levi. "Willow does not know your sister."

"What is 'Willow'?" asked Kat impatiently.

"Willow is my name, you goofooligan!"

Kat raised her stick, but Levi waved her back. "Hi, Willow," he said. "I'm Levi, and this is Kat."

The creature shifted, and Levi noticed how thin it was. He could see its rib cage pressing against its stretched leathery skin.

"Are you hungry, Willow?" He reached into his jacket pocket and found the beef jerky strips Kat had swiped from the mini-mart. He broke off a piece and poked it through the bars.

The creature—Willow—slunk forward, sniffed the offering, and snarfed it hastily.

"Oh, great!" grumbled Kat. "Now we're feeding the little brute! We need that food, Levi!"

"I think Willow needs it more," said Levi. "Did that taste good, Willow?"

"Yessss," agreed Willow.

"You can have more," said Levi, "if you'll help us. We're looking for a monster. Not a monster like you, Willow. A scary monster. Tall. Steals memories."

"Nope. I do not know any monsters."

"Fine," said Kat. "In that case, we'll just have to drag this cage back to the farm and leave you for the farmer to deal with."

"NO!" wailed Willow. "He will kill poor Willow!"

"She's kidding," said Levi. "But please, Willow. Think. You really have no idea what we're talking about?"

Willow seemed to consider this. "Willow does know where to find one monster. One BIIIIIG monster."

"Good," said Levi. He offered Willow another piece of jerky.

"But this is a bad, scary monster."

Kat snorted. "Better pluck up your courage, mister, because big scary monsters are exactly what we're looking for."

"Mister?" Willow's eyes flashed with anger. "Is the goofooligan blind?! Willow is a LADY!"

Levi was surprised to find the corners of his mouth twitching into a smile. "Of course. And a lovely lady, too. Right, Kat?"

"Sure," said Kat. "In fact, there's only one thing that could make her lovelier." She stooped, combed through their stolen supplies, and selected the muzzle and harness. "Lady Willow, welcome to the Monster-Hunting Club."

Chapter 20: HECKBENDER

The air was as crisp as the autumn leaves, and the faint pink of morning was seeping over the horizon.

"Go on, Willow," said Kat.
"Lead the way."

It had been a struggle to get the muzzle and harness on Willow. Ultimately it was the threat of the tranq launcher that did the trick. It was loaded with the single dart recovered from Willow's hide, and Levi doubted it would be any use, but the bluff worked, and Willow had reluctantly allowed Levi to fit her with the muzzle and harness.

Now she led them through the twisted trees and spongy soil.

Levi followed, squeezing the leash until his knuckles glowed white.

Kat came last, brandishing the tranq dart like a TV cop.

Finally Willow stopped. "Almost there. Past the lichweed and mumble stones and then you come to a great sink-pool. There you will find Heckbender."

"Okay," said Kat. "You go first."

"No! I would be a shrimpy-munch for Heckbender! It is time for you to let Little Willow free!"

"Nice try, but not until we beat our monster and save Twila."

"You promised!" whined Willow, but she cringed and obeyed when Kat raised the dart.

They crept through mist and over lichen-encrusted stones to the edge of a dark pool.

"I don't like this," whispered Levi. "We don't really have a plan."

"Same thing we did with Willow," said Kat. "Just working our way up the monster ladder." She crept to the pool's edge. "Hello? Any monsters home?"

Willow pawed Levi's ankle. *"Please, Wise Levi, let Willow go! It is not safe!"*

Levi crouched and stroked her spines. "It's okay. We'll let you go soon."

"Monster!" shouted Kat. "Show yourself!"

Levi could feel Willow's body trembling under his hand. "Kat," he said, "this was a bad idea. Let's get out of here."

Kat spun around and scowled. "And do what? In case you forgot, we don't have many options!"

"Kat-hooligan should listen to Wise Levi."

"Shut up, you!"

"Kat . . ."

"You gotta learn to trust my instincts, Levi! I got this!"

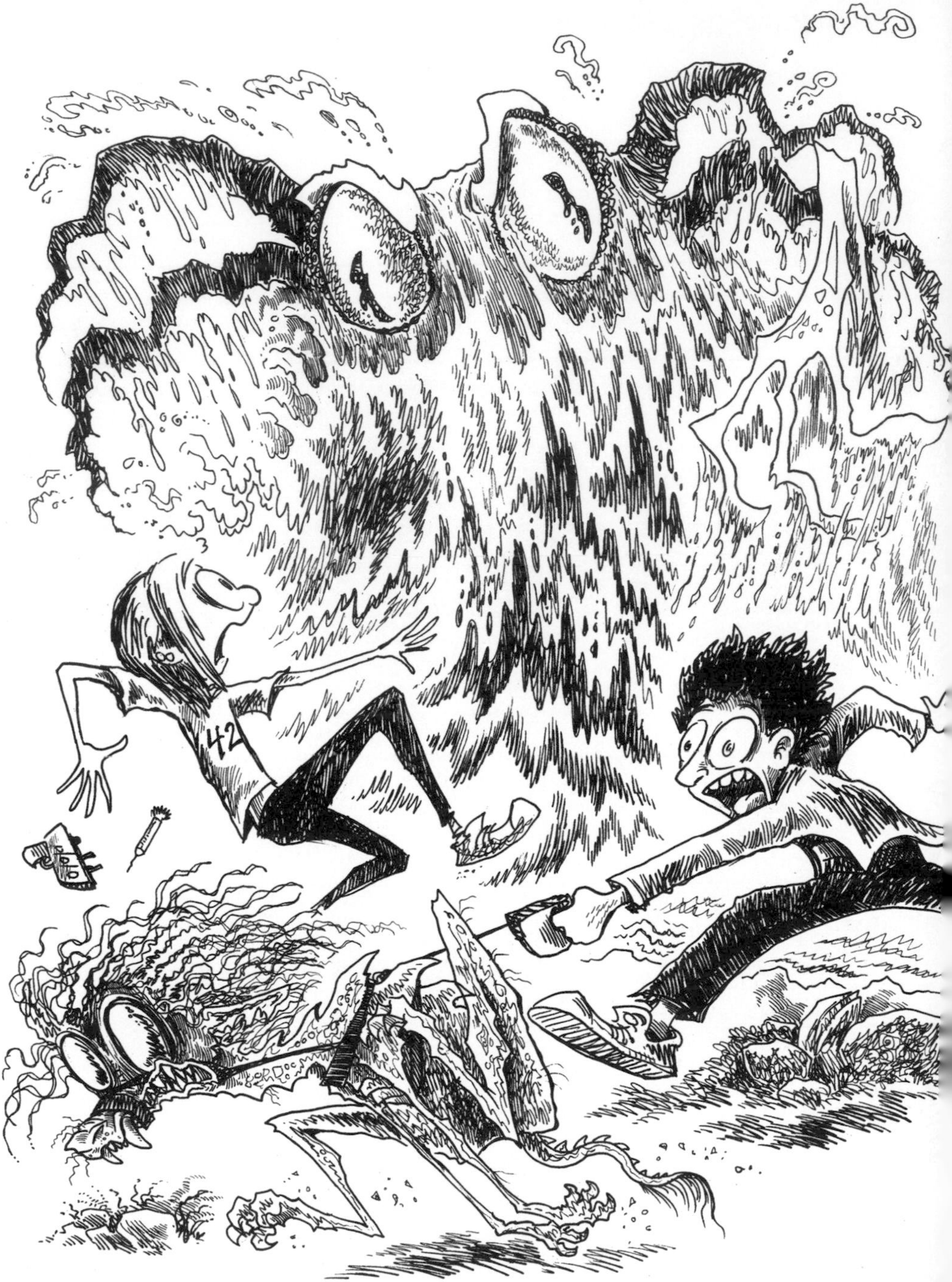
42

Back through the briars and brambles,

over rocks and logs,

behind them the thunder of huge webbed feet.

"Shhh!"

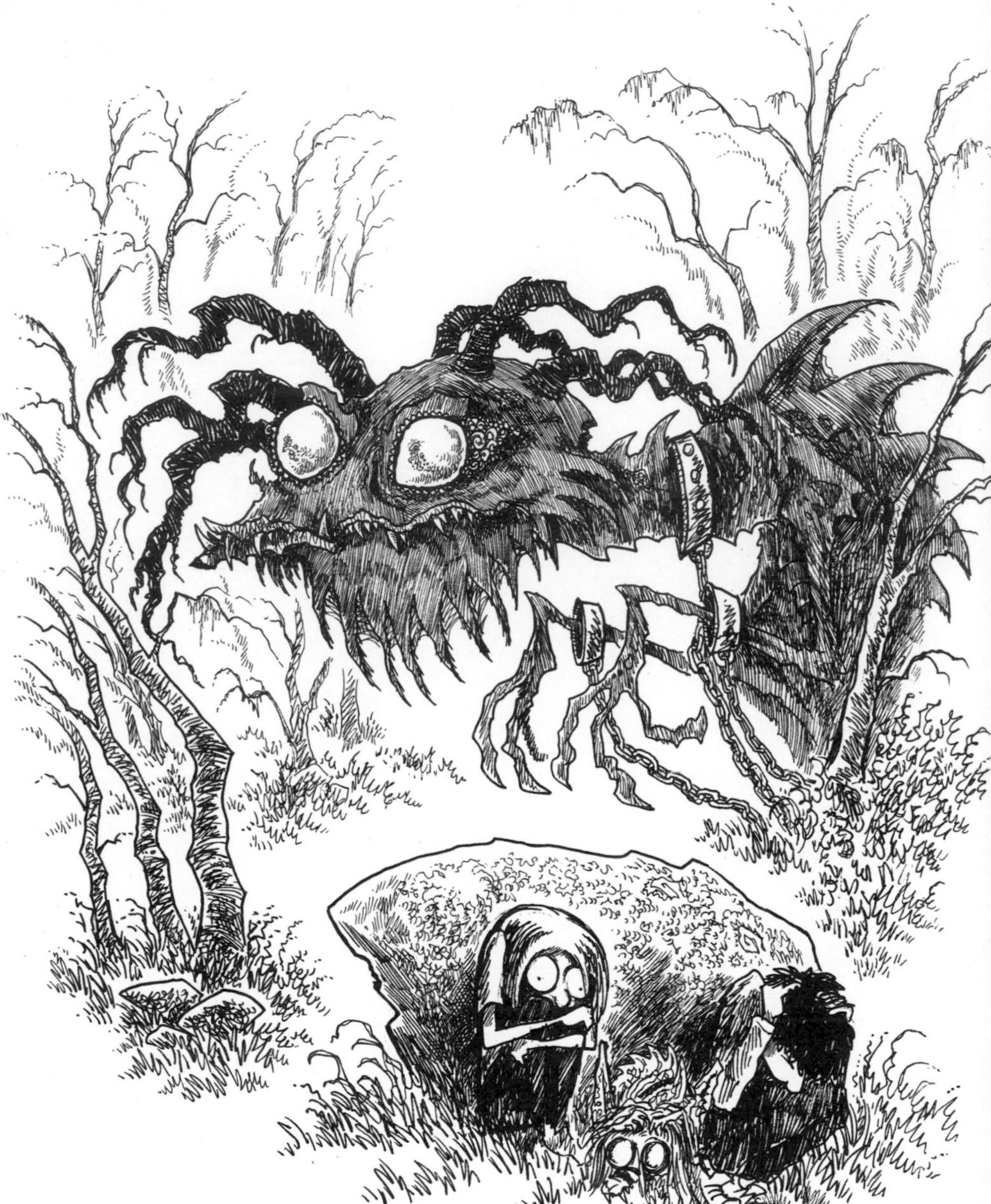

The mist
thinned,

the ground dried,
the day
brightened . . .

171

And then they burst from the woods and into the field on the edge of their neighborhood.

"That . . . that *thing!*" gasped Levi.

"Stupid kiddies!" said Willow. "Willow told you Heckbender is big and scary! We are lucky to be alive!"

"Man!" said Kat. "It had chains around its neck and limbs! Like a big slimy circus animal!" She looked down at her trembling hands. "I lost the tranq. Not sure it would've been any use against that thing, anyway." She turned and saw Levi stalking across the field toward town, dragging Willow along with him. "Levi? What are you doing?"

"What I should have done from the start: going to get real help."

Kat raced to his side. "Aren't you forgetting something? No one knows you anymore! They won't believe your story!"

"So? I'll go to the police. Or I'll go back and talk to my mom, tell her something only family would know."

"Ahem and excuse me," said Willow. "I took Levi and stupid Kat-hooligan to Heckbender. Now it is time to let poor Little Willow free."

"Soon, Willow," said Levi. He didn't want to tell her that he was planning to use her as evidence to support his story.

"We don't know who we can trust," said Kat, struggling to keep up. "Let me come up with a new plan."

"NO!" snapped Levi. He spun around so quickly that Kat froze in her tracks. "I'm done listening to you! You've only made things worse!"

Kat's mouth fell open. "But . . . I saved you."

"Oh, sure, you saved me. After using me as bait for your little trap! Now I'm a stranger to my own family!" The fury in his voice surprised him as much as it surprised Kat. "Then we almost got killed by a giant monster in the woods!"

"I . . . I didn't know—"

"Right! You don't know! You think you do, but you don't!"

"Well, I know more than *you,* you big wimp! You need me!"

"Nobody needs you. You make everything worse. My mom was right about you."

"You've gone crazy, Levi." He couldn't see Kat's face, but the hitch in her voice betrayed her.

"The whole world's gone crazy," he said. "Twila's missing; my family doesn't know me. Boogeymen in the streets, sheepsuckers and swamp monsters in the woods. Nothing makes sense anymore."

A pause. The dry leaves rustled. The tall grass whispered.

Levi gave the leash a tug. Willow whimpered and scampered after him, and Kat followed a moment later.

Chapter 21: The WATCH

"You! Boy and girl with the dog! Stop right there!"

Levi recognized Mr. Lowe and Mrs. Palmer, the neighbors he'd encountered the day he and Kat had rescued the snake.

"I've never seen them before," said Mrs. Palmer to Mr. Lowe. "They fit the description."

"State your names and addresses!" demanded Mr. Lowe.

"Gladly," said Kat. "I'm SpongeBob, he's Squidward, and the address is simply Pineapple Under the Sea."

"Don't get smart with me, young lady!" said Mr. Lowe. "I'm the Acting Vice President of the Cowslip Grove Neighborhood Watch!"

"Chill, Mr. Lowe," said Kat. "We haven't done anything wrong."

"There was a home invasion yesterday at the Bombard house. The perps were a boy and a girl, roughly twelve years old. Sound familiar?"

"In the name of all that is good and decent!" gasped Mrs. Palmer. She pointed to Willow. "What is *that*?"

"Oh," said Levi. "That's . . . that's . . ."

"Our Mexican hairless purebred," interrupted Kat. "Isn't she cute?"

Willow raised her head and glared at them, but thankfully she did not speak.

"It looks diseased!" scoffed Mrs. Palmer.

"I don't see a collar!" said Mr. Lowe. "That's a violation of Ordinance 319: Fraternizing with Unlicensed Animals!"

"We've got her on a leash!" said Levi.

"As Acting VP of the Neighborhood Watch, it's my duty to confiscate this likely dangerous animal." He reached for the leash but jumped back when Willow curled her lip. "That thing tried to bite me! It's rabid!"

"She didn't bite!" stammered Levi. "She's wearing a muzzle!"

"If what you say is true and it's really your dog, your parents can pick it up at the pound," said Mrs. Palmer.

"No!" pleaded Levi. "You can't take her!"

"And you still haven't identified yourselves!" said Mr. Lowe. "You have one last chance to give your address before I'll be forced to make a citizen's arrest!"

"The heck you will!" said Kat. "On what charge?"

"Suspected Home Invasion and Possession of an Unlicensed Animal!" His eyes narrowed. "And Sass-Backing an Acting VP of the Neighborhood Watch."

Kat's face looked firm, but Levi could see her limbs were shaking.

Mr. Lowe's mustache quivered. "Better cooperate. Or I might have to get . . . *tough. Punks!*"

"Walter Lowe!" said a quavering voice behind them. "Lay one finger on those children, and I'll rip that ridiculous push-broom clean off your lip and stuff it up your nose!"

"Mrs. Mushpit," said Mrs. Palmer, "this is a Neighborhood Watch matter. It's none of your business."

"Crab-piffle!" snapped Mrs. Mushpit as she stumped across the street. "When the Watch stoops to harassing my grandchildren, it most certainly is my business!"

"Your grandchildren?" said Mrs. Palmer.

Levi and Kat exchanged baffled looks.

Mr. Lowe straightened and suddenly seemed a lot less intimidating. "And, uh, what about the nasty mongrel?"

"Didn't you hear them, Walter? Or has your mustache grown into your ear canals? It's their darling Chinese crested."

"They said it was a Mexican hairless," said Mrs. Palmer.

"Your rampant eye boogers must be clouding your sight," sniffed Mrs. Mushpit. "It's plainly a Chinese crested."

Mrs. Palmer cleared her throat and tried to recover her dignity. "The Bombards reported a pair of home invaders yesterday. These children fit the description."

"Impossible!" said Mrs. Mushpit. "My grandchildren didn't arrive in town until this morning. But if the police need to start somewhere, I suggest they question *your* charming hooligans, Marybeth."

"*My* kids?" Mrs. Palmer huffed. "My kids are honor-roll students!"

"*Humph!* Seems academic standards slip lower every year," clucked Mrs. Mushpit. She turned to Levi and Kat. "Come along, dears. The Neighborhood Inquisition must resume patrolling the sidewalk for crabgrass and stray animal droppings."

Levi and Kat stood still as statues, too dumbfounded to move.

"NOW!" squawked Mrs. Mushpit, and they scuttled after her, Willow in tow.

"This isn't over yet, Olga Mushpit!" shouted Mr. Lowe. "There will be an investigation!"

"Investigate your head soaking in a bucket of ice water!" called Mrs. Mushpit over her shoulder. She snapped her fingers at Levi and Kat. "Hustle your bustles, you two. You're in danger—and I'm not talking about the Neighborhood Watch."

Chapter 22 : Trust

"Are we really trusting her?" whispered Kat to Levi.

"*I* am," said Levi. "You can do what you want." They followed her up the front walk, carefully avoiding the garden.

A lump on the porch rocker stirred and adjusted its glasses. "Olga? You found them?"

"Obviously I found them! Dust off your wits and peepers, Emmet!" She turned to Levi and Kat. "My husband, Mr. Mushpit. Emmet, meet Levi Galante and Katherine Bombard: former fence wreckers, current fugitives."

"Charmed," said Mr. Mushpit.

Levi looked at Kat and saw her face was full of shock. Then it dawned on him. "You remember us!"

"The Boojum didn't snitch our memories, if that's what you mean," said Mr. Mushpit. "Come inside and we'll explain."

Levi started to follow them indoors, but the leash jerked him back. He looked down and saw that Willow had planted herself at the end of the walk.

"Please, Kind Levi," Willow pleaded, "Willow took you to Heckbender. Then Willow almost got grabbed by the hairy lip man. PLEEEZE—it is time to set Poor Willow free."

Levi knelt beside her. She cringed, but she relaxed when he gently ran his hand along her spines.

"You honestly know nothing about the missing children?" he asked. Willow shook her head. He reached to undo the muzzle. "And you won't bite me when I take this off?"

185

Kat turned and saw what he was doing. "Levi, don't! We need her! I think she knows something she's not telling us!"

"That spindly thing?" Mrs. Mushpit gave Willow a good squint. "Bah! Turn her loose! She won't be any use."

"But we can't just let her go!" insisted Kat. "Maybe she didn't take Twila, but she could be a spy for the monster that did!"

"Don't be a dunder-noodle!" snapped Mrs. Mushpit. "She might be a spy for the Boojum, and she mightn't. Doesn't matter either way. The Boojum already knows everything about you. Let the little cur loose—we've no reason to keep her, and I could do without the odor."

Levi unfastened the muzzle and harness. He expected Willow to bolt, but when the final strap came away, she continued to stand obediently still.

He reached into his pocket and pulled out the last piece of jerky. "For you," he said. "I'm sorry for the trouble."

Willow leaned forward, sniffed the jerky, and took it gently in her teeth.

"Yes, yes, all very tender," said Mrs. Mushpit, "but let's move past the heartstring-tweaking, shall we? We've business to discuss. Dark business, I'm afraid."

Levi followed Kat and the Mushpits indoors. Willow lingered a bit longer. Then she turned and slipped down the sidewalk, away from the ivy-strangled house, away from the quiet neighborhood, to the shadows at the edge of town.

Chapter 23: When the World was Wild

"I won't sugarcoat it," said Mrs. Mushpit. "Your sister was taken by the Boojum."

"By the what?" asked Levi.

"The Boojum," said Mrs. Mushpit. "It also took all the memories of you from your families and cohorts."

"That's what the Boojum does," added Mr. Mushpit. "Steals away children, filches memories, leaves families with false recollections and a vague sense of emptiness."

Levi's stomach lurched. "You mean Twila's . . . Twila's . . ."

"Dead?" said Mrs. Mushpit. "No, no. Not yet, at least. The Boojum has her tucked away in its lair, alive and likely asleep."

Alive. The word alone lifted a great weight from Levi's chest.

"Aye, asleep," said Mr. Mushpit. "But not safe. The Boojum will sap her, feed off her mental energy."

"We saw it!" said Kat. "It came into Levi's room at night! It was tall and shadowy! I shot it with a rocket!"

"Bah!" said Mrs. Mushpit. "That wasn't the Boojum! Just one of its many underlings. The Boojum is fond of rallying the rabble to carry out its bidding while it hides in its lair."

"Lair?" said Kat. "So it's in the forest! I knew it!"

"Don't be daft, girl!" snapped Mrs. Mushpit. "The forest is just a husk of its former greatness, but it's still too wild for a calculating thing like the Boojum."

"But we saw a monster in the woods!" insisted Kat. "This morning! Back by the marsh—something huge and horrible!"

"Ah. That was probably just Heckbender," said Mr. Mushpit. "Pay him no heed. If you stay away from his bog, he won't be a bother."

"He seemed pretty dangerous to me!" said Kat.

"Naturally. He'd crunch your bones to paste if given the chance," said Mrs. Mushpit. "So don't give him the chance. He's a tragic specimen, really. A relic."

"But where are these monsters coming from?" asked Levi.

"Oh, there've always been monsters," said Mrs. Mushpit. "There used to be a lot more of 'em, too. Sadly the world's moved on, been sanitized. No room for anything strange in this modern era. And all that's left are old fossils like Heckbender and miserable stowaways like your little goatsucker friend— eking out a sad living on the edge of existence."

"And the Boojum," added Mr. Mushpit.

"Aye, the Boojum," said Mrs. Mushpit. "But the Boojum is a different sort of monster." She saw the confusion on their faces and sighed. "I see. You're young. Sheltered. Mayhaps we need to start further back.

" Back when the *World* was still *Wild*...

191

People who think the world was made for them have forgotten how it used to be...

A Wild place.

Life. Survival.

They go back a long way.

Not as far back as oceans or stones or magma, but certainly further back than I can remember.

Yet I can recall an earlier time.

A different age.

When the nights were dark and the forest deep and full of what you'd call Monsters.

Teeth and beaks,

claws and talons,

venom and tendrils...

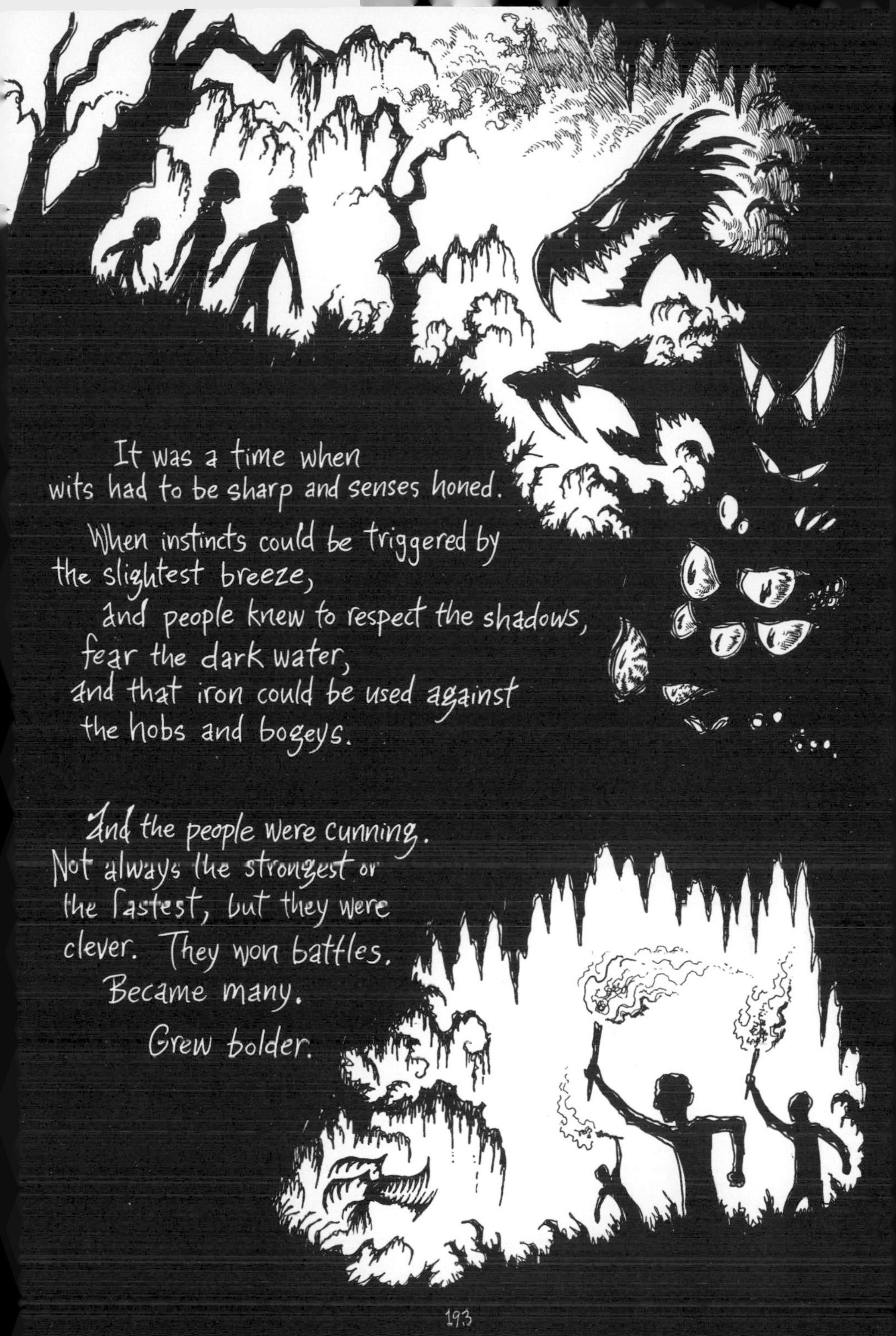
It was a time when wits had to be sharp and senses honed.
When instincts could be triggered by the slightest breeze,
and people knew to respect the shadows,
fear the dark water,
and that iron could be used against the hobs and bogeys.
And the people were cunning.
Not always the strongest or the fastest, but they were clever. They won battles.
Became many.
Grew bolder.

They cut down the forests and drained the swamps and burned the jungles to make room for houses and roads.

They wiped out the most fearsome beasts, and those that remained were tamed and reduced to living plush toys.

Then came the electric lights, exiling the surviving shadows, herding and clipping them to the outskirts of society.

Young minds may still fear the shadows. Perhaps it's instinctual, as if some part of the brain remembers when the darkness ran deeper.

But today the shadows are too shallow for true danger, and the monsters are gone.

Or... Perhaps not.

No one was expecting the *Boojum*.

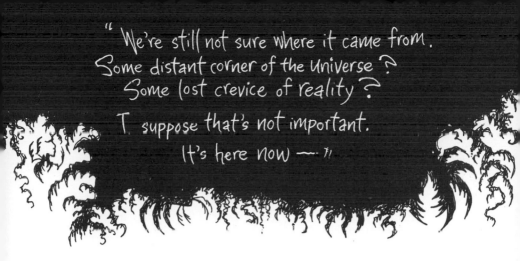

"We're still not sure where it came from.
Some distant corner of the universe?
Some lost crevice of reality?

I suppose that's not important.
It's here now —"

"Funny," interrupted Mr. Mushpit. "The sense of safety and order is likely the very thing that drew the Boojum here. It's like with diseases: a vaccine may wipe out ninety-nine percent of a strain, but there's always that one percent that survives, immune. Then as soon as everyone's let down their guard, it swoops in to fill the power vacuum."

"Don't interrupt my elegant storytelling with your clunky metaphors!" snapped Mrs. Mushpit. She cleared her throat, opened her mouth, then scrunched her face in annoyance. "Ah. I guess that was all I had to say. Never mind."

"Okaaay," said Kat. "But you still haven't told us what the Boojum *is*."

Mrs. Mushpit's beady eyes flashed. "Didja not hear a word I just said? It's the one monster that thrives in safe, sleepy suburbia!"

"But what does it look like?"

"Hmm. There's the rub," said Mr. Mushpit. "As far as we know, it doesn't look like anything. It's seemingly non-corporeal."

"Weird," said Kat. "But *where* is it? If not the woods, then—"

"Think, girl!" clucked Mrs. Mushpit. "Under your very noses!"

"Don't blame them, Olga," said Mr. Mushpit. "It's not like it's some big scaly monster stompin' down Main Street. It's subtle. Invisible unless it wants to be found."

"But what about Twila?" said Levi. "And the other children? Are they somewhere in town too?"

"Quite likely," said Mr. Mushpit. "Stashed in its lair, where it can feed off the electrochemical pulses their minds produce."

Levi's brow furrowed.

"Well," said Mrs. Mushpit, "you weren't expecting it to chow down on burgers and soda pop, eh?" She paused and sighed. "Have we covered everything?"

Levi raised a timid hand. "Um, I was just wondering why, if this Boojum thing can steal and change memories, why—"

"Why you're immune to the Boojum's trickery? Why you remember what others have forgotten? Yes, that's a noggin-scratcher." She tented her fingers and fixed them with a piercing stare. "Why do *you* think you remember the taken?"

"Because," said Kat slowly, "we are . . . *the chosen ones.*"

Mrs. Mushpit snorted. "That might just be the stupidest thing I've ever heard. You've been poisoned by Hollywood, girl. Don't buy into prophecies, and don't flatter yourselves. Keep thinking. What's something you both share? A trait? An experience?"

"The garden?" said Levi in an unsure voice.

Mrs. Mushpit twitched an eyebrow. "Go on."

"Um, so, both me and Kat got tangled in your garden. We got wrapped in ivy, scratched by thorns, breathed in the pollen. I still have a weird rash." He pulled down his shirt collar to reveal the purple welts on his collarbone.

"Me too," said Kat.

"Hmm," said Mrs. Mushpit. "Our garden *is* different. None of those tacky retail-chain flowers you see in other yards. Our plants go back."

"And plants have a certain magic," added Mr. Mushpit. "Not a spells-and-wands-and-glitter magic. The magic of stars and water and life itself. Something the Boojum can't fully grasp, despite all its cunning and calculation."

"Spider-Man got his superpowers when he was bit by a radioactive spider," said Kat. "We got beat up by a wacko garden."

"An interesting hypothesis," said Mr. Mushpit.

"Aye. So we've identified the situation," said Mrs. Mushpit. "Now we move on to the best possible solution to your problem."

But at that moment, there was a knock on the Mushpits' front door.

149

Chapter 24: VIOLATIONS

"Stay in the back room," hissed Mrs. Mushpit to Kat and Levi.

Both Mushpits shuffled to the door and opened it.

"Hello, Mr. and Mrs. Mushpit."

"Hello, Braxton. Walter. Marybeth," said Mrs. Mushpit. "To what do we owe this visit?"

Kat crept to the side window and peeked outside.

"Can you see anything?" whispered Levi.

Kat went pale. "Uh, nothing," she said quickly. "Just some neighbors."

Levi peered over her shoulder. He saw three people on the Mushpits' front walk. His heart jumped as he recognized Mr. Lowe and Mrs. Palmer. The third was a man who looked vaguely familiar.

"I told you already," Mrs. Mushpit was saying, "they're our grandchildren. They arrived last night."

"You said they arrived this morning!" barked Mr. Lowe.

"If so, I misspoke," said Mrs. Mushpit. "Regardless, they've been with me and Emmet the entire time. They most certainly are not your home invaders."

"We still must speak with them," said the vaguely familiar man.

"Can't," said Mrs. Mushpit. "They've gone back to Nagspeake."

The man pulled some papers from his briefcase. "Fine. But that's not the only reason we're here."

"Oh? Well, I hope you're not after my famous apple coffee cake. Emmet polished that off last night."

"We're here on behalf of the Cowslip Grove Homeowners' Association. As president, it's my duty to inform you that you've violated several bylaws. Let's start with your yard. The plants—"

"Lovely this time of year, aren't they?"

"—do not meet our standards. There's a list of plants acceptable for yard display. These include tulips, marigolds, and three types of tasteful shrubs."

"Bah! Bush league!"

"And your house," said the man. "It's an eyesore. It's covered in ivy. Again, a clear violation of HOA guidelines."

"We've lived here long before those blasted guidelines were set in place by dull-witted suburbanites with too much time on their hands!" ranted Mrs. Mushpit.

The man was still calm, but his face reddened and filled with terrible anger. "Mrs. Mushpit, you don't have a choice."

Levi recognized him now. He'd seen him just yesterday—chasing Kat across his lawn, screaming threats and curses.

"Remember," continued Mr. Bombard, "that I'm also the County Representative and Town Supervisor. Follow the rules, or you'll be evicted."

"It's our home!" sputtered Mr. Mushpit. "You can't evict us!"

"Legally we can," said Mr. Bombard. He closed his briefcase and turned to leave, adding, "You have two weeks to get your property up to code."

Mr. Lowe and Mrs. Palmer nodded approvingly and followed him back to the road.

The Mushpits closed the door and shuffled back inside.

"We try to open their minds," spat Mrs. Mushpit, "help them see the real world beyond their yards, and for what? To be attacked and belittled!" She suddenly looked impossibly old and tired. "It's no wonder the Boojum can live among them and snitch their children without them even noticing. And Braxton Bombard is the worst of them all. A cruel, shallow bully."

Levi watched Kat from the corner of his eye. She had her arms behind her back to hide her trembling hands.

"Let it go, Olga," said Mr. Mushpit.

"No, I will not let it go, Emmet! We were better off when the world was wild. The *old* monsters knew how to keep people in shape."

"Olga, please!"

"Let the Boojum take 'em all! Especially that two-faced warthog Braxton Bombard!"

Kat turned, stalked across the room, and disappeared out the back door.

"He's her father, Olga. Remember?" said Mr. Mushpit quietly.

"Ah, yes," said Mrs. Mushpit. "Seems my tongue is looser than an eel in a stork's gullet."

Levi stepped out the back door. Kat was sitting on the porch, picking at the splintered wood.

"You okay?"

Silence.

Somewhere in the overgrowth, a cicada trilled.

He sat down beside
her and drummed his
fingers on the wood. In the garden,
a katydid rasped.

"Getting chilly," he said. He'd noticed Kat's arms
were shaking. He pulled off his jacket and offered
it to her. "I don't need this. I got a sweater
underneath."

Cicada trilled.

Katydid rasped.

Kat took the jacket
and slid her arms into it.

Levi plucked at a vine that was twining up from between the wooden planks. "I'm sure your dad's a nice guy once you get to know him."

Cicada trilled.

Katydid rasped.

Cricket chirped.

"I haven't seen my dad for a long time," he added. "Don't even have his number." He twirled the stray vine around his finger and wondered how far the Boojum's power reached. Would his dad remember him? Did it matter?

The back door squealed open. Levi jumped, and the vine between his fingers snapped.

"Are you kids hungry?" asked Mr. Mushpit.

"We're making sandwiches."

"Thank you," said Levi, tucking the severed vine into his pocket before Mr. Mushpit could see it.

"Wait," said Kat when Mr. Mushpit turned to leave. "We never talked about our next step. How do we fight the Boojum?"

Mr. Mushpit paused. "The next step is getting you two as far from Cowslip Grove as we can."

"*That's* your big plan?" said Kat. "To run away? But our families are here!"

Mr. Mushpit's face quivered. He was struggling for words.

"Mrs. Mushpit is right," he said at last. "Perhaps the world needs monsters. But the Boojum . . . there's something not right about the Boojum. The way it takes people, leaves no trace, no memories.

"Perhaps that's less painful than the alternative. But sorrow, grief . . . that's part of what makes you human. Taking it all away, it's like plucking the wings off a butterfly and setting it free again." He sighed. "I guess that's why Olga and I want to do something. We just don't always know what that something should be."

Cicada trilled.

Katydid rasped.

Cricket chirped.

A stomach growled.
Levi wondered if it had
been his own stomach.

"We'll talk more over lunch."
Mr. Mushpit shuffled back inside.
Levi and Kat sat on the porch a bit longer,
listening to the insects and watching the garden.

Chapter 25: Out of the Night

"Psst! Levi!"

Levi's eyes fluttered open and looked around blankly. After a moment, he remembered where he was: the Mushpits' house.

"We must've nodded off after lunch," said Kat. "It's dark out now." Her eyes were wide and anxious. "I think I heard something outside."

Levi sat up and looked out the window. The sky had dimmed to a deep purple.

"We should wake them," said Kat, nodding to the Mushpits. "In case Mr. Tall, Dark, and Creepy pays a visit." She gingerly tapped Mrs. Mushpit on the shoulder. "*Psst!* I heard something outside."

Mrs. Mushpit did not move.

"C'mon," said Kat. She jostled Mrs. Mushpit's shoulder. "Wake up! It's night!"

A cold shiver prickled down Levi's spine.

Kat gave up on Mrs. Mushpit and went to Mr. Mushpit. "Hey! Wake up!"

Mr. Mushpit did not wake up. Kat pulled back, her lip curling in horror. "They're dead!"

"No, they're not," said Levi, studying Mrs. Mushpit. "They're asleep. See? They're breathing."

"But why won't they wake up?" Kat leaned close to Mr. Mushpit's ear. "HEY!"

Mr. Mushpit did not flinch.

"This is bad!" moaned Kat. "It's like what happened to us when the tall man attacked us in your room! A sleeping spell!"

"Shhh!" said Levi. "I . . . I think I heard . . ."

skritch skritch

They froze.

Waited.

Listened.

skritch skritch skritch

"It's outside!" said Kat, her voice a panicked whisper.

SKRITCH SKRITCH SKRITCH

"No," moaned Levi. "I think it's under the house!"

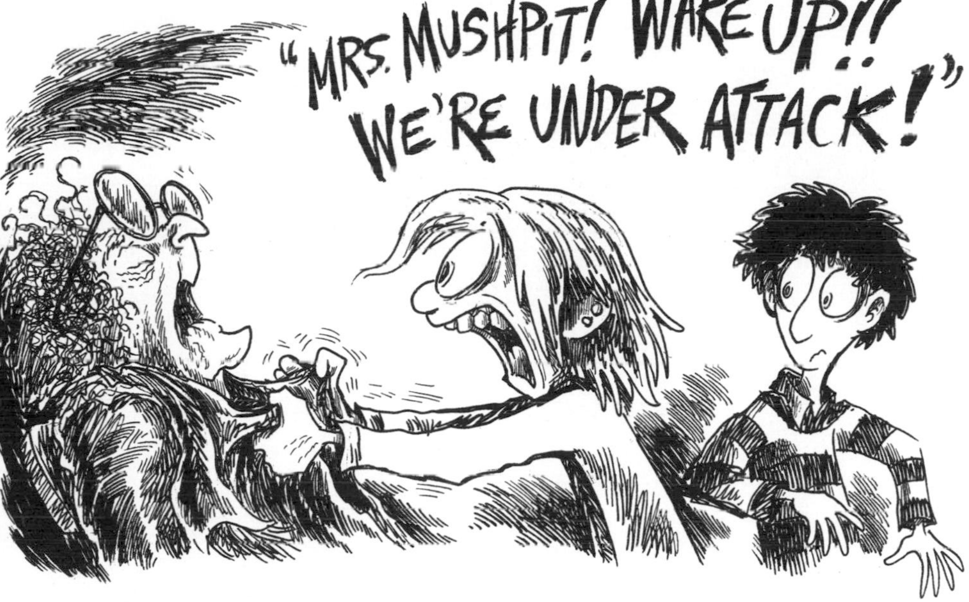
"MRS. MUSHPIT! WAKE UP!!
WE'RE UNDER ATTACK!"

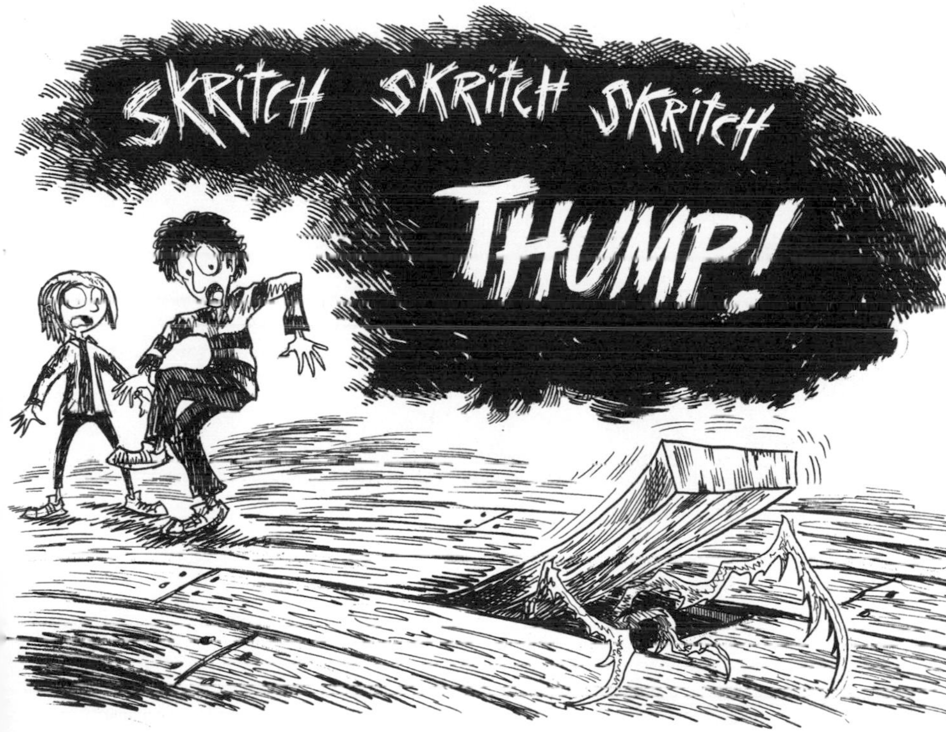
SKRITCH SKRITCH SKRITCH
THUMP!

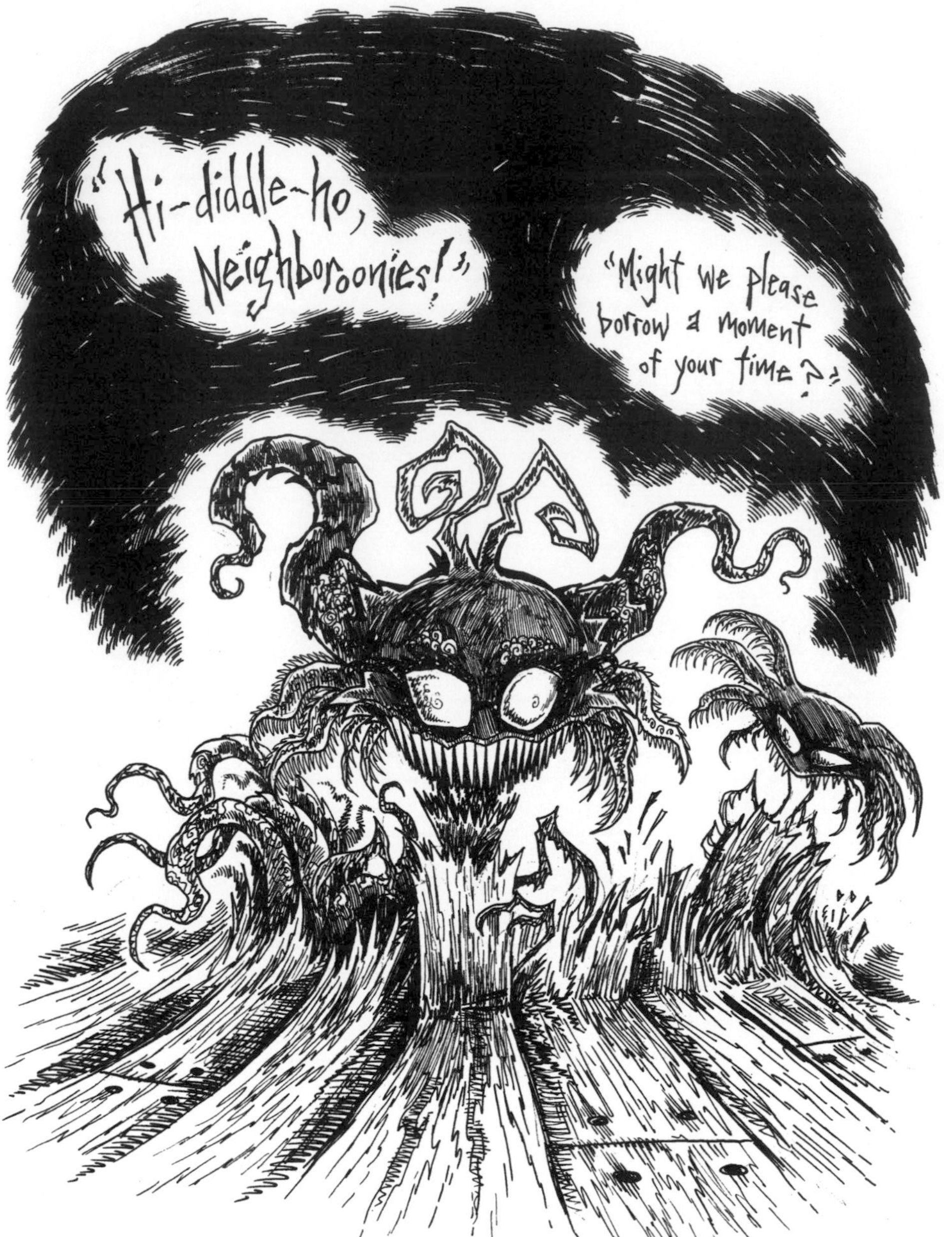
"Hi-diddle-ho, Neighboroonies!"
"Might we please borrow a moment of your time?"

"Wait! Look at the garden!"

The ivy shivered.

The vines writhed.

They looked over their shoulders. The floorboard creatures had not followed them outside into the yard.

"What *were* those things? Not the monster that attacked us in your room!"

"The Mushpits! We can't leave them inside with those creatures!"

But neither of them could find the courage to go back into the house. They stood in the middle of the walk while the overgrowth twisted around them.

"Willow!" gasped Levi. "What are you still doing here?"

"Came back to warn Kind Levi! The Boojum—he wants you!"

"The things in the house?" said Kat.

"No. They are only the Boojum's bogeys."

"Oh, jeez!" cried Kat. She pointed past Willow, across the street. Misshapen shadows skittered just beyond the streetlight's glow. "They're everywhere!"

"They will not come here in the garden. They are scared of the snaggy-plants."

Kat glared at Willow. "You said you didn't know anything about the disappearing kids! You lied!"

Willow cringed. "But you must trust Willow now! The scary tall man is coming! Levi and Kat-hooligan must run!"

Headlights lit up the road, and Willow yipped and shrank back into the shadows. An engine approached. But not just an engine—there was also a tinkling, musical sound. A song. A familiar song.

"The ice cream truck?" said Kat.

The shadows retreated as the headlights swept across the yards. The truck pulled up to the curb and the ice cream man opened the passenger door. "Sorry, kids. My shift's done." He squinted at them. "You all right? You look like you've seen the boogeyman."

He continued: "You know it's past curfew? If the Neighborhood Watch catches you—"

"We're not worried about that," said Levi. He could still hear the garden rustling and, beyond that, the sound of something chittering in the darkness. He looked for Willow, but she was gone.

"I guess I could give you a ride home," said the ice cream man.

Both Levi and Kat were silent, unsure of what to do.

"No?" The ice cream man shrugged and pulled his head back into the truck. "Suit yourselves."

The truck started down the street. The moment its headlights turned away, the shadows filled with the scritching sound. A manhole cover lifted, and an insectoid limb scratched at the pavement.

"WAIT!" screamed Levi.

The truck stopped. Levi raced to the driver's window. "Can you give us a ride to the police station?" He saw the ice cream man's confused face and added: "There's something bad out here."

"Bad? Here?" The man chuckled. "Okay. Sure. Hop in."

Levi hesitated. He turned and looked at Kat. Their eyes held a private conversation:

Something gibbered from the storm drain next to their feet, and that settled it. Both Levi and Kat hopped through the passenger door, and the truck drove slowly down the road.

After a minute, the chittering in the shadows fell silent. The Mushpits' garden stopped rustling.

Willow emerged from her hiding place behind a shrub and watched the ice cream truck's taillights turn right. Her eyes blinked in the darkened street like troubled lightning bugs. Then she sprinted down the road and across lawns, racing after the truck.

Chapter 26: I Scream, you scream

"What were you doing at the Mushpits' house?" asked the ice cream man. "When I was a kid, people said they were a witch and a warlock."

Levi waited for Kat to respond—she was the talker. But after a pause, he realized she wasn't going to answer, so he said, "Just visiting."

"They'd say Mrs. Mushpit once lived in a house that walked on chicken legs. And Mr. Mushpit owned a magic flute and had used it to drown all the rats and children in a town across the ocean." He chuckled and strummed his fingers on the steering wheel. His fingers were very long. So were his fingernails. They were poking through his latex gloves.

"How far to the station?" asked Levi.

"Less than a mile."

The truck passed under a streetlight, and for a moment, the driver's face lit up enough for them to see the purpled skin around his left eye.

"How'd you get that bruise?" asked Kat in a low voice.

"Space debris," he said, rubbing the discolored spot with a long, bony finger. "I was out for a night walk, and something fell from above. Maybe a piece of the moon." He gave her a friendly smile. "You seem on edge, little lady."

"I guess I'm just a little weirded out," said Kat. "You know, riding in the Mr. Frosty truck. At night."

"Afraid of your friendly neighborhood Mr. Frosty?" He chuckled again. "Of course, Mr. Frosty isn't my real name. Not exactly . . .

"My real name is Mr. Frost.

Rafer Frost . . .

"And believe me, I know what it's like to be lost...
Lost in safe little suburbia...
"So sweet and sunny.
"...On the Surface.
"Which is perhaps what makes it so dangerous..."

A loose thought in Levi's mind clicked into place: the stranger who'd chased him down the street had been whistling a song.

The ice cream truck song.

"I could have put you to sleep with the Mushpits. Could have sent a little tendril of the dust your way at any time."

Levi felt something squirming in his pocket. He thought it was Kat trying to warn him, but no—Kat was sitting rigid in the seat.

The ice cream man pulled a vial of sand from his coat.

"This is the really special mix. Pure sandman formula. Far stronger than the nip of nap I gave the old folk. One little breath and you'll sleep forevermore."

The thing in Levi's pocket squirmed again, and then he realized what it was—the little piece of ivy he'd accidentally broken off while sitting on the Mushpits' back porch.

" It could have been easier for both of us. It would have all been over by now — you'd be dreaming with the Boojum.

Oh, but after the trouble you've caused me, I don't want to make it easy. I really just want to hear you scream.

So please, before you sleep,

Scream for me. "

Kat screamed and grappled with the passenger-door handle.

Levi screamed, pulled the thrashing little vine from his pocket, and threw it at the ice cream man.

The vine latched onto the ice cream man's face and lashed with budding thorns.

The ice cream man screamed.

He let go of the steering wheel and clawed at the attacking vine.

The wheels screamed as the truck skidded off the road. The headlights lit up an old tree.

Metal crunched.

Glass shattered.

Kat recovered first. She whipped off the seat belt and shook Levi. "Levi! You all right?"

"Yeah!" He groaned, only half aware of what was happening.

"C'mon!" Kat found the lock and snapped the passenger door open, hauling Levi out of the truck with her.

They staggered away from the wreckage.

A stone caught Levi's foot, and he fell hard.

Kat rushed to his side and pulled him up.

"Is he following us?" wheezed Levi.

Kat peered into the darkness. "I don't think so. Maybe the crash finished him off. His side of the truck got the brunt of the tree."

Levi moaned and rose to his feet. "We need to go back. He's the one who took Twila."

"Can't go back," said Kat. "He was going to put us to sleep."

"We need to know where he was taking us!"

Kat stopped and stared ahead. "I think we already know."

234

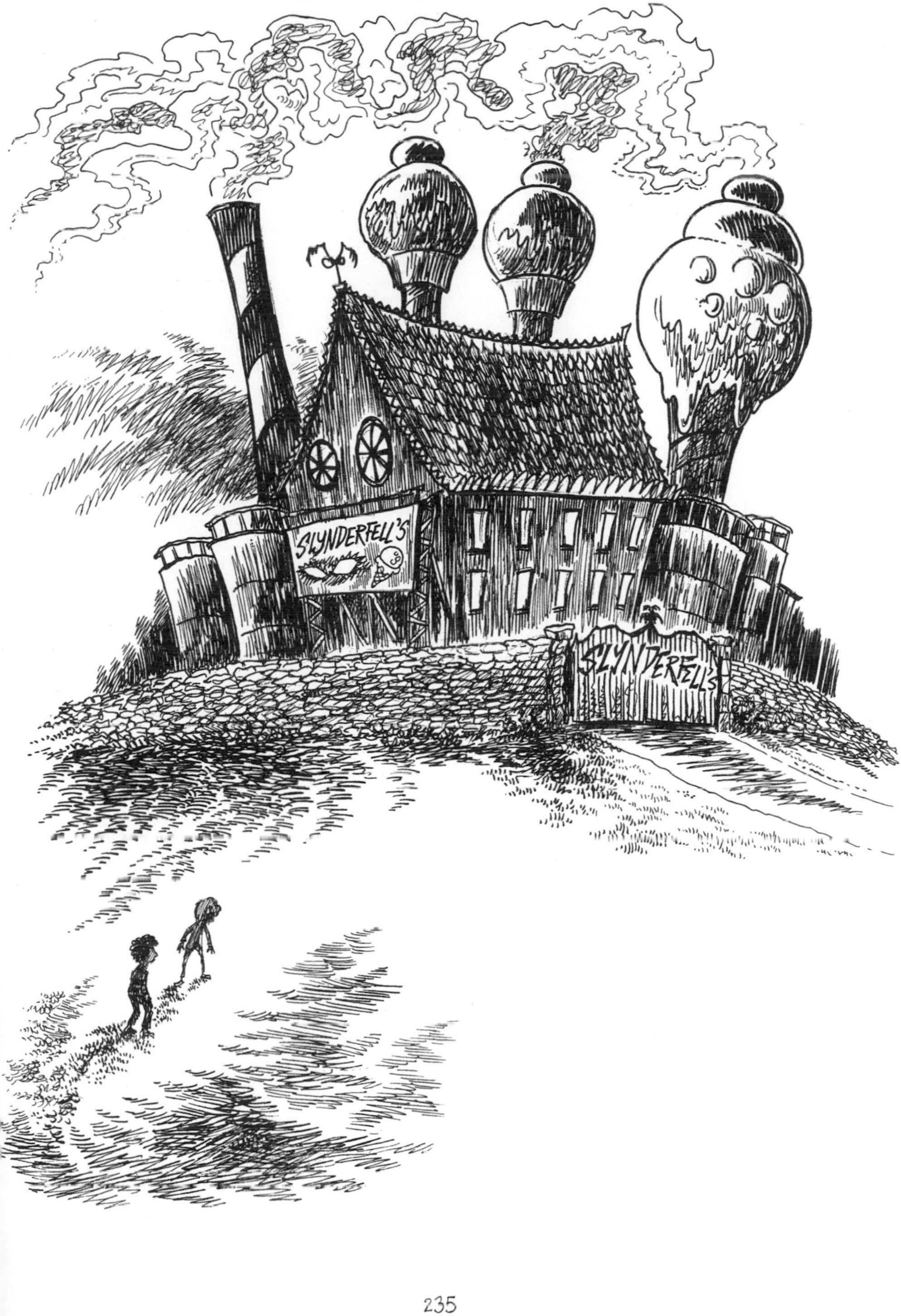
SLYNDERFELL'S
SLYNDERFELL'S

Chapter 27: Following

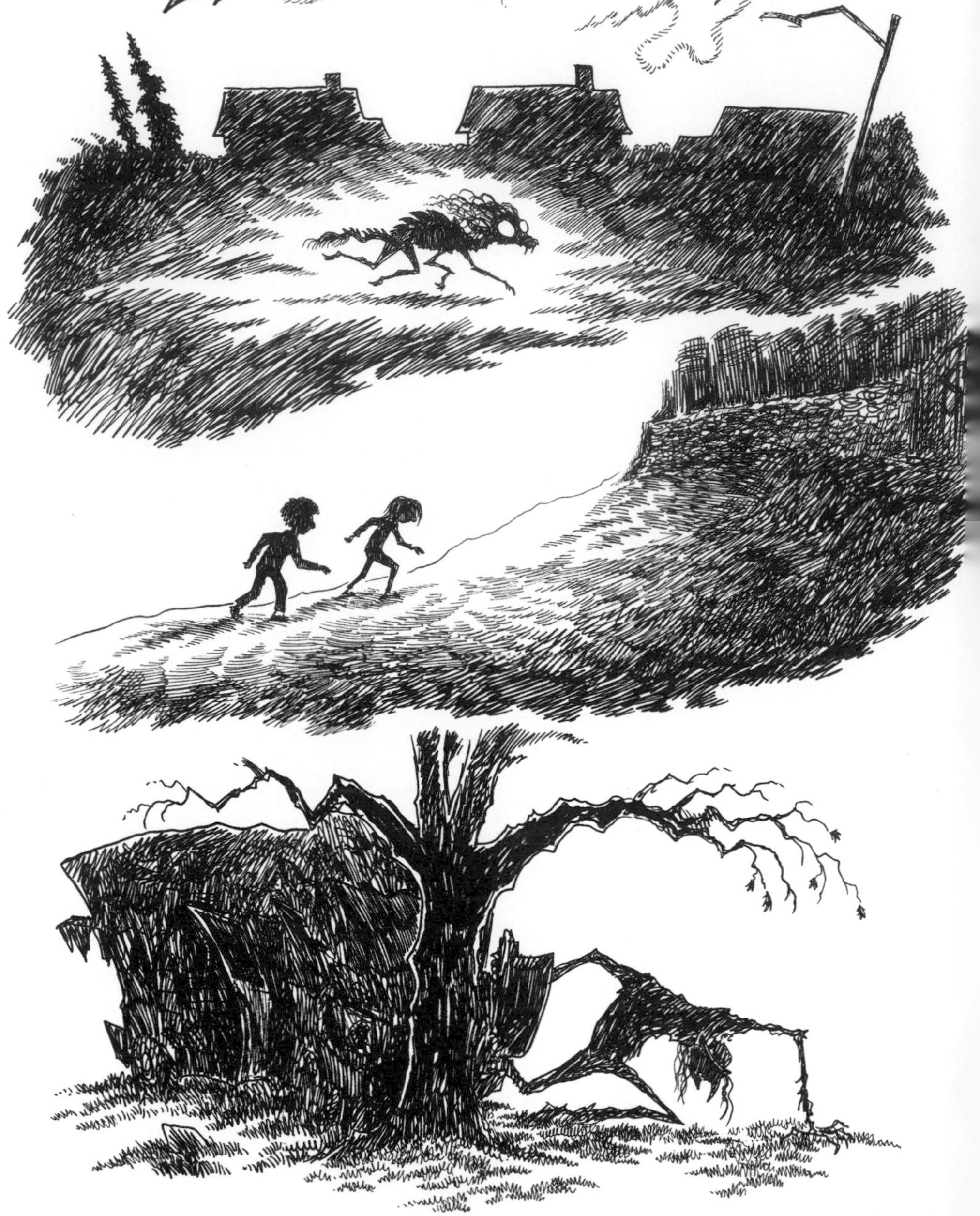

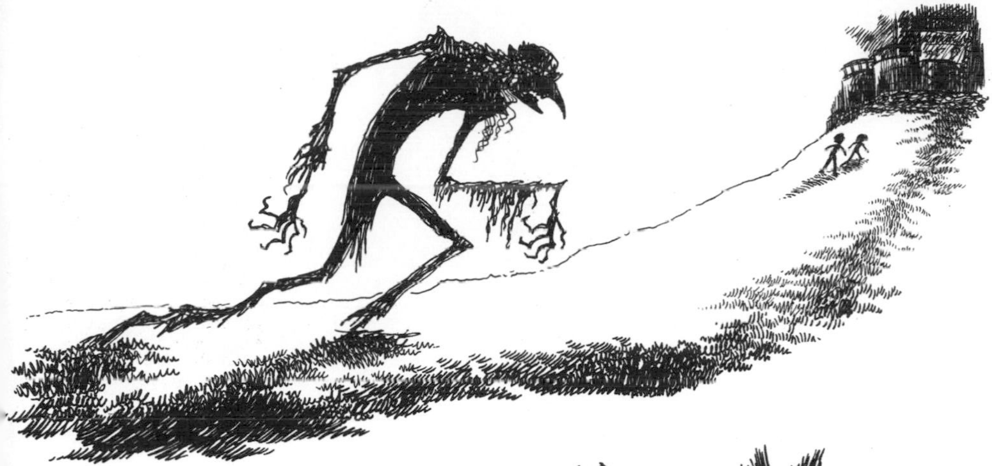

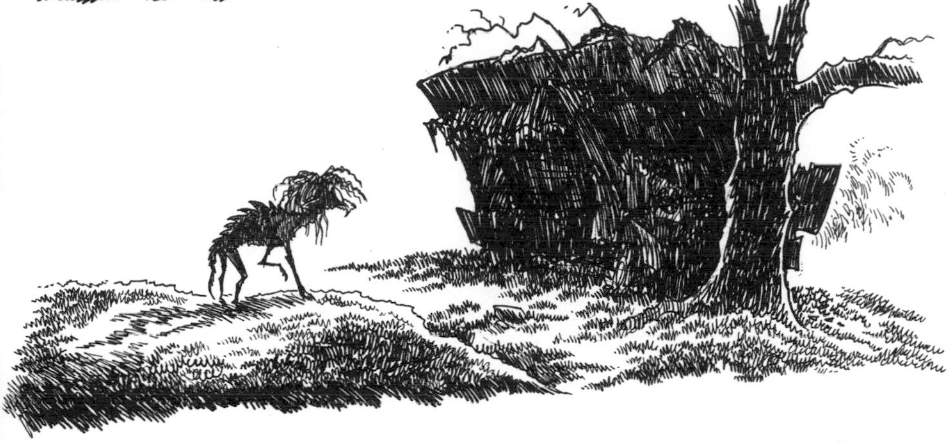

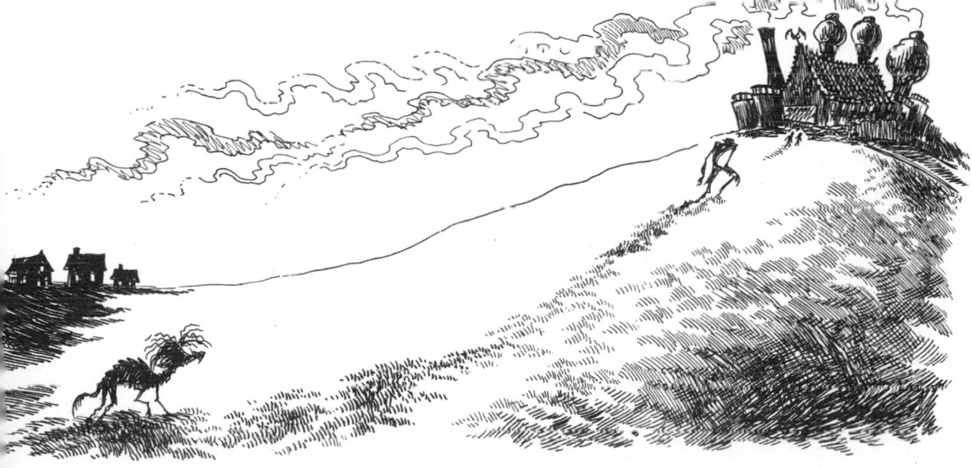

Chapter 28: The Surface

"It's . . . it's . . ."

"Just a warehouse."

They slipped through the loading-dock door and made their way through the warehouse, hiding behind crates to avoid being spotted by the work crew.

"They keep weird hours," said Kat. "And it's cold."

"Of course it's cold. It's ice cream," said Levi.

"There's gotta be clues around here," said Kat, "if this is where they're keeping the missing kids." She started to climb a steel shelf loaded with crates of Slynderfell ice cream cartons.

"Careful," said Levi, pulling her down from the shelves. "If those crates come loose and spill, we'll be buried under twenty tons of ice cream."

They tiptoed through the crate maze, toward the incandescent glow of the offices.

"There's got to be more to this than meets the eye!" said Kat.

"Maybe. But I feel like my mom would have noticed if there was anything fishy."

"Well, your mom didn't notice anything fishy when her own kids disappeared." She looked back and saw the hurt on his face. "Sorry. It'll be okay, buddy. We're close. And after what we just went through, I gotta believe the worst is . . . behind . . . us . . ."

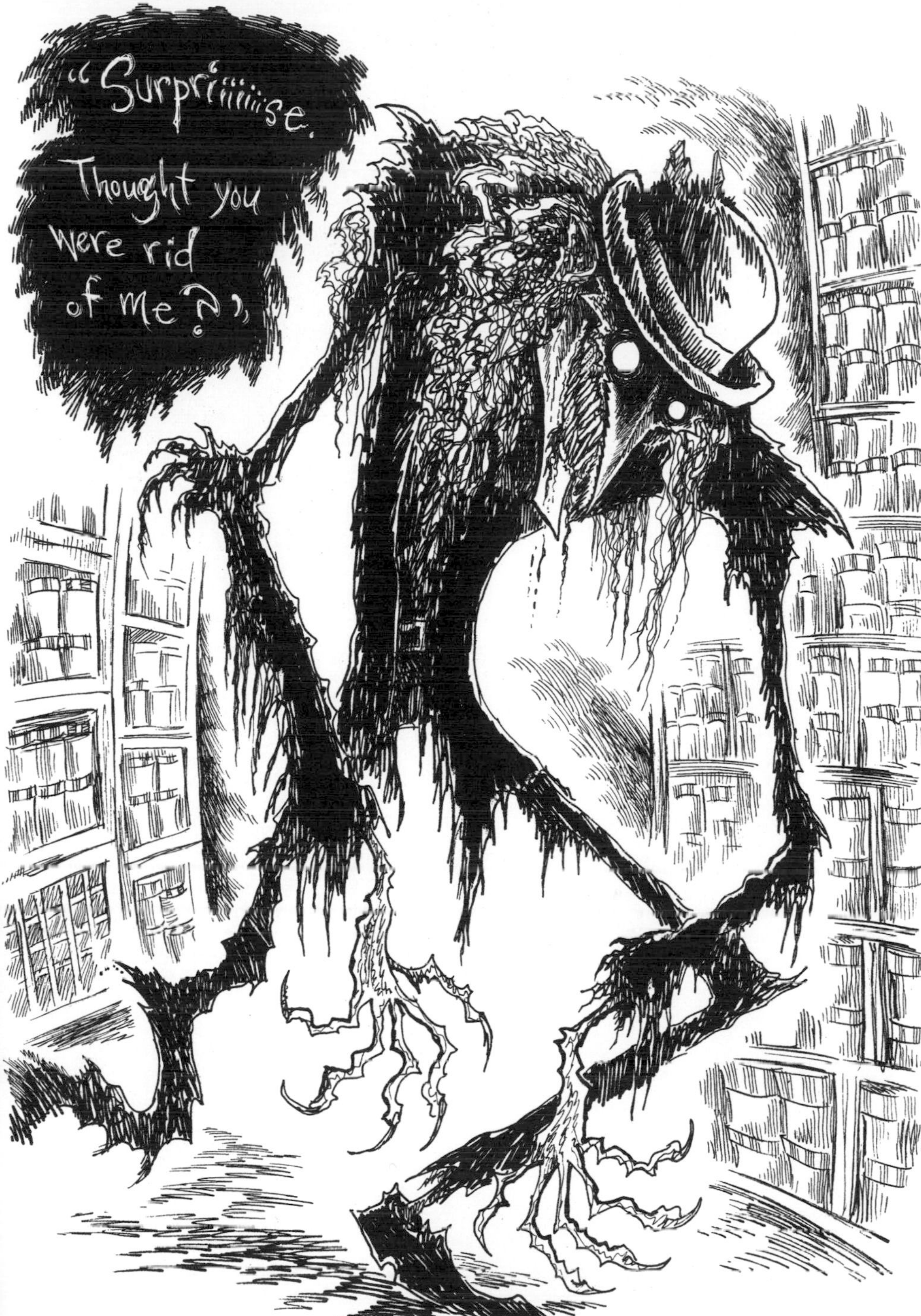
"Surpriiiiiise.
Thought you
were rid
of me?"

Chapter 29: ICED

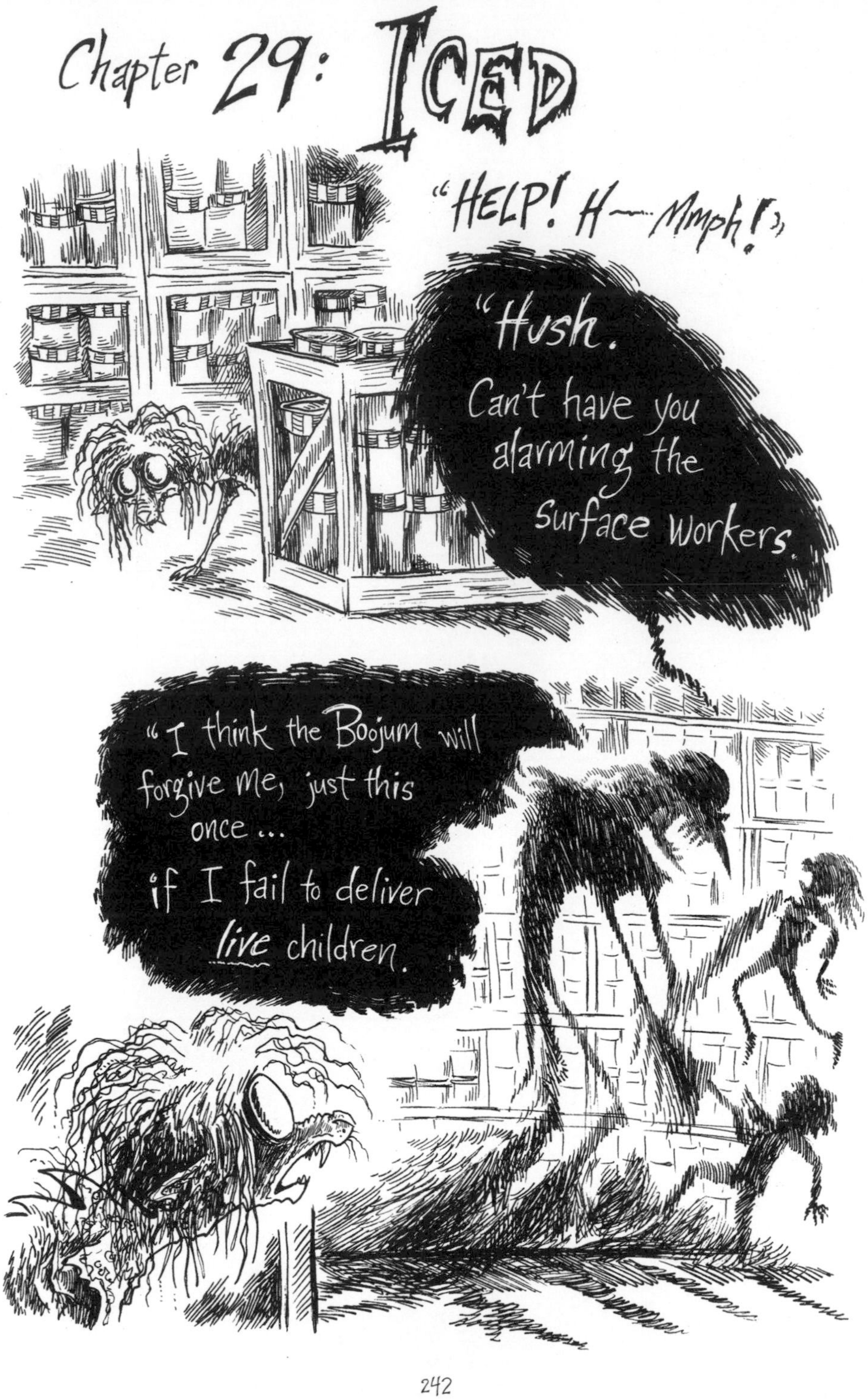
"HELP! H—Mmph!"
"Hush.
Can't have you alarming the surface workers.
"I think the Boojum will forgive me, just this once...
if I fail to deliver live children.

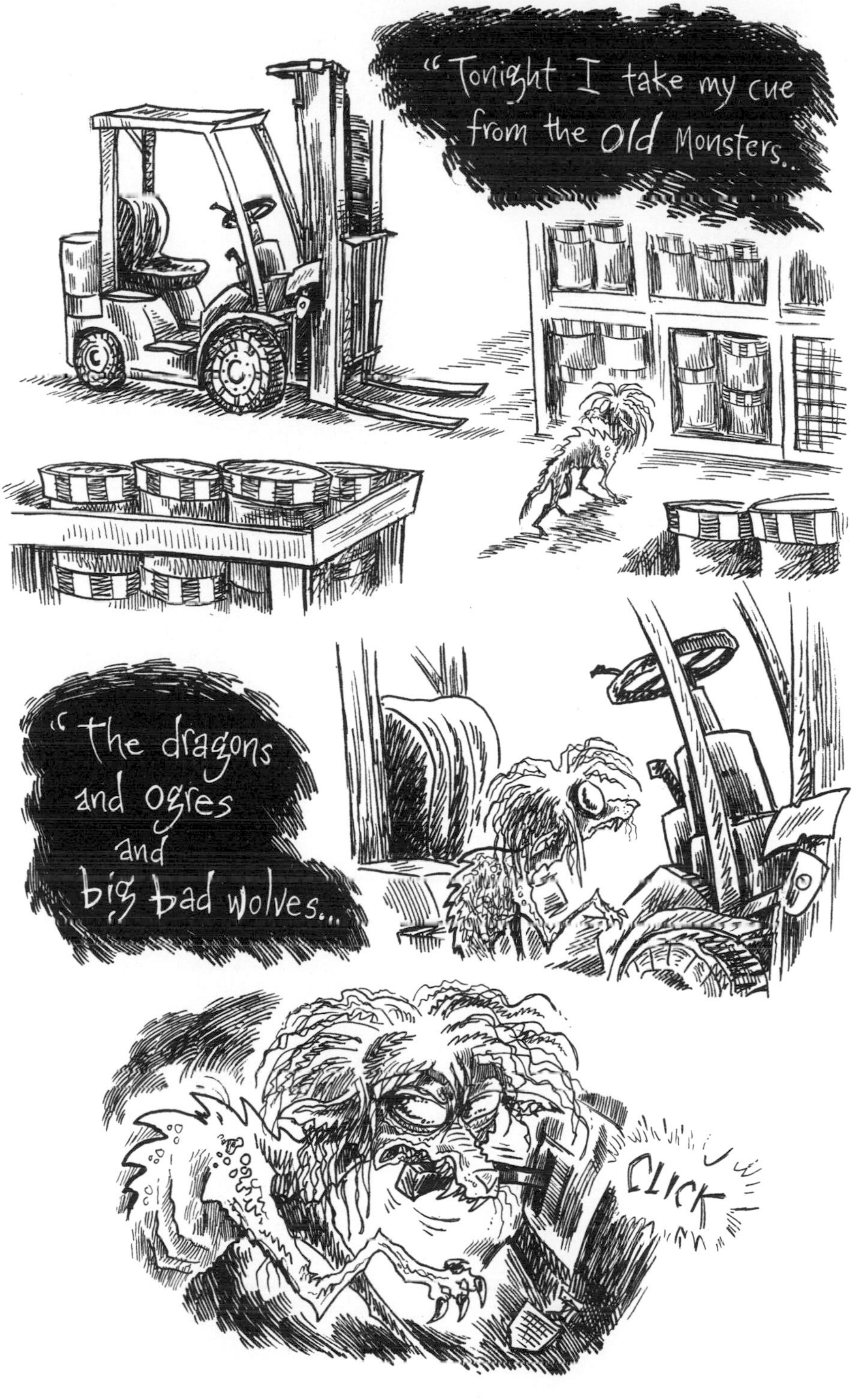
"Tonight I take my cue from the Old Monsters...
"the dragons and ogres and big bad wolves...
CLICK

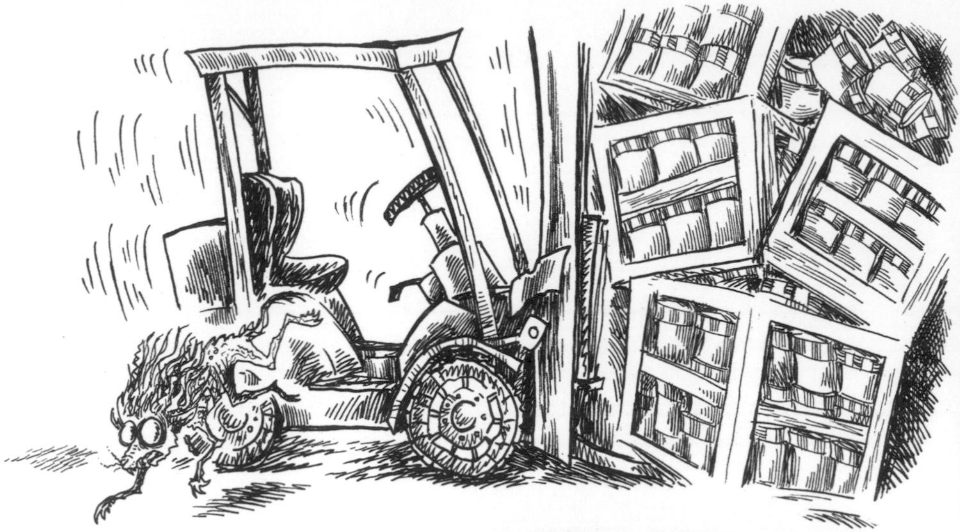

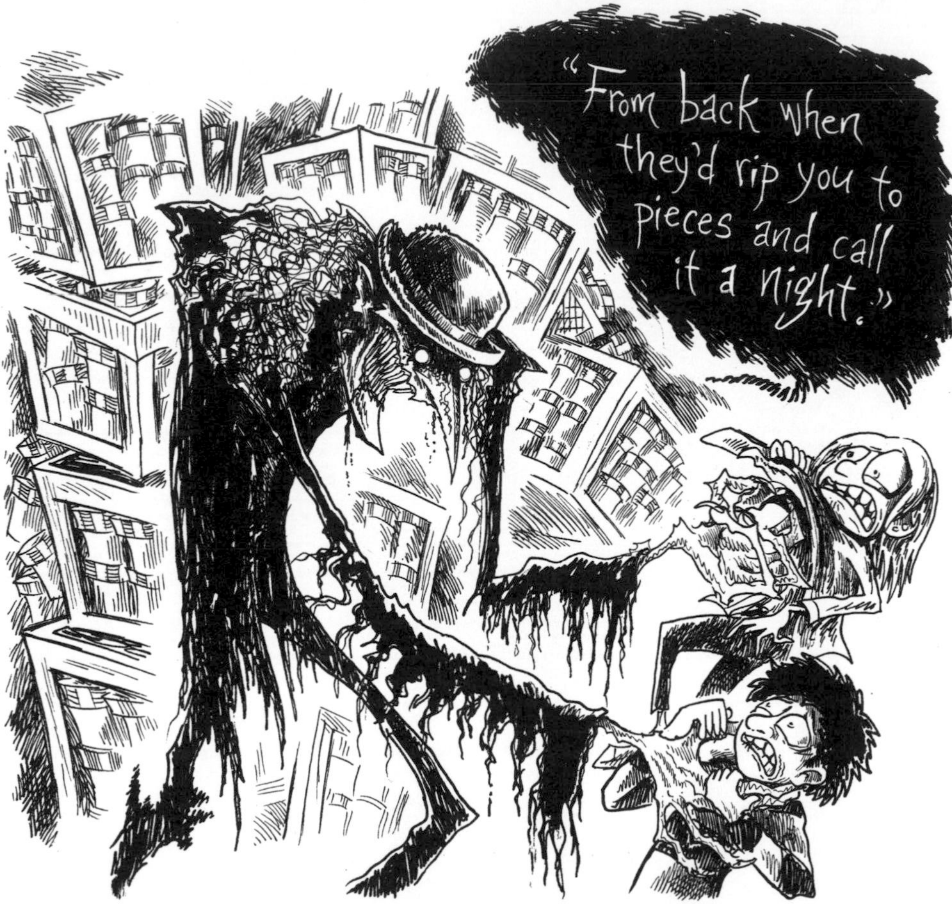
"From back when they'd rip you to pieces and call it a night."

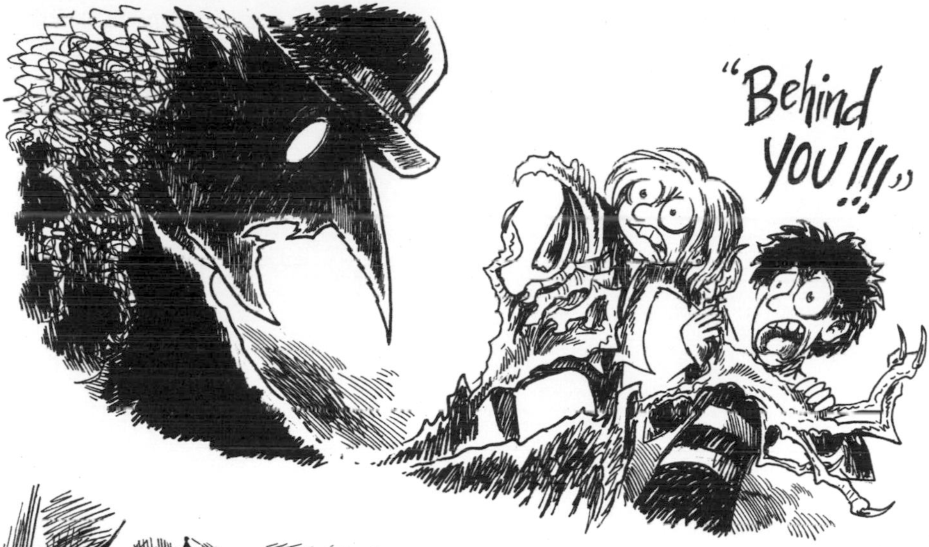
"Behind YOU!!!"

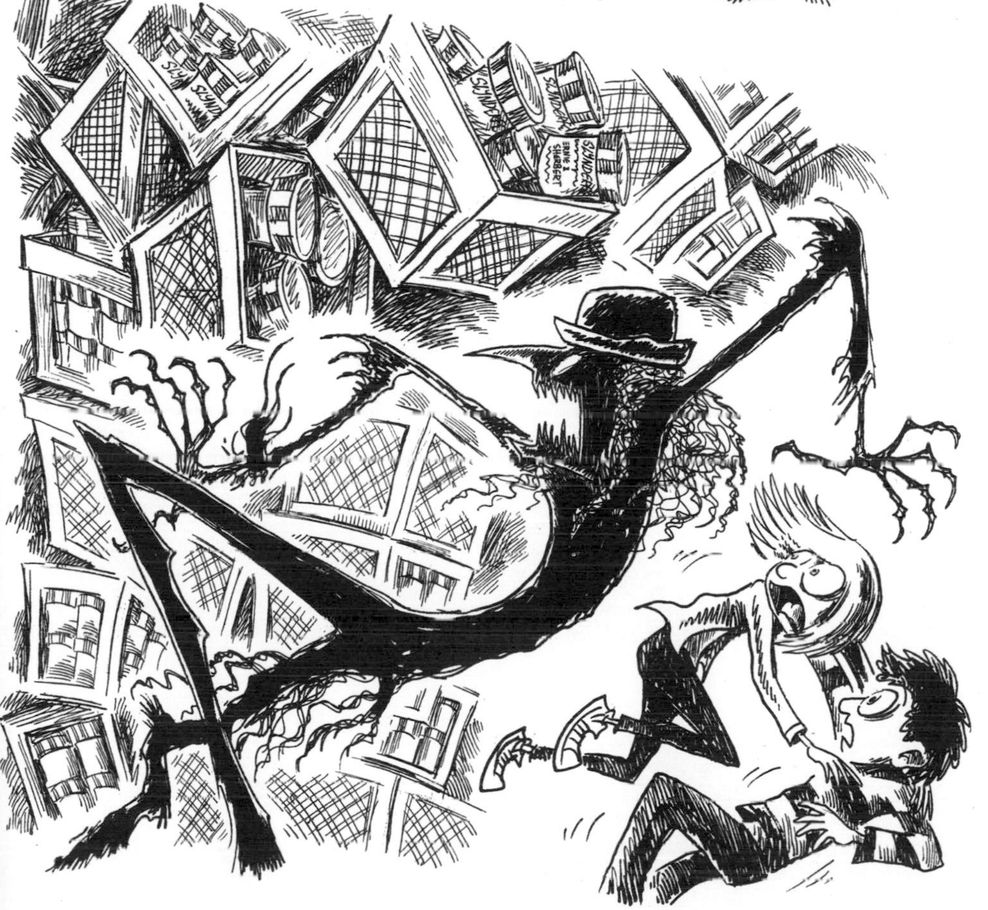
ERNIE & SHERBERT

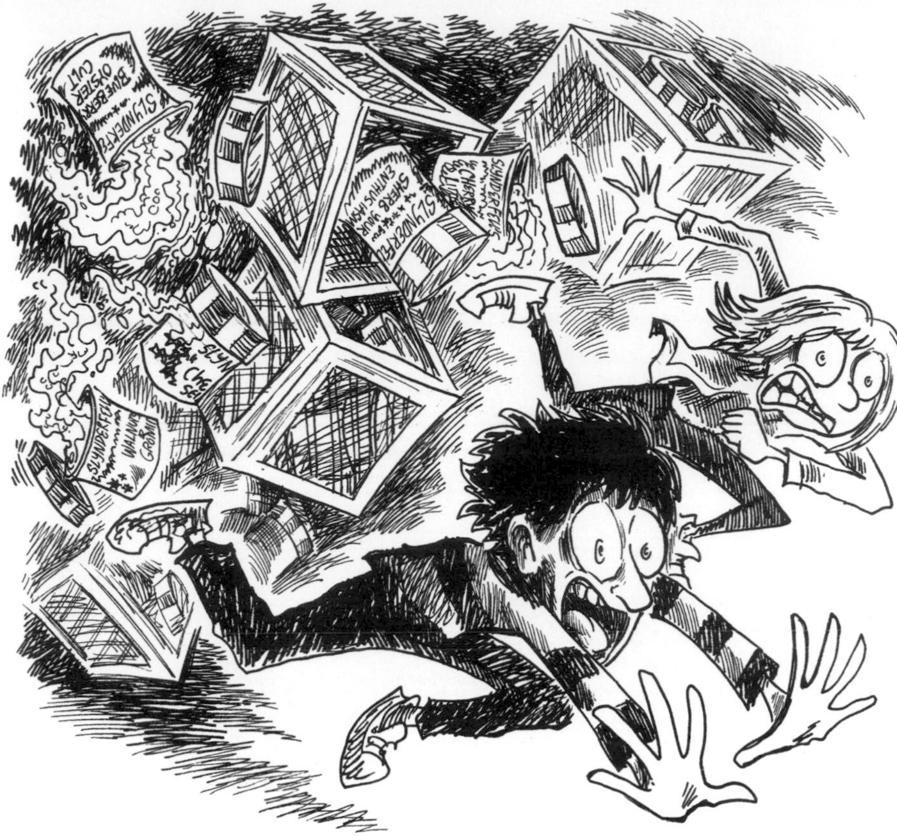

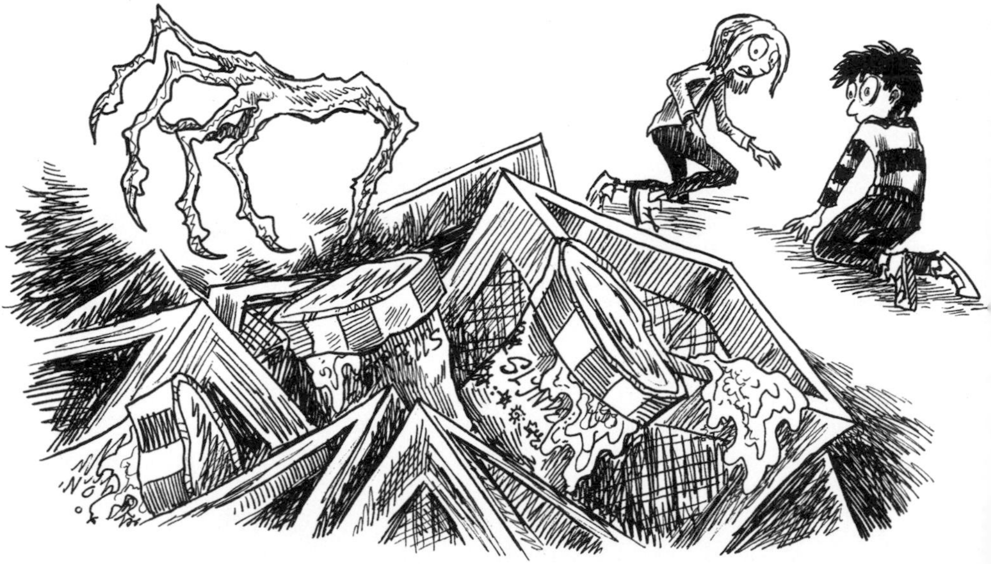

"Look!" said Levi, pointing to something small and spiny scurrying away from the collapsed shelves. "Willow?"

Footsteps approached. "What was that?" said a voice.

"It's the warehouse crew!" hissed Kat.

They jumped up and started back through the crate maze.

"Willow, wait for us!" called Levi.

They rounded a corner just in time to see the spiny thing slip through the gap in the warehouse door.

"Hurry!" said Kat. "Before she gets away . . ."

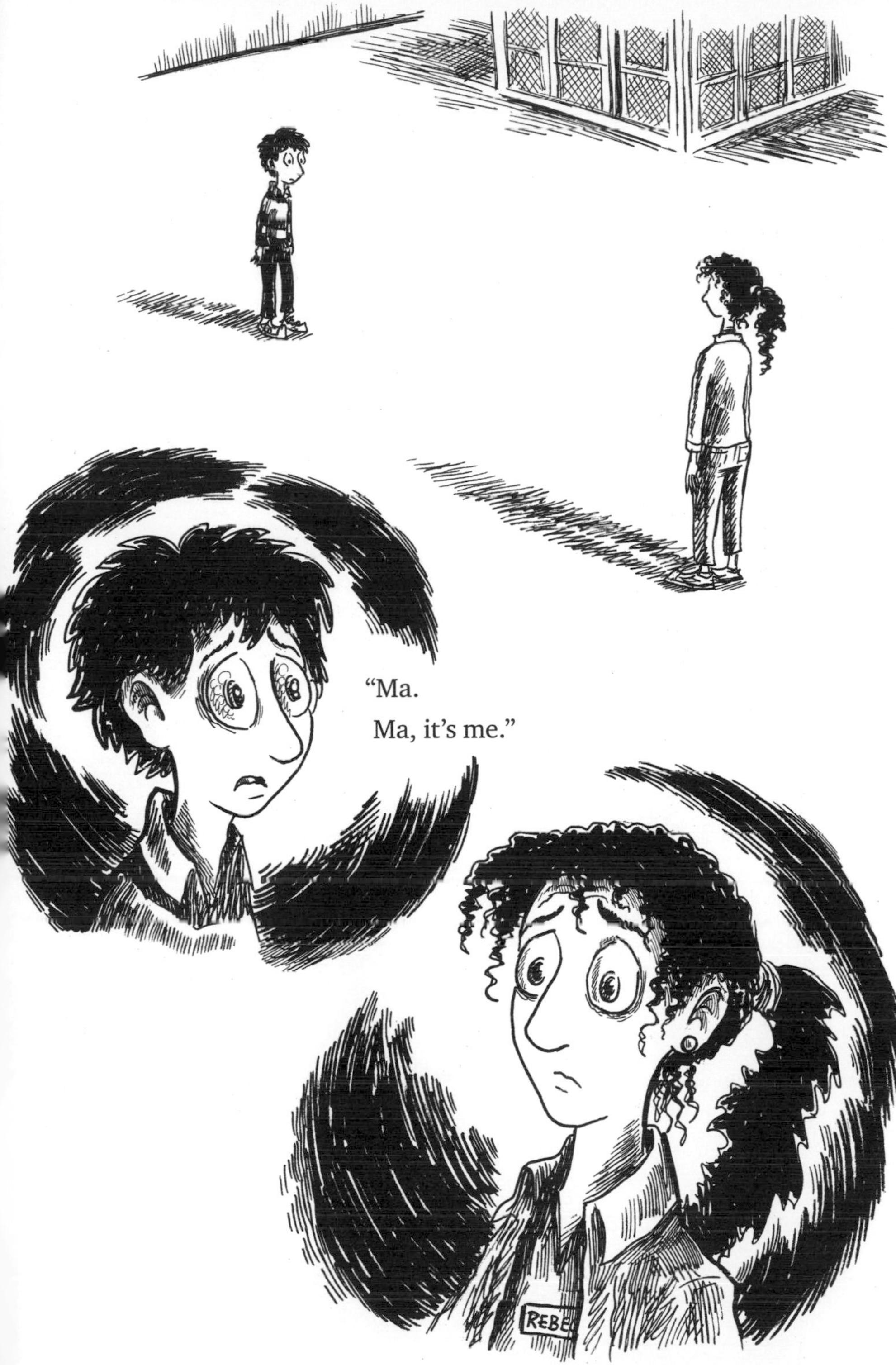
"Ma.
Ma, it's me."
REBE

"Rebecca!" called one of the workers. "You'd better get over here! The forklift crashed into a whole shelf—it fell on someone!"

"I think it's the truck driver!" said another. "He's hurt bad! Rebecca, call an ambulance!"

"Come on, Levi," said Kat, gently taking his arm and leading him out the door.

"She remembered me!" said Levi as they raced along the side of the main building. "Some part of her did!"

"Levi, get a grip! She's probably telling security right now!" panted Kat. "We've got to catch up to Willow! She's keeping something from us! There's got to be more to this factory than the warehou—!" Her train of thought was cut short when she slipped and skidded down the muddy slope.

She landed next to an immense drainage pipe, rusty and slimy and coated in lichen, its mouth yawning out from the slope like a monster leech.

Kat chewed her lip. "You don't think—"

"No," said Levi. He'd been building a tolerance for the uncanny over the last few days, but seeing his mother in the warehouse had been an emotional gut punch.

A skittering noise echoed from somewhere deep in the pipe.

"Willow?" called Kat. She turned to Levi. "I think this is what we've been looking for. The secret part of the factory." She started forward.

"No!" moaned Levi. "This . . . it's too much!"

"What about Twila?" said Kat. "Do it for Twila. Right?"

He paused. Took a deep, ragged breath.

"Right. Okay. For Twila."

She took his hand.

And together they stepped into the pipe.

Chapter 30: Slynderfell

"Careful! It's slippery.
Ew! And sticky! Like . . ."

"Melted
ice cream?"

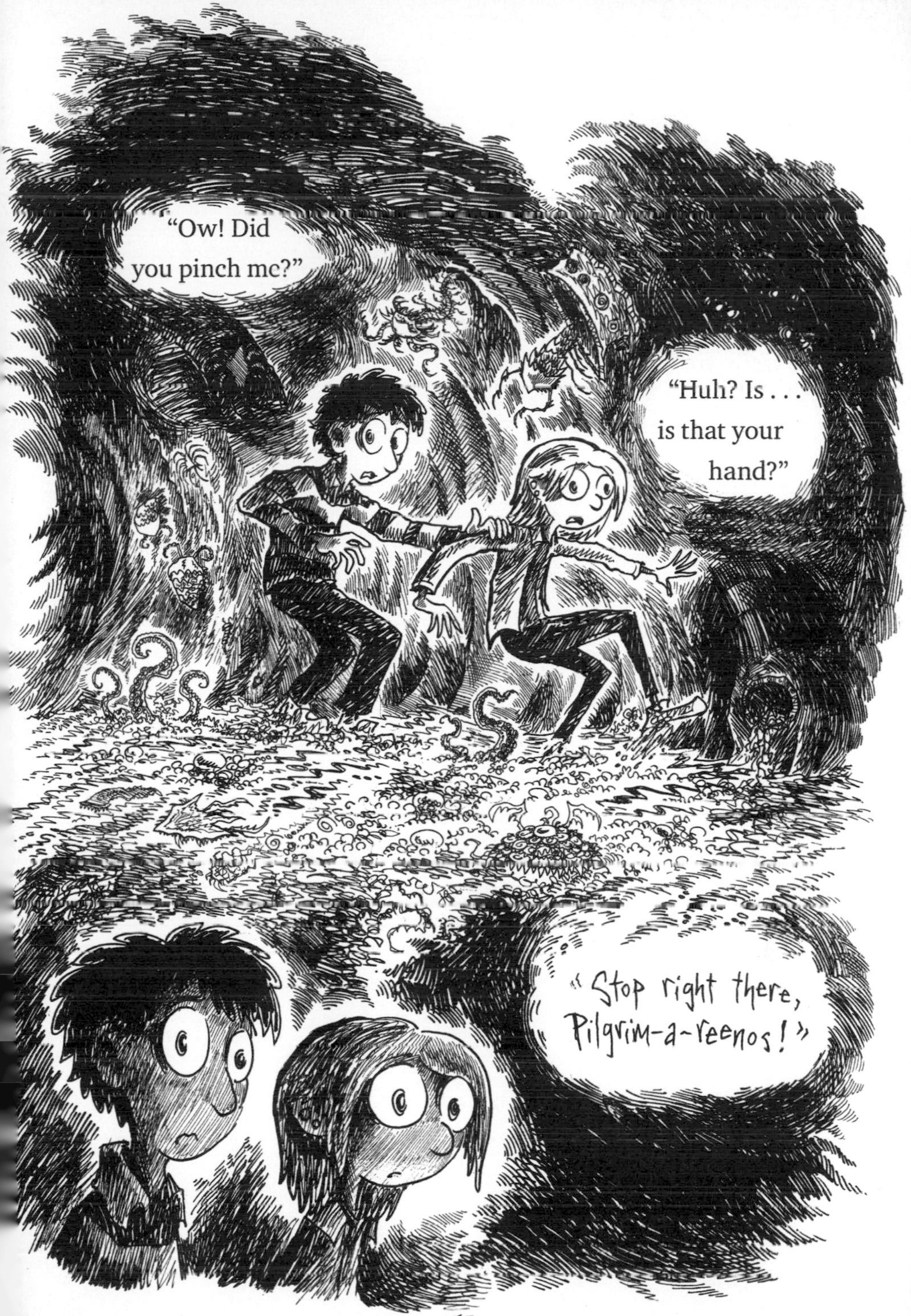
"Ow! Did you pinch me?"
"Huh? Is . . . is that your hand?"
"Stop right there, Pilgrim-a-reenos!"

"It's a violation of Ordinance 391 to enter without stating identification!" The voice may have sounded human, if not for the ticks and rasps.

"Wait, are you Galante and Bombard?" said a second voice, equally strange.

"Um," said Levi, "maybe."

"Ohhhh! The boss is expecting ya!" Two very inhuman shapes appeared in front of them.

"Follow us!"

"Should we?" whispered Levi to Kat.

"Do we have a choice?" Kat whispered back.

They followed the sound of the voices. The pipe expanded and became the gritty stone of an underground tunnel lit by bioluminescent fungus.

"We weren't expecting you to be awake," said the first creature. "Mr. Frost usually escorts sleeping guests. Where is Mr. Frost, anyway?"

"He had a little accident," said Kat. Her bugged eyes were fixed on the creatures. "You're bogeys, aren't you?"

"Bogeys? What a hateful term! We got names, ya know! I'm Officer Gerber and this is Inspector Skeebs."

"We met about an hour ago," said Skeebs. "At the Mushpits' house."

"Righto," said Gerber, "though that wasn't a proper introduction. Sorry for that. Didn't mean to scare ya."

"Actually we *did* mean to scare ya," corrected Skeebs. "That was the plan. Mr. Frost sends a breeze of snooze dust through the window and puts the geezers to sleep, and we rip through the floor and scare the kiddies out of the house so Mr. Frost can scoop them up in his truck."

"Seemed needlessly complicated," said Gerber. "We are busy enough with our regular responsibilities: removing the evidence, forging the documents . . ."

Levi's spine prickled. "Removing evidence?"

"Exactively positulutely!" chirped Skeebs. "Mr. Boojum erases the memories, Mr. Frost collects the forgotten kiddies, and we take care of the rest."

"The hard job," grumbled Gerber. "Altering the photos, pitching rooms full of clothes and furniture. And the toys—kids today have sooo many toys! And then there's the paperwork that comes with it all."

"Hark!" trilled a voice ahead. "Gerber! Skeebs! Is that you?"

"Crickety!" said Skeebs. "It's Mr. Slynderfell!"

"Ooo! Can we pretend we captured you?" asked Gerber. "That would look great on our Performance Reviews!"

Before Levi and Kat could object, the creatures seized their arms.

"Mr. Slynderfell, we got the kiddies!"

An otherworldly figure materialized in front of them.

"Splendiferous!" said the creature. "I am the infabuloso Mr. Slynderfell! You may shake my hand!" Slynderfell offered a gloved appendage to a nearby rock.

"Erm, Mr. Slynderfell, sir," said Gerber, "we're over here."

"What? Where the ditzies are my eyes?!" Slynderfell spun about blindly. "Eyes! Report to my head!"

Two glowing orb creatures scurried from a crevice, scuttled up Slynderfell's coat, and perched on his head.

"That's better!" said Slynderfell. He turned the glowing orb creatures on Levi and Kat. "These are the children? The ones who thwarted Rafer Frost and resisted the Boojum's memory-snitchery?"

"Yez, indeedy!" said Skeebs. "We got 'em!"

Slynderfell rolled his eyes (or his eye creatures did a literal somersault). "Since you're here—and awake—I may as well give you a tour of the ice cream factory."

"Uh," sputtered Levi. "Okay."

Slynderfell ran a glove through his head tentacles and twirled a cane topped with a silver sundae and a gemstone cherry.

"Down to the Keep of Slynderfell! Where wonders swirl and lost dreams dwell."

They followed him down a spiraling passage, past lichen-encrusted pipes and fossil-studded stalactites.

"This is the factory's basement?" asked Kat.

"Don't be a sluggonaut," said Slynderfell. "This is the factory proper."

"But what about the warehouses up top?"

"Decoys to beeboozle the simpletons.

This... Down here... is where the Magic happens..."

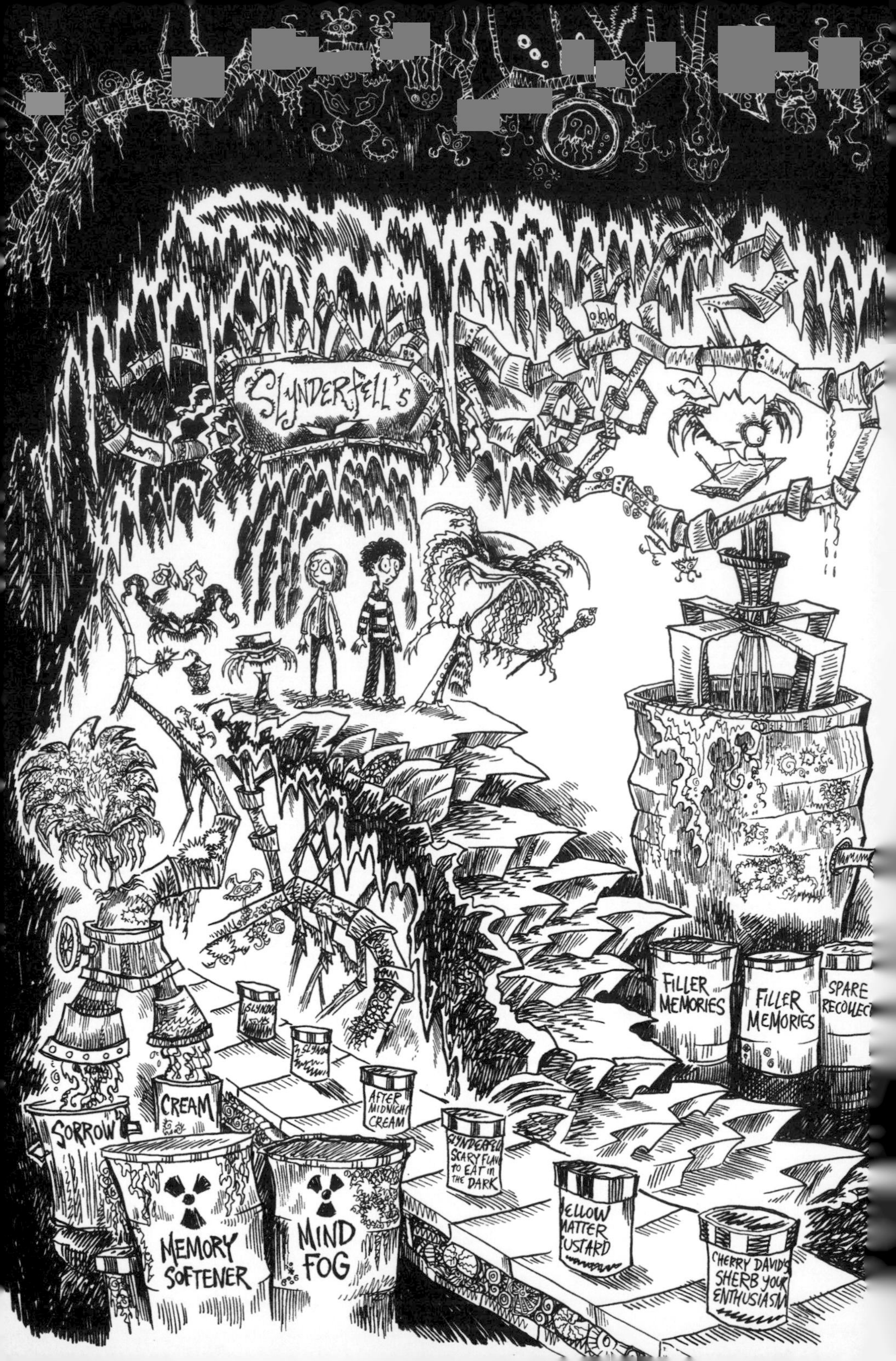
SLYNDERFELL'S
SORROW
CREAM
AFTER MIDNIGH CREAM
SLYNDERFEL SCARY FLAV TO EAT IN THE DARK
MEMORY SOFTENER
MIND FOG
ELLOW MATTER USTARD
CHERRY DAVID'S SHERB YOUR ENTHUSIASM
FILLER MEMORIES
FILLER MEMORIES
SPARE RECOLLECT

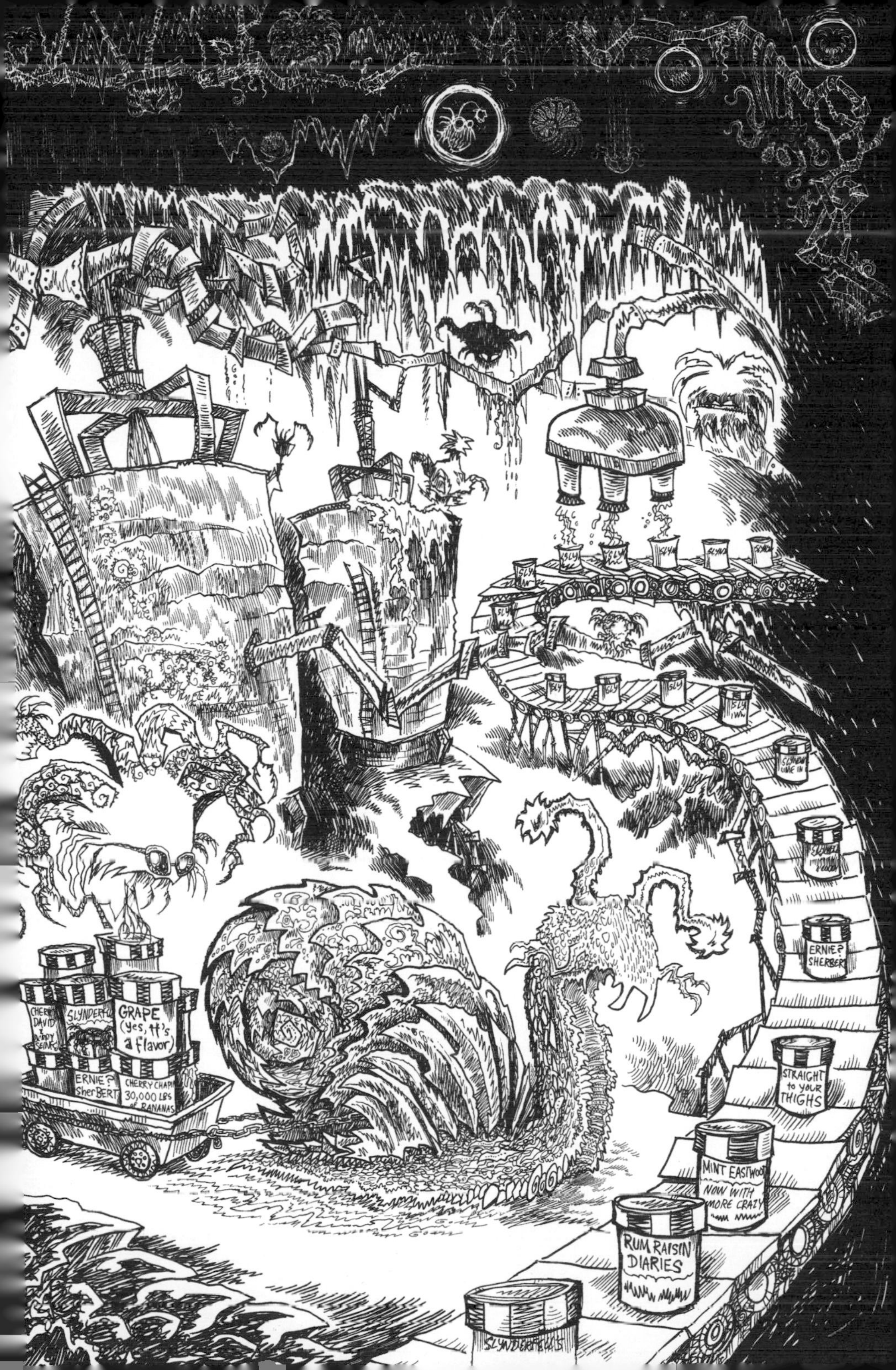
GRAPE (yes, it's a flavor)
ERNIE? SherBERT
ERNIE? SHERBERT
STRAIGHT to your THIGHS
MINT EASTWOOD NOW WITH MORE CRAZY
RUM RAISIN DIARIES

Chapter 31: Beneath the Surface

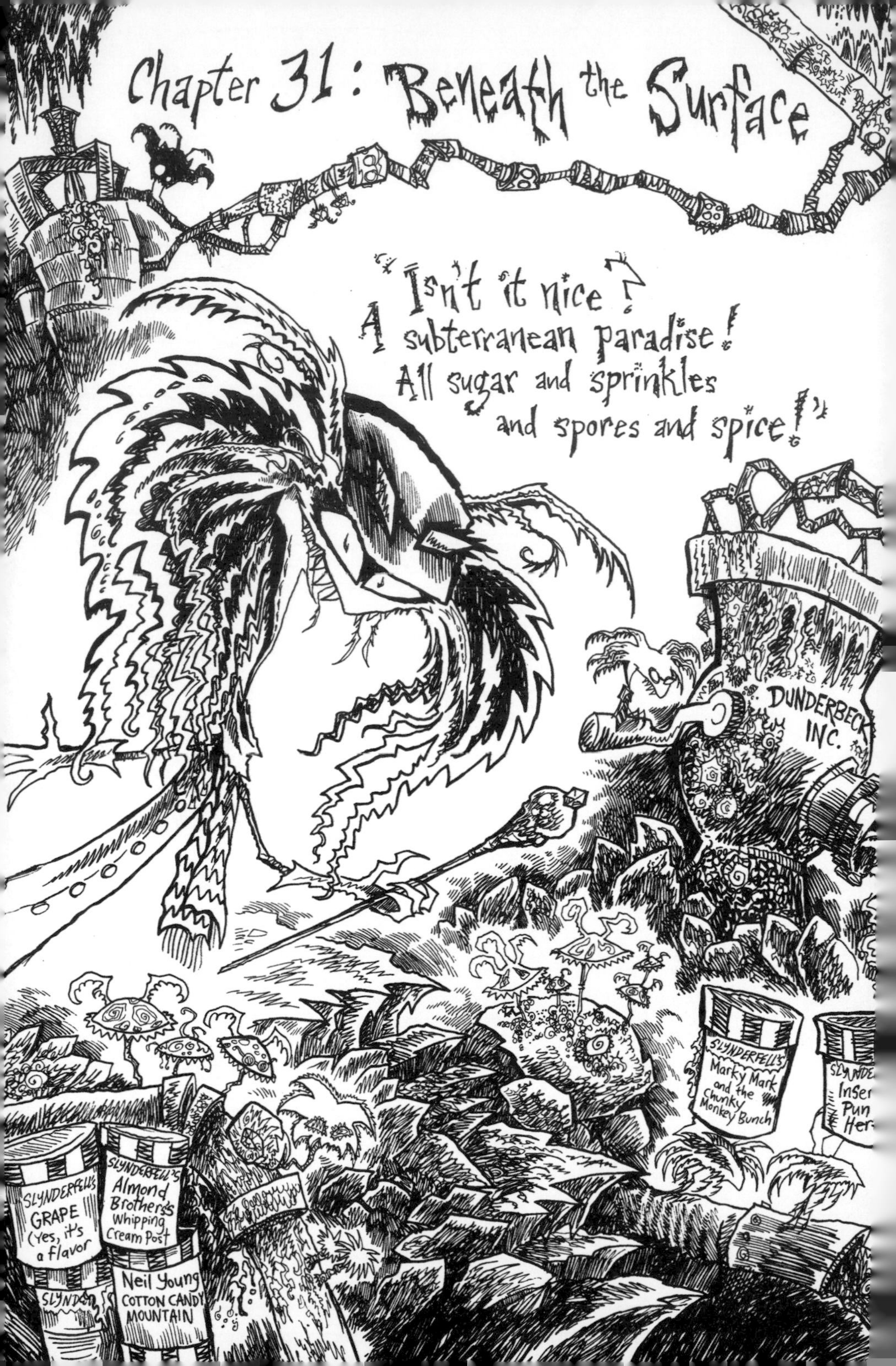
"Isn't it nice?
A subterranean paradise!
All sugar and sprinkles
and spores and spice!"
DUNDERBECK INC.
SLYNDERFELL'S
Marky Mark and the Chunky Monkey Bunch
SLYNDE
Inser
Pun
Her
SLYNDERFELL'S
GRAPE (Yes, it's a flavor
SLYNDERFELL'S
Almond Brothers's Whipping Cream Post
Neil Young COTTON CANDY MOUNTAIN
SLYND

PUN DEPARTMENT

CELEB PUNS:
Fudge Judy
Blue-barrymore

SONG PUNS: Bad Moon Raisin
Build Me Up Butterscotch
Call Me Maple
~~Walk the Lime~~

EXPIRED PUNS

HANG IN THERE

"If we had more time, we'd offer a free sample of Konked by a Coconut. It's quite scrumlishy-us, or so I'm told. I wouldn't know personally. I don't eat ice cream, or any physical food, for that matter. None of the true Slynderfellians do."

"If you can't eat it, then why do you make it?" asked Kat.

"Why, to feed the livestock."

"What livestock?"

CALL BLYME

GUITAR LESSONS

FALL HARVEST GRID

FIELD 1A
(3 OFFSPRING BUMPER CROP) ★

FIELD 2A
(FALL HARVEST)

FIELD 2B
(SPRING HARVEST)

12 YR
6 YR

13 YR
7 YR
2 YR

MUSHPITS

"Patience, little jibber-gob. Now we move away from the ice cream and to the core of our operation."

"What's that grid back there?" asked Levi.

"Oh, just a diagram of the farm."

"Farm?" said Kat. "You mean factory."

"No, no. The factory is just the processing plant."

"Upper Dwellers?" interrupted a tentacled creature. It adjusted its glasses (though it had no eyes). "If you've a moment, I'd like to discuss some embarrassing inaccuracies in this text."

"Hey! That's my book!" exclaimed Kat. *"Cryptopedia!"*

"A-hoim! Leaflet 112 describes a living pliosaur in a Highland loch. Impossible. The last pliosaurs went extinct about 66 million years ago."

"LaMantia!" snapped Slynderfell. "Get back to the Inventory Storerooms!" He swung his cane at the offending worker, sending it scurrying into a darkened chamber. "Apologies. The bean counters forget their place."

"It had my book!" said Kat. "Does that mean all our stolen stuff is down here somewhere?"

"Questions and confuddlements will be addressed at the end of the tour."

COMPANY MOTTO:
• BE PROACTIVE
• BE SYNERGETIC
• WORK SMARTER, NOT HARDER

SUPPORT the NEIGHBORHOOD WATCH
KEEPING THE SHEEP IN LINE

NIGHTLY GRACE
Hail to the Boojum, GOD of the HARVEST, HE who creeps beneath the rows, Savior of the Slynderfellians... Deliver us from extra dimensional Void.

SLYNDERFELL'S Fifty Flavors of Gray

Kat nudged Levi. "Look!" She pointed to a colossal monster chained to a nearby vat.

"Ol' Heckbender," snickered Slynderfell. "Our beast of burden. Hauling carts and machinery, mixing the cream, that sort of work. Can't let him to the surface. He'd terrorize the livestock."

"But we *did* see him outside!" said Kat. "He was in the woods this morning! He almost got us!"

"We let him out from time to time for walkies, though never off his leash." Slynderfell nodded to the great iron shackles and chains clamped to Heckbender's neck and limbs.

A thought was creeping to the front of Levi's mind. "Is Willow down here?" he asked.

"Willow?" Slynderfell's eye creatures tried their best to look puzzled.

"Small, spiny, looks like a shriveled coyote," said Levi.

"Oooh, the chupacabra!" He rapped his cane against a pipe. "Sheepdog! Report!"

Levi scanned the caves until he spotted two fluorescent orbs gleaming in the shadows. "There she is! Willow, over here!"

Willow did not move.

"Wretchitty bloodsucker!" sneered Slynderfell. "Although I suppose it serves its purpose."

Levi felt cold. "What purpose?"

"Sheepdog. Her duties include patrolling the perimeters, keeping track of wayward livestock, and assisting our shepherd."

"Told you we couldn't trust her," Kat whispered.

Levi said nothing.

"Oh, cuttlepish!" said Slynderfell cheerfully. "Let's sidle on. We've reached our tour's last stop." He gestured to a small room. "Our Bibble-Babble Room! Or what you might know as a 'conference room.'"

Their feet made a squelching sound as they stepped into the darkened room. Something cold and slimy was covering the floor. Kat wrinkled her nose. "Ugh! What kind of conference room is this?"

No answer. They turned and saw too late that Slynderfell was still standing outside the doorway.

The trap's bars fell down with a clang, sealing them inside the slimy chamber.

They threw themselves against the bars, pulling and clawing like caged foxes.

"Let us out!" cried Kat.

Slynderfell cackled. "So sorry, little slubbermuffins. If you'd only cooperated with our shepherd Mr. Frost. You'd be dreaming peacefully with the Boojum right now, like the other kiddies."

Levi tried to bring his foot up to kick at the bars, but it was caught in the slimy mess. The slime made a sucking sound as he pulled free, but a moment later the ooze reached up and seized his foot again. "What is this stuff?"

"The factory's garden," said Slynderfell from the other side of the bars. "You can thank your own parents and neighbors for the contribution. They saturate their lawns with pesticides, weed killers, chemical fertilizer. All those nitrates seep into the ground and collect here.

"Normally we send kiddies to the Boojum for dream milking, but you are just a bit too feisty to keep around, so into the ooze you go. It's a living garbage disposal: it'll dissolve your skin, your innards, your bones. There's no place for restless rabble on our farm."

"Farm?" spat Kat as she tugged at the bars. "You bug-eyed mutant! Why do you keep talking about a stupid farm?"

Levi felt himself go numb. "The farm. It's . . ."

"Go on," crooned Slynderfell.

"It's the *town*," said Levi softly.

"What?" said Kat.

"That grid we saw: it was the whole town," continued Levi. "Cowslip Grove is a *farm*. And the livestock . . ." He thought of Twila and couldn't finish his sentence.

"It's giddylish," sneered Slynderfell as the factory workers assembled around the cage and chattered anxiously. "For millennia, humans have thought themselves the undisputed victors. The planet's spoils ripe for the taking. Oh, but they forgot us, the Underground Dwellers, hiding just below the crust, watching the human-folk grow soft and dull."

"You creepy Morlocks!" gasped Kat. "Humans aren't like sheep!"

"Ah, yet they are!" chortled Slynderfell. "They guzzle our ice cream and stay soft in body and mind."

"They'll fight back!"

"WHO will? The Neighborhood Watch is too busy fussing over black lambs to notice us."

"But why do you need livestock? You said you don't eat, so—"

"True, but we are very fond of electrochemical pulses, especially the sort produced by dreams. It's the energy that sustains us. And the dreams of children are the cherry on top!"

Slynderfell continued: "The Boojum insists there's something especially powerful about a child's dreams. Potent, rich, untouched by the muddle of reality and the toxins of adult worry. It's a shame you won't meet the Boojum. No, this is where your story ends."

The slime tendrils wrapped around Levi's shoulders, and he felt them pulling him down into the bubbling mess. He gagged as his lungs filled with the chemical fumes. He heard Kat scream as the killer bloom dragged her from the bars.

With his last bit of strength, he wrenched his body up and slammed against the bars. His eyes scanned the chittering workers until they settled on a small, spiny shape crouched near the back of the crowd. "Willow. *Please!*"

"She was never your friend!" Slynderfell twittered. "She'd been instructed to lead you into the wild, where Heckbender would be waiting."

Levi ignored this. He fixed his eyes on the fluorescent orbs. "Please . . . Willow . . ."

The tendrils found Levi's neck, and he felt himself going down.

Suddenly there was a great commotion among the workers.

"My cane!"
shrieked Slynderfell.

Willow scurried past the gawking workers to the bars of the cage with the silver sundae cane clamped between her jaws. She forced the gemstone cherry into the lock, and the bars swung open.

"Kat-hooligan! Catch!" cried Willow as she flung the cane into Kat's free hand. Kat jammed the cane into the writhing algae, prying tendrils from her body.

Willow sank her fangs into the knot of slime surrounding Levi, ripping and snarling like a caffeinated terrier at a rat convention. Levi felt the coils falling away from his limbs.

"Gawklers! Don't just stand there bug-oggled!"

The worker horde chattered feverishly, though none seemed willing to approach the toxic garden and its escaping victims.

"Seize them, or answer to the Boojum!"

That did it—the workers lunged forward, waving insectoid appendages and spouting alien obscenities.

"Run, Goofooligans!"

Chapter 32:
Where the WILD THINGS Are NOW

Down the tunnels, dodging stalactites, jumping pipes. The clicks and jabbers of the bogey horde behind them. The fugitives ducked behind a rock wall.

"No time to doodle-dwaddle," whispered Willow. "Willow will lead you back to the surface."

"No!" heaved Levi. "I'm not leaving without Twila!"

"You must!" pleaded Willow. "She is with the Boojum! Your minds will melt to brainy-goo in the Boojum's lair." Her voice stopped short when she saw the determination on their faces.

"Then so it be. Willow will lead you to the Boojum. Oh, mercy."

"THERE'S the kiddies! Get 'em!"

"Go! Keep going down! Down!
To the Arches!"
"FASTER! Don't look back!
Almost there! Almost—"

"Willow!"

Levi started to run back to her, but the bogey horde engulfed her tiny body.

"Look out!" screamed Kat, grabbing his shoulder. They dove behind a vat and hugged its metal walls as the workers dragged the struggling Willow back up the tunnel.

"We have to help Willow!" Levi said.

"Not now!" hissed Kat. "We've got bigger problems!"

A voice boomed
above them:

"*BIGGER PROBLEMS INDEED!*"

They looked up in horror at the familiar gargantuan monster chained to the vat they were hiding behind.

"FEAR NOT," said Heckbender. "I AM NOT GOING TO EAT YOU."

Levi and Kat looked unconvinced.

"SO, OKAY," agreed Heckbender. "I TRIED TO EAT YOU IN THE SWAMP THIS MORNING, TRUE. BUT SLYNDERFELL HAD LET ME TO THE SURFACE, AND I WAS CAUGHT UP IN THE THRILL OF THE HUNT. HERE, IN THIS CLAUSTROPHOBIC LABYRINTH? FRANKLY, I FAIL TO SEE THE SPORT IN IT."

Kat pointed to Heckbender's shackles. "Ha! You couldn't get us even if you wanted! Slynderfell has you chained!"

Heckbender sighed. "TRUE. A SAD LIFE, MINE. THE BOOJUM'S FOLLOWERS KEEP ME ON A SHORT LEASH."

"Speaking of the Boojum," said Levi gingerly, "would you, uh, maybe—"

"POINT YOU IN THE DIRECTION OF ITS LAIR AND THE MISSING CHILDREN?" Heckbender combed his gill filaments reflectively. "PERHAPS. IF YOU WILL DO OL' HECKBENDER A FAVOR IN RETURN." He pointed to a giant padlock attached to his shackles. The keyhole was hexagon-shaped. The shape of a gemstone cherry.

Kat hefted the cane, then paused. "How do we know you won't gobble us up once we free you?"

"IT IS A GAMBLE." Heckbender grinned. He waited, then sighed again. "DOWN THIS TUNNEL, TURN LEFT, RIGHT, LEFT, PASS THROUGH THE STONE ARCHES, AND DOWN INTO THE BLACK. NOW, THE PADLOCK, PLEASE?"

They were interrupted by an ear-hair-singeing cry: "There they are, Mr. Slynderfell! Hiding by Heckbender's mixer!"

"SEEMS YOU HAVE BEEN SPOTTED," groaned Heckbender.

Slynderfell and a platoon of workers emerged from an adjacent tunnel.

"Sneacherous Worms!
Tear them to tatters!
Scoop their gray matters!
Pickle their bladders!"

Kat plunged the cane's gemstone cherry into the keyhole. Slynderfell and his underlings stopped cold as Heckbender's chains went limp and his shackles fell to the ground with a clang.

"OHHH . . . THAT FEELS DIVINE!"

Heckbender turned his bulging orbs on Levi and Kat. He blinked his left orb. He blinked his right orb. He blinked his rudimentary peripheral orb clusters.

Levi and Kat held their breath.

Heckbender turned to the factory workers.

"FELLOW LOST ONES!" he boomed. "WHAT PATHETIC CREATURES YOU HAVE BECOME! WHAT HAPPENED TO STALKING SWAMPS AND CHASMS AND PRIMORDIAL OOZE? HAVE YOU GIVEN IT ALL UP FOR *THIS*? TOILING UNDERGROUND, SERVING BUREAUCRACY AND BUZZWORDS?"

"Don't listen to that fossil," said Slynderfell, though his voice sounded less confident. "Go on. Seize the kiddies."

"YES," said Heckbender. "DO NOT LISTEN TO AN ANCIENT RELIC LIKE ME. LISTEN INSTEAD TO YOUR OWN INSTINCTS."

There was a pause. Finally Skeebs spoke: "You know, I've never felt comfortable wearing ties and suits. I don't even have a body."

"Seems like my whole life is now paperwork," mumbled Gerber.

"I used to be the Terror of the Mauve Lagoon," said LaMantia. "Now I just fuss over ice cream flavor puns."

"Slugganoids!" screeched Slynderfell. "Have you forgotten what's happened to the world? There is no place for bogglers like you! The humans would wipe you off the planet! The wild things and wild places are gone! Extinct!"

"IT IS A CHANGED WORLD," said Heckbender. "BUT IS THIS LIFE OUR ONLY ANSWER?"

"The Boojum has allowed us to turn the tables!" snarled Slynderfell. "The humans have been reduced to livestock!"

"And what happens when the humans are all used up?" asked Kat abruptly. She elbowed Levi.

"Uh, right," added Levi after a moment. "Who will be the Boojum's prey then? Maybe the Boojum is already grooming his next flock of sheep."

The factory workers chittered nervously and fumbled with their ill-fitting clothes.

"I GROW TIRED OF TALK!" bellowed Heckbender. He swung a shackle over his head and slammed it into a sherbet vat.

The vat exploded. The workers cheered.

Heckbender roared:

"LET the WILD RUMBUS COMMENCE!"

"C'mon," whispered Kat, tugging Levi's arm. They slipped past the rioting workers, dashed down the main tunnel, veered left, darted right, slipped left, and dove through the stone arches Heckbender had described.

"Willow's still up there somewhere!" panted Levi.

"She'll have to fend for herself," said Kat. "Plus she was working for the bad guys, remember?"

"She saved our lives!"

"Going back now won't save Willow," said Kat at last. She turned toward the descending black. "Only one thing to do."

The air rattled in Levi's chest as he inhaled.

"I know," he whispered.

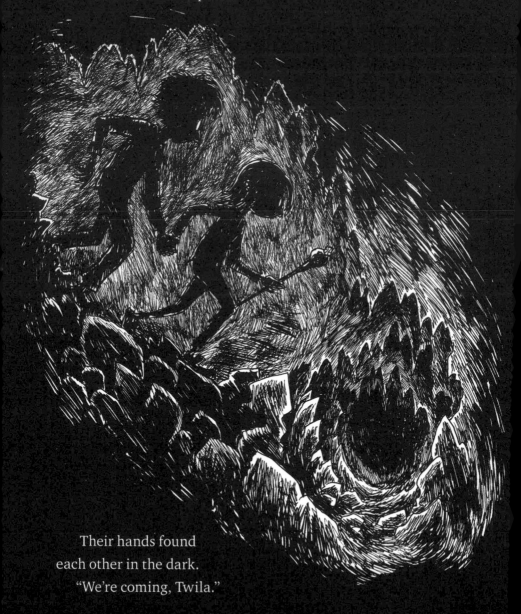

Their hands found each other in the dark.

"We're coming, Twila."

Chapter 33: The Boojum

"Mrs. Mushpit said certain metals can be used against bogey-things," said Kat. She brandished the sundae cane. "Maybe we can use this against the Boojum."

"When did Mrs. Mushpit say that?"

"When she was talking about the olden days. Surprised I remembered?"

"I'm surprised you were even listening," said Levi, his voice oddly close to a laugh. "You weren't the best listener in school."

"I listen more than you might think," said Kat. She was quiet for a moment; then she chuckled. "I guess I was kind of a pain sometimes. Poor Ms. Padilla. She really was a good teacher. Remember the story she read us about the monster in the cave that eats elephants and rhinos for lunch?"

"Sorta."

"And then the monster turns out to be a little caterpillar."

"Yeah."

Another pause. The silence loomed.

"If we get out of this," said Kat at last, "I'm going to make some changes. I'll stop fighting and lying and making up stupid stories."

"Stories?"

"You know, the alien abductions and Bigfoot and all that conspiracy baloney. You didn't really believe any of it, did you?"

"No. But if you'd told me now, I guess I'd have to."

"Yeah," she said. "Thanks for being a buddy."

Levi would have said more, but at that moment he saw something ahead of them.

Or, more accurately, he saw nothing ahead of them.

Nothing. An emptiness.

Kat raised the cane and inched to the edge of the emptiness. "Hello?" she said.

The emptiness surrounded them. The walls of the cave
faded to nothing.

"Stay close," said Kat.

Levi's eyes searched
the emptiness. For a
moment, he thought he
saw something pulsing
amid the nothing, but
then he blinked and
realized it was
only the blood
vessels in his eyes.

"Twila?" he
called.

He turned to Kat.
"What's happening?" he
asked.

Kat didn't answer.

Kat wasn't there.

He spun around
in the emptiness,
calling for Kat,
calling for Twila.

No one. Nothing.
Even the ground was
gone.

"Hello, child," said a voice. "I'm so happy you've finally come home."

It sounded nothing like a caterpillar.

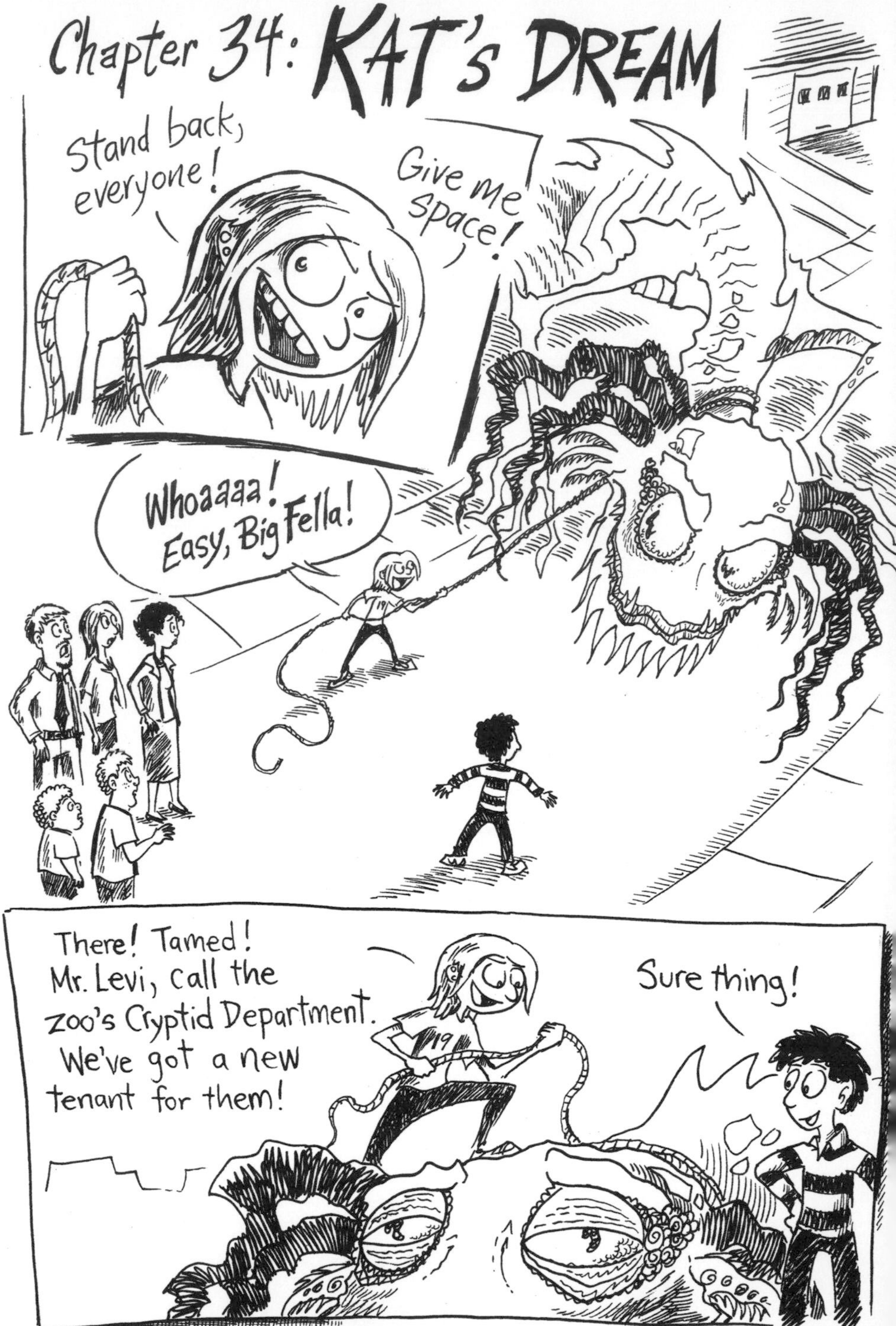
Chapter 34: KAT's DREAM
Stand back, everyone!
Give me space!
Whoaaaa! Easy, Big Fella!
There! Tamed! Mr. Levi, call the zoo's Cryptid Department. We've got a new tenant for them!
Sure thing!

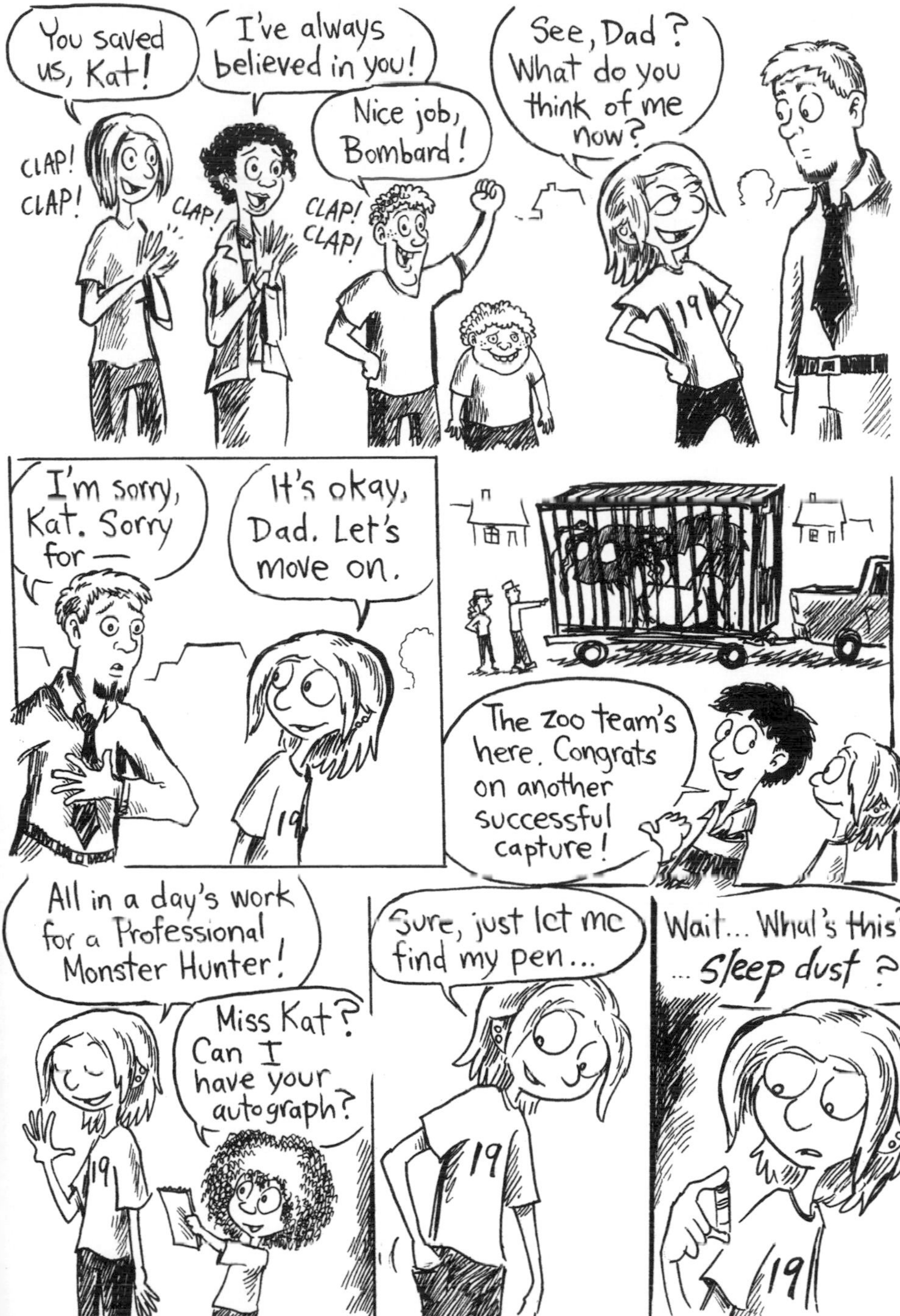

You saved us, Kat!
I've always believed in you!
CLAP! CLAP!
CLAP!
Nice job, Bombard!
CLAP! CLAP!
See, Dad? What do you think of me now?
I'm sorry, Kat. Sorry for —
It's okay, Dad. Let's move on.
The zoo team's here. Congrats on another successful capture!
All in a day's work for a Professional Monster Hunter!
Miss Kat? Can I have your autograph?
Sure, just let me find my pen...
Wait... What's this? ... Sleep dust?
19

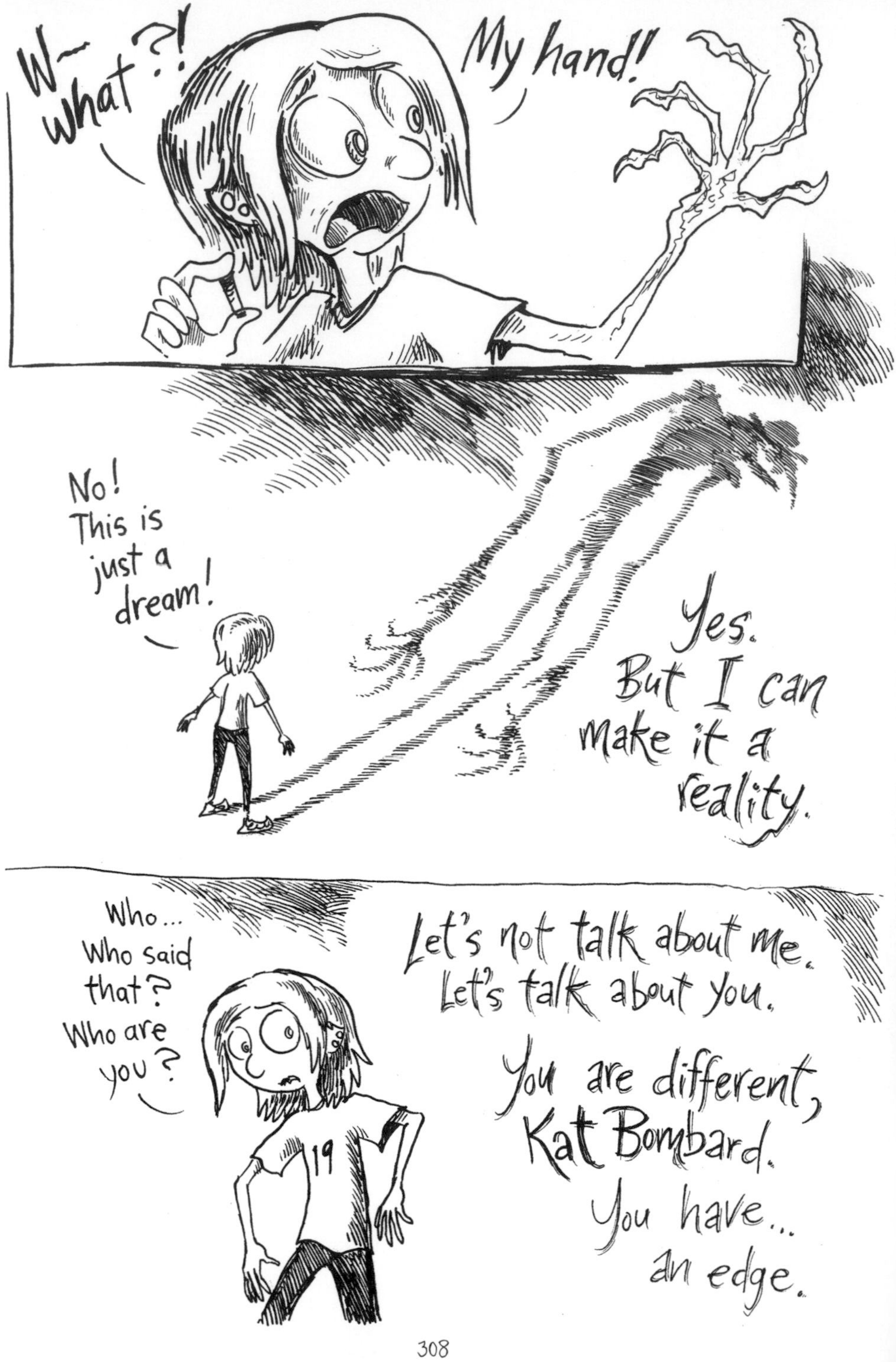
W— what?!
My hand!
No! This is just a dream!
Yes. But I can make it a reality.
Who... Who said that? Who are you?
Let's not talk about me. Let's talk about you.
You are different, Kat Bombard.
You have... an edge.
19

Rafer Frost had it too.
He was like you — a black sheep.
Couldn't fit in.

Rafer Frost used to be a *kid*?

Years ago. He's human, after all. My bogeys serve their purpose, but I prefer that actual human touch when working with children.

I'm nothing like Rafer Frost!

You don't have to be a boogeyman. That was *his* choice.

You can instead be **Kat** the Cryptid Hunter. They'll respect you. Believe your stories. I'll make it happen.

... And in return:
Once in a blue moon, you bring a sleeping child down into this cave. No one will miss the child, And the child will forever dream, And you'll be everything you've always wanted.

> I...

Most of the children I take just sleep until their dreams run dry. I'm offering you a chance to be my new shepherd. A special deal for a special girl.

So **Kat Bombard**, what say you?

Be the hero. Prove them all wrong.

No. No, I wouldn't be a hero.

I can make them *think* you're a hero.

But deep down *I'd* know the truth. I wouldn't be a hero, I'd be a monster.

Do you know why my magic doesn't work on you?

Katherine, dear. You *are* a Monster...

Because of the Mushpits' garden.

No. That's what the Mushpits told you...

In truth, my magic doesn't work, because you do not matter. You are not a part of the world above. You have no friends...

Shut up!

Your classmates and teachers and neighbors will never love you. Even Levi— if he had a spine, he would have told you off long ago...

And of course your father. We know how he sees you. I'm the only one who will accept you for who you are...

Because without me, there is no place for Monsters.

Well?

hmm hmm heh heh

Hee hee heh HEH HEH! HA HA! Oh man!

Why are you laughing?

Oh, just 'cause we've been so afraid of you. But it turns out you're just a bully who likes stupid mind games. Like Joey Downey. Or my dad.

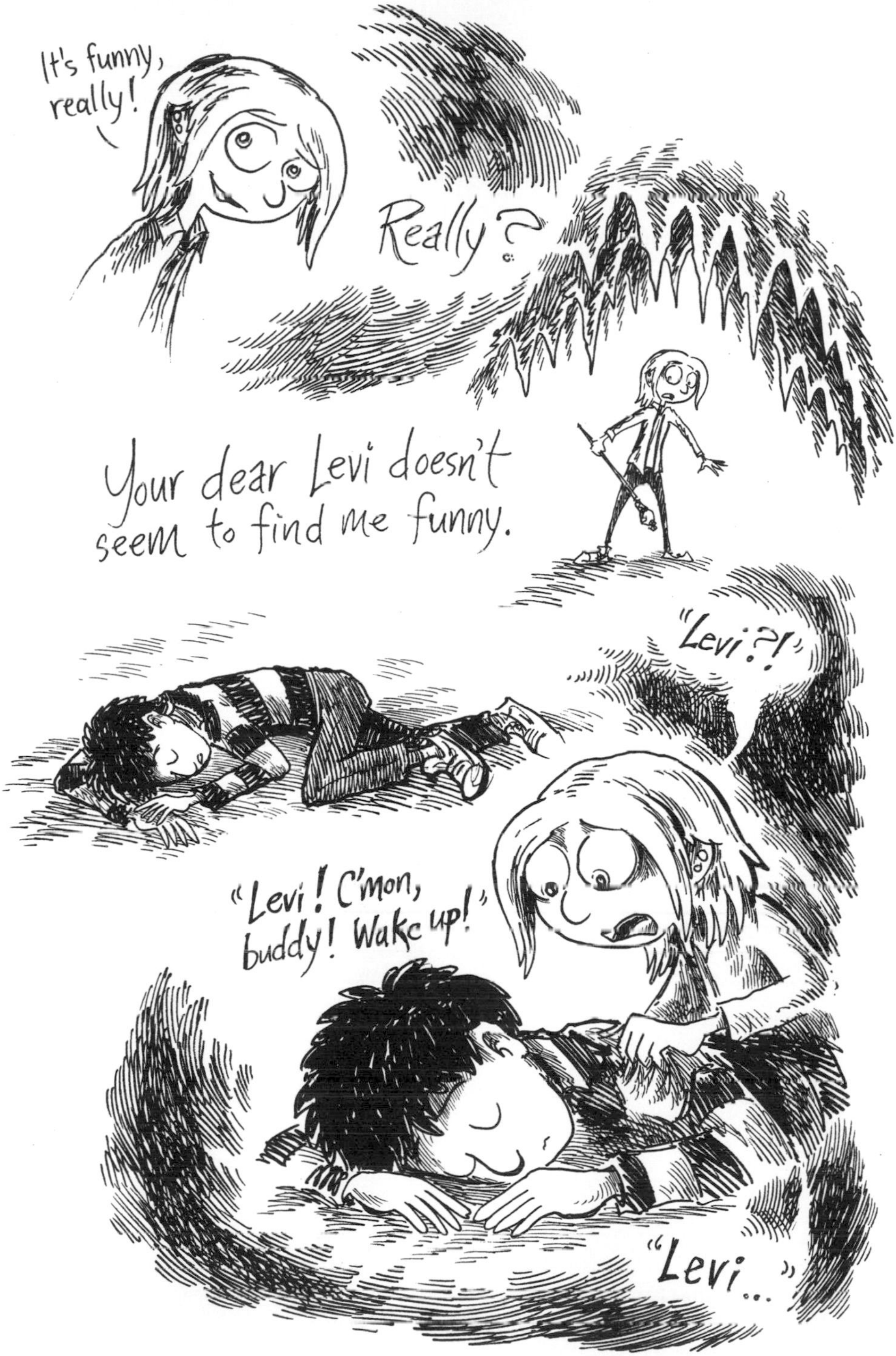
It's funny, really!
Really?
Your dear Levi doesn't seem to find me funny.
"Levi?!"
"Levi! C'mon, buddy! Wake up!"
"Levi..."

Chapter 35: Levi's Dream

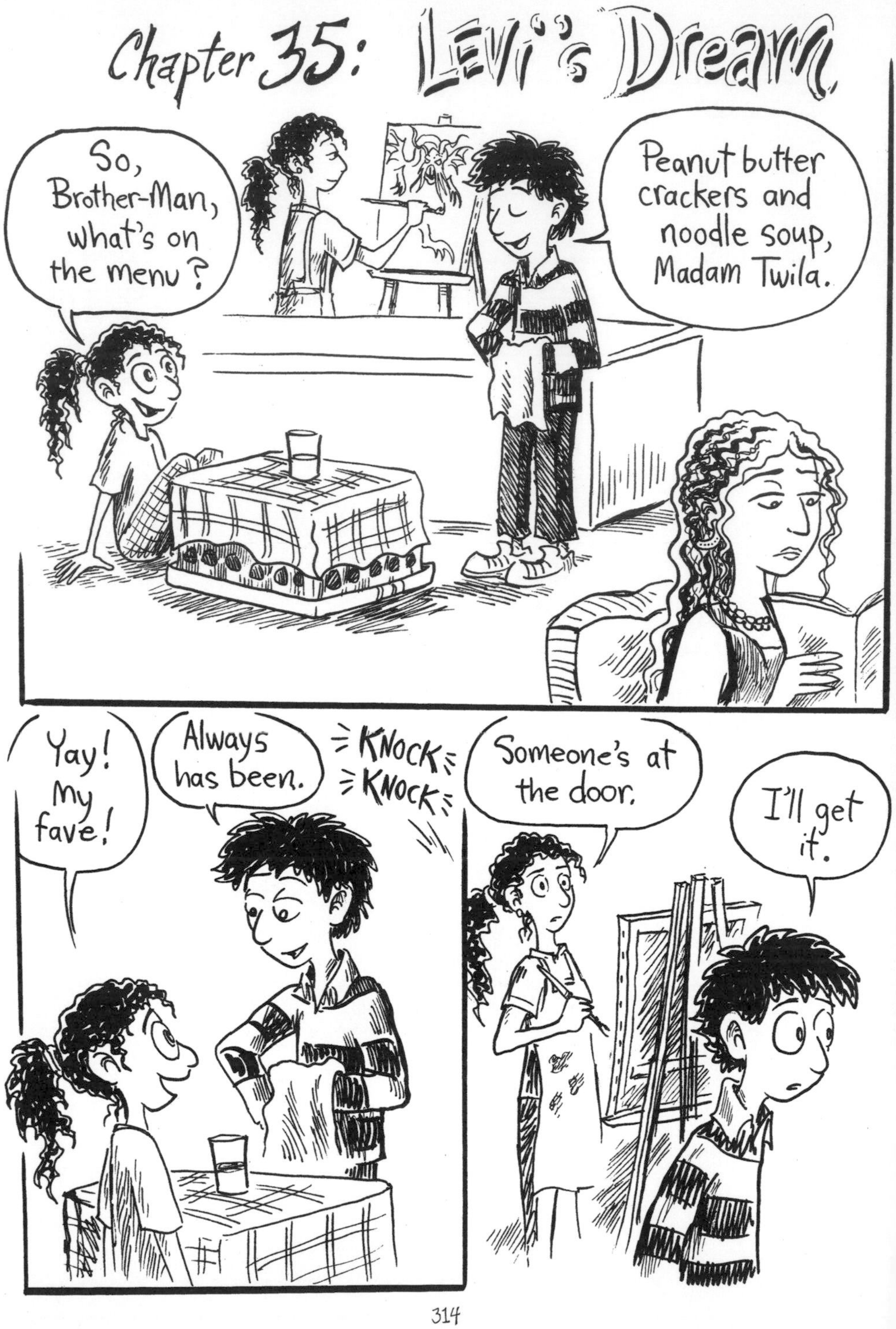

So, Brother-Man, what's on the menu?
Peanut butter crackers and noodle soup, Madam Twila.
Yay! My fave!
Always has been.
KNOCK KNOCK
Someone's at the door.
I'll get it.

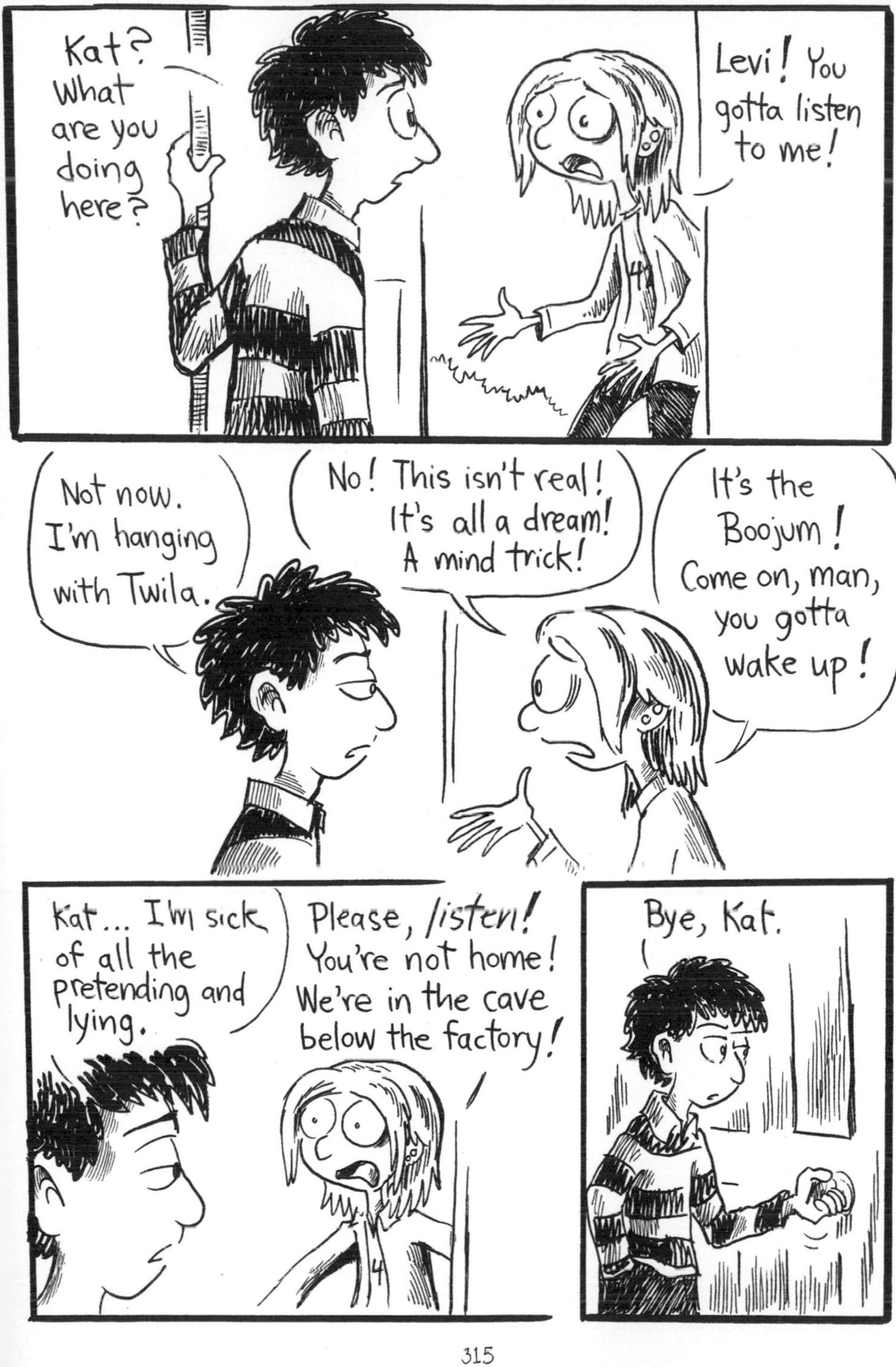
Kat? What are you doing here?
Levi! You gotta listen to me!
Not now. I'm hanging with Twila.
No! This isn't real! It's all a dream! A mind trick!
It's the Boojum! Come on, man, you gotta wake up!
Kat... I'm sick of all the pretending and lying.
Please, *listen*! You're not home! We're in the cave below the factory!
Bye, Kat.

Who was that?

Oh, uh, someone from school.

That weird girl no one likes?

Kat.

Yeah. I'm glad you didn't let her in. She's creepy.

C'mon, Levi. I'm waiting for my soup and crackers.

Levi?

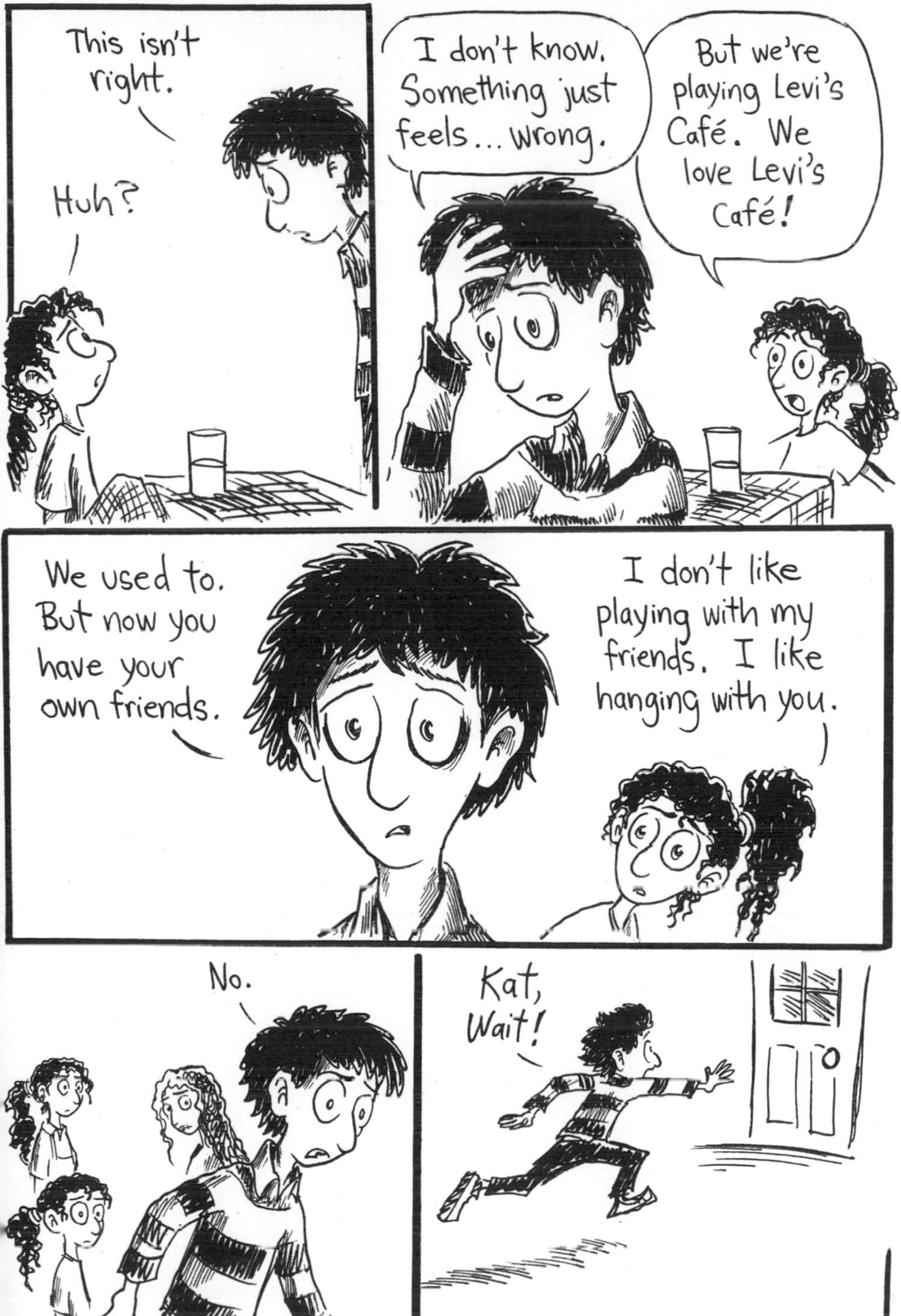
This isn't right.
Huh?
I don't know. Something just feels... wrong.
But we're playing Levi's Café. We love Levi's Café!
We used to. But now you have your own friends.
I don't like playing with my friends. I like hanging with you.
No.
Kat, Wait!

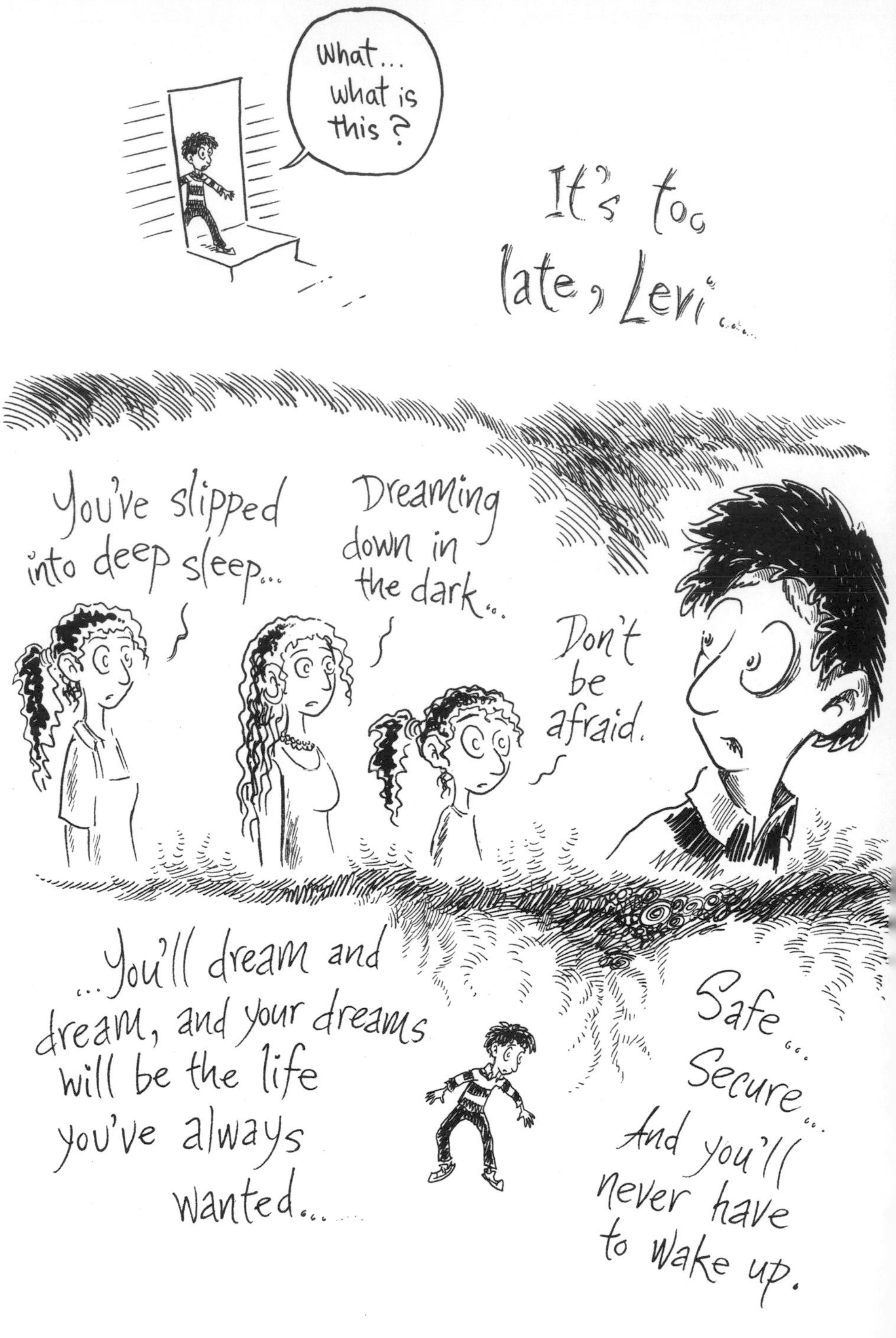
What... what is this?
It's too late, Levi...
You've slipped into deep sleep...
Dreaming down in the dark...
Don't be afraid.
...You'll dream and dream, and your dreams will be the life you've always wanted...
Safe... Secure... And you'll never have to wake up.

Chapter 36: Waking

"Levi! Come on, wake up!" Kat brandished the silver sundae cane at the emptiness. "What have you done to him?"

"He saw the safe little dream and slipped right into eternal slumber," said the Boojum.

"He always was weak. Sheltered. Given time, he would have fit into the neighborhood very neatly. As you said about him earlier: a mama's boy."

"I didn't mean that!"
She swung the cane at the
nothingness, and for a moment,
the nothing seemed to flinch
and flicker.

"Don't you see how good I have been to both of you? Levi will never have to face the unpleasantness of the Wild World. And you had the adventure you've always wanted."

"I never wanted this!"

"We both know you did. You were always along for the thrill, not for Levi or Twila."

"No."

"Yes. I know every corner of your warped little mind, Kat Bombard. So ... Reconsidering my offer?"

"No. But let *me* make *you* an offer. Let Levi and Twila go, and take me instead."

"Oh, how you jest," said the voice. It was suddenly full of static.

"I'm not." The cane slipped from her hands and clattered to the ground. "I will never help you take children. I won't be your shepherd like Rafer Frost. But if you need someone, need dreams to sustain you, please take me instead of Levi and Twila. I'll sleep. I'll dream. I have lots of dreams. Bad dreams. Sad dreams. Sweet dreams that will never come true."

The nothingness
rippled. It sparked and
swirled with startled
color.

Levi's eyes fluttered open.

He saw Kat, her arms outstretched, her hair swaying as if underwater. Around her, the nothingness strobed and blistered.

He saw something. Not just a trick of his eyes this time—a thing of twisting threads in the nothing.

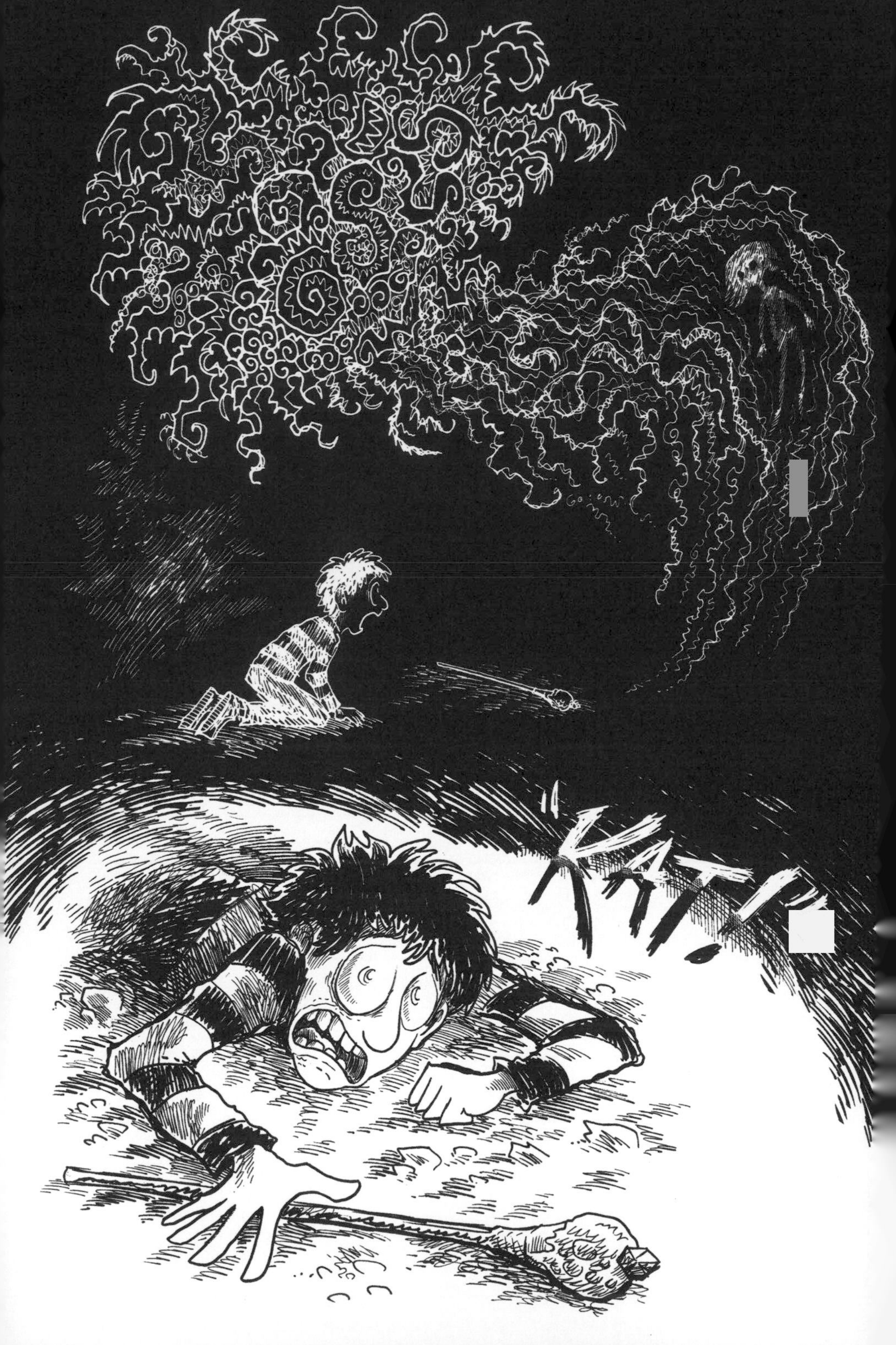
KAT!

He reached the nearest veil of nothing-threads and swung the cane.

The threads sizzled and flared.

The cane flashed again and again.

The thing writhed. Sparks blazed and exploded.

It was moving now, twisting and lurching into the dark of the cave, away from Levi. He dove at it, swinging and screaming, the cane a white torch.

He felt the cane fly from his hand, a searing cold comet.

The thing gave one final pulse and launched itself down the tunnel.

Sparks whirligigged, faded, and then there was only black.

Levi collapsed to the cave's floor, his limbs numb, palms blistered, eyes dazzled by afterimages.

"Kat!" he wheezed.

His voice echoed in the black:

Someone answered. Not Kat. A young child's voice in the darkness. Crying. Calling for its mother.

Another voice joined. And another.

The emptiness was gone. The stone walls were solid. Whimpering shapes huddled against them. Levi rose on unstable legs and staggered across the cave, squinting at each of them, listening to their voices, searching . . .

He found her curled beside a rock. It was too dark to clearly see her features, but he knew it was her immediately. Perhaps it was the scent—the faint smell of familiar laundry detergent. He knelt beside her, his eyes stinging with tears. For a moment, he wondered if it was another trick. But no—his hand brushed her forehead, felt her warmth, and he knew she was real.

"Twila," he whispered. He shook her gently. "You have to wake up."

"Hmm? . . . Levi?"

He lifted her.

Something groaned—something old and deep. Not the children. *The cave.* Debris trickled from the ceiling. Children wailed. Some were crawling or trying to stand.

"Levi?" said Twila, her voice no longer foggy. "What is this?"

"Later," he said as he helped her to her feet. "Now we've got to move."

He darted back
and forth, waking
the other children,
hauling them upright.
There weren't many—
under ten, all Twila's
age or younger.

The cave shook.
Pebbles streamed
from above.

"LEVI!" cried Twila.

"It'll be okay!" he
called back. "We're
getting out of here!"

*Just as soon as I
find her.*

He scrambled
to the back of
the cave, to the
endless black.

Rocks rained down and filled the back of the tunnel, sealing the thread-thing's exit.

"LEVI!" sobbed Twila.

Levi stood paralyzed, his eyes searchlights in the dark. "Up the tunnel! Go!" he said at last. He scooped up a little girl who was not yet fully awake and started after the children. He cast one final look over his shoulder.

"Kat! I'll be back! I promise!"

Chapter 37: ESCAPE

The children burst from the tunnel in a sobbing, sniveling
pile. Levi pushed his way through them, the
petrified little girl still in his arms. Behind,
he could hear the clatter of stones as the tunnel
collapsed.

"Stay close," he told Twila.
"Follow me."

Something was happening in Slynderfell's factory. When they passed through the arches, the riot was in full view.

"Wild things!" gasped Twila.

And they were. They'd shed their trappings—the ties and shirts and clipboards—and gone back to their true nature.

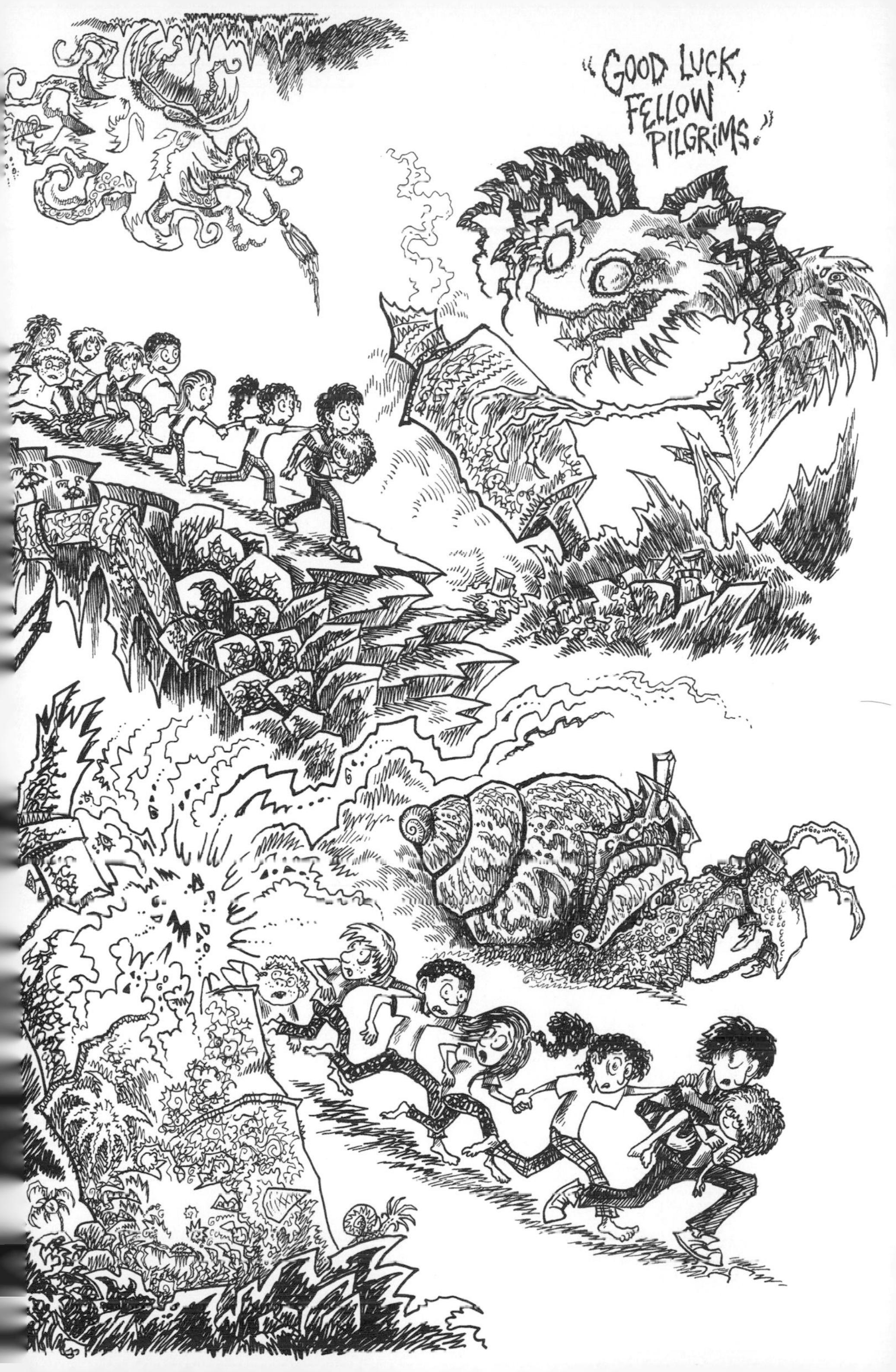
"GOOD LUCK, FELLOW PILGRIMS."

Pipes burst. Vats exploded. A root beer soda grenade leveled the Marketing Department, taking a host of bad flavor puns with it.

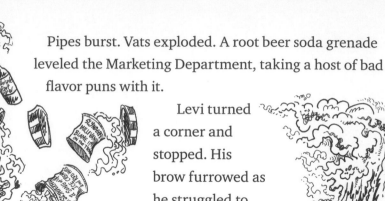

Levi turned a corner and stopped. His brow furrowed as he struggled to remember the route to the surface.

"Side-snicking remora!" shrieked a disturbingly familiar voice. Slynderfell loomed over him, a flaming ice cream cone torch in his hand.

Something small and spiny collided with Slynderfell, and his eyes were thrown from his head.

"My eyes!" screamed Slynderfell as he blindly chased after his retreating sight creatures. "Come back, you skitterish peepers!"

"Quickly, kiddies!" yipped Willow. "Follow Willow to freedom!"

Up, up through the corkscrew labyrinth.

The cave walls narrowed . . .

became the rust of the drainage pipe . . .

and then they spilled into the crisp air of the night outside.

Levi ushered the children down the slope to a scrubby field. He lowered the crying little girl into a patch of old dandelions and did a quick head count. He looked for Willow, but she had once again disappeared.

"Levi?" said Twila in a small voice. "Is this just a bad dream?"

"Yeah," he said after a moment.

Twila nodded, knelt, and hugged the little girl Levi had rescued. "Shhh. It's okay," Twila whispered. "What's your name?"

"Cindy," sniffled the little girl.

"You'll stay here and keep them safe?" Levi asked Twila softly.

Twila looked up. "Why? Where are you—"

"Whatever you do, don't follow me," he said. He started back across the field, ignoring Twila's protests, but before he reached the slope, he heard a murmur sweep through the children. He looked back.

They materialized slowly, gradually taking shape as they emerged from the mist. They were slouched and shuffling, but at that moment, they somehow managed to be *majestic*.

"Mushpits!" he cried as he ran to them. "The Boojum! It was below the factory! With lots of monsters and lost wild things working for it! With the . . . children . . ." His voice trailed off as he saw their faces. "You knew all along, didn't you?"

They were silent. Mr. Mushpit pushed his hands into his pockets and cleared his throat sheepishly.

"If we'd told you, you would have charged headlong into that horrible abyss," said Mrs. Mushpit at last. "Alas, it seems our caution was moot."

"Not to mention our treaty with Slynderfell," muttered Mr. Mushpit.

"Bah!" spat Mrs. Mushpit. "All regulations were whipped out the window the moment those creepers sleep-sanded our wits and demolished our floorboards!"

"We have to go back!" interrupted Levi. "It took Kat!"

Mrs. Mushpit's face went gray. "The spitfire girl? She's still down there?"

"Yes! Somewhere! We have to help her! NOW!"

Mrs. Mushpit sighed deeply. "We'll do everything we can," she said, "but you need to stay here with the others."

"NO! I'm going with you! You won't know where to go! You—"

"Shhh," said Mrs. Mushpit. She placed a hand on his shoulder, and for the first and only time, he heard her voice become gentle, the voice of a favorite grandmother. "You're tired," she whispered. "It's been a long, long day. There's a difficult path ahead, but it's for us to walk. There's only one thing for you to do now: sleep. Sleep, Levi. You've earned it."

He didn't want to sleep. *How* could he sleep? But a sudden warmth filled his body. His limbs were like iron, his eyelids lead. He felt his body staggering back to the field, kneeling, lying in the cool, inviting grass.

"Levi?" whispered Twila. "Will we remember this when we wake?"

He gazed up at the night sky, saw the stars glittering above, saw the autumn constellations, felt the cool breeze prickling his skin.

The sleep overtook him before he could answer.

Chapter 38: Fading Memories

Sometimes, in children's stories, the young hero wakes at the end and wonders if the adventure had all been one wild dream.

This did not happen to Levi.

Morning sunlight streamed through his bedroom window, turning the dancing dust motes to gold.

His mother's voice fluttered down the hall: "Levi! It's after seven."

345

His family was in the kitchen.

"I overslept," said his mother. "We'll have to hurry."

Regina was shoveling cereal into her mouth and looking quite averse to the sunshine, and sitting at the far end of the table was Twila. She looked up from her breakfast and beamed.

"Feeling better?" he asked her as he took his seat.

"Yep! Slept like a bug in a shag carpet."

It was cool outside. The summer had surrendered at last. Levi and Twila wore jackets as they walked to school (although Levi's favorite jacket was mysteriously missing). They talked the whole way, though of nothing important.

He took his seat in Ms. Padilla's room and watched and waited as the other students trickled in. He peeked inside the desk next to him. It was neatly organized. The pencils were unchewed.

"Why are you searching through my desk?" asked Lydia Schnell behind him.

"Uh," said Levi. "Sorry."

The school day sailed along. Ms. Padilla was full of enthusiasm as she discussed latitude and longitude and *Call It Courage.*

Lunch was uneventful. The Table of Isolation remained uninhabited, although Mrs. Robacher threatened to banish the Downey brothers.

The final bell rang, and Levi walked home with
Twila. "You're acting weird," she said with a smirk
when she caught him staring at her sideways.

Partway home, Levi told her he had to go check with some
friends about . . . something. She gave him a confused look but
didn't question him.

The plants in the Mushpits' yard were brown. Hadn't they been in full summer health just days ago?

He peered through the dark, filmy windows and tapped on the door. No answer. He hadn't been expecting an answer. Had been mostly hoping there would be no answer.

Then he looked down and saw the note.

To Any Fence-Wrecking Gahoonigans foolish Enough to Seek Truth in Strange Places:

Please know we did our best—finding the right homes for the lost children, reconstructing their lives, clearing/resetting the damaged memories, fabricating fillers to make up for the lost time.

The work took its toll, and Emmet and I are ready to leave this petty place and go home. To our _real_ home.

And please, understand we did everything we could to find your friend. We searched the caves high and low, but the Boojum had fled, taking that poor girl with it.

Yet take comfort in this : She hurt it badly. Shocked it from its comfort zone. Made it physical. And vulnerable.

It is gone now, and will likely never resurface.

If this note fails to scratch that lingering itch, please cast it aside with the cobwebs.

Regards,

Olga Mushpit

PS: Should this note fall into the hands of the Neighborhood Watch/HOA, kindly understand these words were never meant for your mold-infested melons.
Go soak your heads!

He sat on the porch and read and reread the note. His brow creased as he struggled to make sense of it, or why he'd even come here at all.

To apologize for the fence. That's why you came. You tripped and fell into their fence, and you needed to apologize.

A snake poked out from the ivy and inched toward Levi, taking in his scent with its flickering tongue.

A cool breeze rustled the dry garden. Somewhere in the undergrowth, a katydid rasped.

Finally he stood, tucked the note back under the door, and started for home. There was a weight in his chest, a clog of emotion and confusion, but he sensed there was nothing left to do about it.

The sun had already slipped below the western horizon when he arrived home. Twila was sprawled in the living room, homework spread across the floor.

Levi sat on the couch and offered assistance. He was especially good at the science.

"Thanks, Brother-Man!" said Twila when the work was through. She flashed her crooked smile—her Twila smile— and any lingering doubts and worries were gone.

Chapter 39: Triggered

A few days passed.

Twila was busy again with her friends.

Levi worried about his concentration. At school he was fine, but at home, his thoughts seemed unfocused. He started a journal and filled it with writing and sketches while lying in bed at night, but his scribblings seldom made sense in the morning.

At school, while skimming through a marine wildlife book, his eyes were held captive by an illustration of a man-of-war.

Portuguese Man-of-War:

A siphonophore. Not a true jellyfish, but a colony of polyps acting as a single organism drifting in the sea. Its attractive sail rests above the water, but beneath the surface are the stinging cells that can deliver a deadly sting to prey or enemies.

Hadn't he done a report on the man-of-war a few weeks ago? Was that why it seemed so eerily familiar?

He started taking walks after school. One day his wanderings led him to the Slynderfell Ice Cream Factory. The factory had been closed for several days. Part of its foundation had collapsed, and an employee—an ice cream truck driver— had been hospitalized. Levi's mother had been working in the warehouse the night of the accident, and Levi was thankful she'd been unharmed.

But now there were whispers of misconduct or some other conspiracy, and rumors that the factory would never reopen.

His mother almost seemed relieved, even though she'd soon have to find a new job. She admitted she'd never felt comfortable working at the warehouse, although she couldn't explain why. It had just been a weird feeling.

His stroll around the factory revealed an old drainage pipe facing away from town. He stared into it and shuddered, feeling a crazy urge to crawl inside, to search for something lost, something—some*one*—that had meant a great deal. But then he saw the pipe was full of rocks, impassable, and the urge faded. He walked back to town and never returned to the old factory again.

The next day his walk took him past the biggest house in the neighborhood—the Bombard house, according to their mailbox. He saw a man and woman unloading groceries from their car.

Another crazy urge hit him—the urge to introduce himself, ask them if they remembered . . .

Remembered what?

He watched them from the sidewalk until Mr. Bombard glared at him suspiciously, and he wondered about them the whole walk home.

On Thursday he was surprised when his mother asked if she could join him on his walk. She even brought along her sketchpad, in case inspiration struck. They followed the usual route, passing spotless lawns and trimmed hedges. But Levi had started to notice wild stowaways: a praying mantis on a fencepost, a toad crouched below a shrub, and a snail with a sinistral shell on a fossil-studded rock.

"You know a lot about weird creatures," said his mom as she sketched the snail.

By the weekend, his strange thoughts had dwindled to a faint itch in the back of his mind. An itch that may have vanished completely, if not for what happened on Saturday.

He and Twila were on the front lawn. Twila was juggling an apple with her new lacrosse stick, and Levi was about to set off on another neighborhood stroll.

That's when they heard it.

It was a warm day, warm enough to be mistaken for summer again, so the tinkling music shouldn't have seemed too out of place. And it wasn't a Slynderfell truck, and it wasn't Rafer Frost behind the wheel, thank goodness.

But that song . . .

"It's still here," said Twila in a distant voice.

"What's still here?" he asked, though he knew the answer.

"Here . . . close to us." Her lacrosse stick, the crisp autumn apple still cradled in its mesh, hung limply from her hand.

"The Mushpits' note said it was gone," he said before his mind could fully register what he was saying.

"They're wrong. I can feel it. It's close. The Mushpits didn't know it like I did." She was trembling all over. The apple bobbled in the lacrosse stick's mesh. "I was with it. Was part of it. Could feel it . . . leeching me."

Levi took a deep breath, swallowed his panic. "Stay here. I'm going to the Mushpits' house to see if there's a way to contact them."

"I'm coming with you."

"No! Get inside with Ma."

He started down the sidewalk. *The Mushpits said it was gone,* he told himself. *They would have felt its presence if it were still in town.*

But Twila was right. It was not gone. Not completely. He'd find a way to contact the Mushpits, and they'd come back, and maybe it wouldn't be too late to save . . .

Pangs of grief and guilt shot through his body. His walk turned into a run.

"Oi! Kind Levi!"

A pair of fluorescent green eyes peeked out from behind a bush.

"Willow!" Something in him wanted to hug her spiny little body to him, the way one loves a lost dog, but another memory clicked into place. "You betrayed us," he said flatly. "You were the Boojum's spy."

Willow cringed. "Willow did not want to help the Boojum. But what else could Willow do? Where to go? The human-folk would never understand. No place safe. Had to turn to the Boojum."

A car horn blared nearby, and Willow shrank back to the bush. She paused, then stepped into the open, and her fluorescent orbs locked with Levi's eyes.

"But Willow was wrong. The Boojum does not save. Only uses. I should not have lied to Levi, for Levi is not like the Boojum. Levi is kind. Levi cares."

Levi studied the miserable little thing, and in that moment, she seemed neither miserable nor little. She seemed *majestic*.

"It's still here," he said. "The Boojum. It's still in town somewhere."

"No, Kind Levi," said Willow. "Not in town. Not now."

"But Twila can feel it. *I* can feel it."

"Not in town," repeated Willow. "But not in the Wild, either. The Boojum was never a thing of the Wild."

Not in town. Not in the wild. Somewhere close.

Close to his mind. Close to his heart.

He understood.

"Wait here," he said. "I'm going to try to contact the Mushpits."

"No. If the Boojum senses danger, it will flee for good, for spite, and then there will be no chance to save the hooligan girl."

"Her name is Kat."

And as he said it, he realized they were running.

Chapter 40: Where Sidewalks End

"Beware, Kind Levi," said Willow as they approached the old car.

He peered through the fogged windows. Someone was slouched in the back seat. He rubbed the glass with his sleeve, trying for a better look. The someone—the some*thing*—reached slowly, awkwardly, and opened the door. Levi stepped back.

What emerged from the car was the worst
thing he'd ever seen.

Worse than the empty rooms. Worse than Rafer Frost,
Heckbender, the wild creatures in Slynderfell's factory, the
emptiness.

"Kat?" he said in a small voice.

It was Kat . . . but it wasn't Kat. It had Kat's shape, but the features were wrong. It took a moment for him to realize that the face, the entire body, was covered in the opaque threads of the nothing-creature. Or what remained of the nothing-creature.

The man-of-war, said his mind.

Willow was growling beside him, her spines bristled in fear.

"Kat, it's me," he heard himself say.

The thing took a shambling step forward. Willow crouched low, but Levi forced himself to stand firm, to push back his horror, to look past the threads and find the thing's true form.

"It's Levi," he said. "Do you remember me?"

The thing stopped. It swayed. It gradually lifted its hand.

"I remember you," he continued.
"You were my true friend."

The hand wobbled, as if
two minds were fighting for
control.

"It will be all
right now." He
offered his arm.

The thing seized his hand.

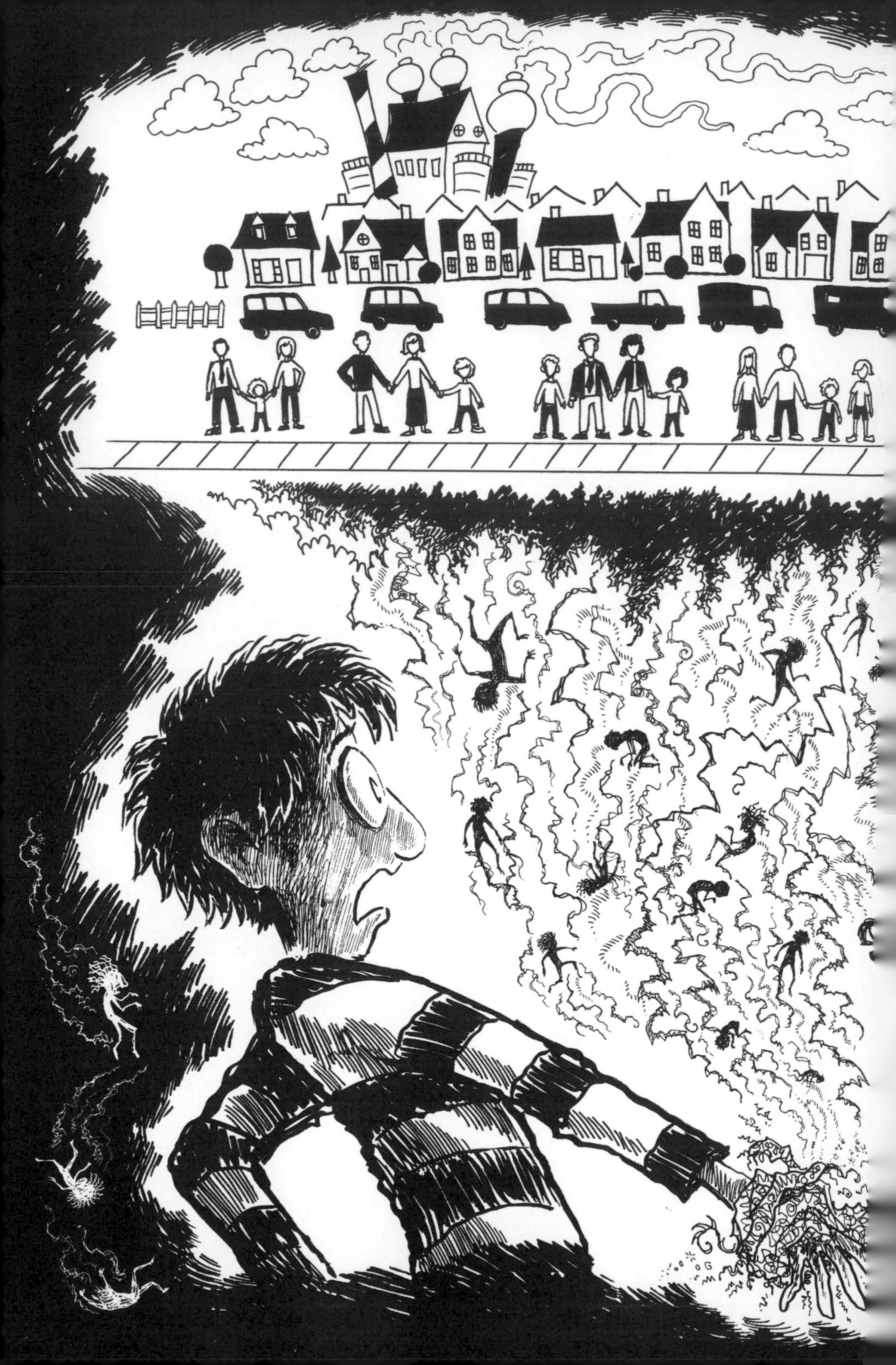

And he saw it all:
The beautiful sail of the man-of-war.
Every child who'd ever slipped through
the cracks in the sidewalk.

His hand prickled, and he felt the
stinging cells, deadly weapons of the man-
of-war, working into his skin. He didn't have
time to react—they would strike, flood him
with their fatal toxin, in less than a second.

But a lot can happen in under a second.
A fly's wings may beat 200 times.
Light may travel over 200,000 kilometers.

And in that split second, something flashed past Levi's vision and cracked across the thing's dome. It released his hand and collapsed in a messy heap.

Twila stood in the middle of the field, her lacrosse stick in hand. Levi looked and saw what she'd thrown: the ripe fall apple lay in three pieces amid the grass, its juice droplets sparkling in the daylight.

"Look!"

cried Willow.

The thing—the remnant—was oozing away from the body and squirming on the ground. It was no longer a man-of-war. Now it was small. Larval. The threads sizzled and curled like dry sticks on a fire.

"The apple," whispered Levi. "From the Mushpits' garden?"

"No," said Twila. "From the tree outside our house. That's all."

The residue on the body was dissolving, the shape becoming more and more recognizable. Levi knelt and carefully turned the body over. Its face was wet, its hair plastered flat, but through the mess, he could make out its features. Its true features.

"Kat?" He gently lifted the upper body. "Can you hear me?"

"Levi?" Her voice was faint and raspy, a voice that had been asleep for a long time.

Levi took a deep breath, felt Twila and Willow standing beside him.

"It's okay, Kat. We've got you now. You're safe."

Kat's eyelids fluttered open, winced in the daylight, closed again. "Thanks, buddy . . . bro . . . dude-man-pal." Her voice sounded stronger now. "We make a great team, don't we?"

"Yeah. We do."

"Levi?"

"Yeah?"

"Think anyone will
believe our story?"

"I don't know.

But . . . I guess . . .
Well . . .
We know.
You, me,
Twila, Willow.

We'll
remember."

"Right.

We'll remember."

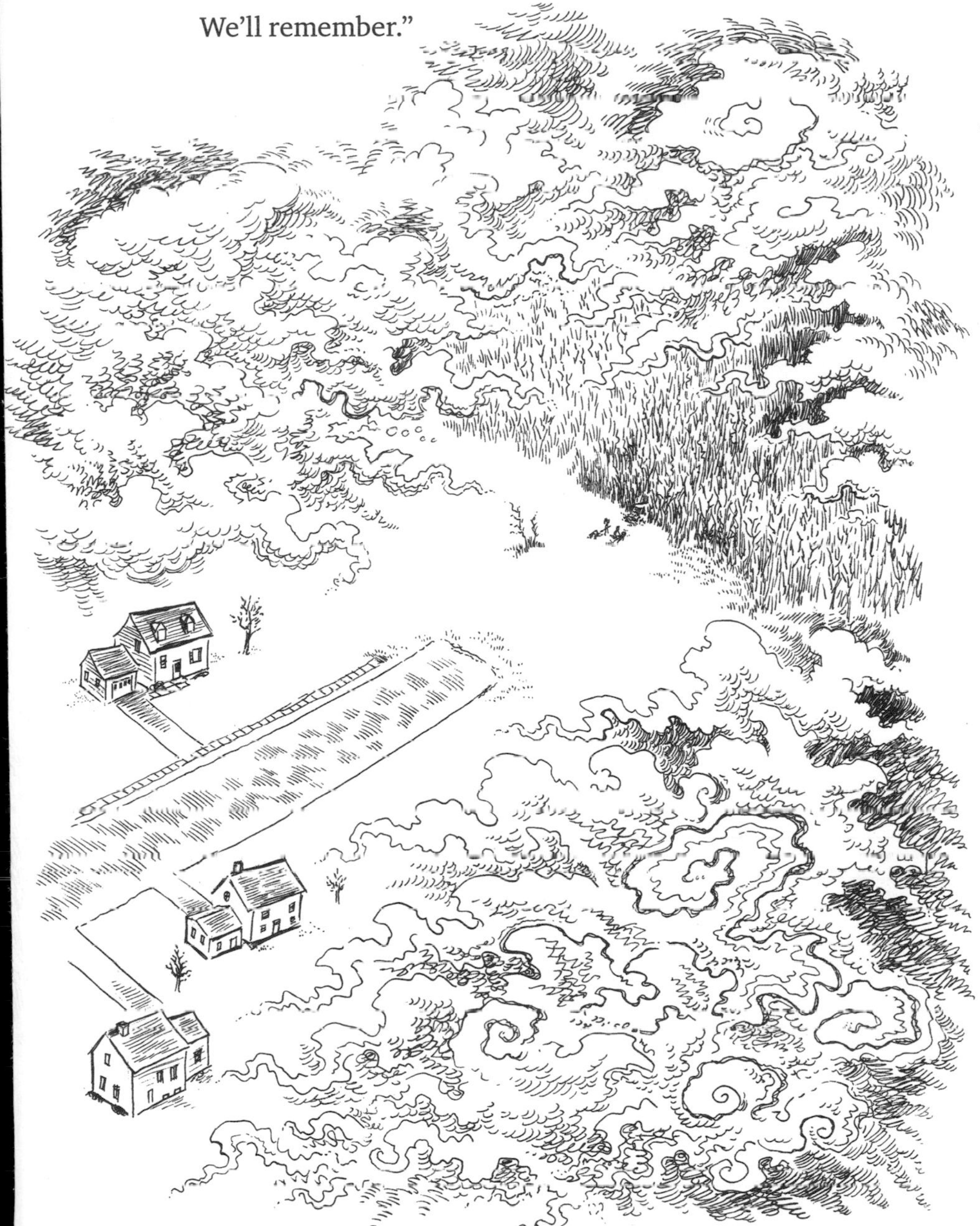

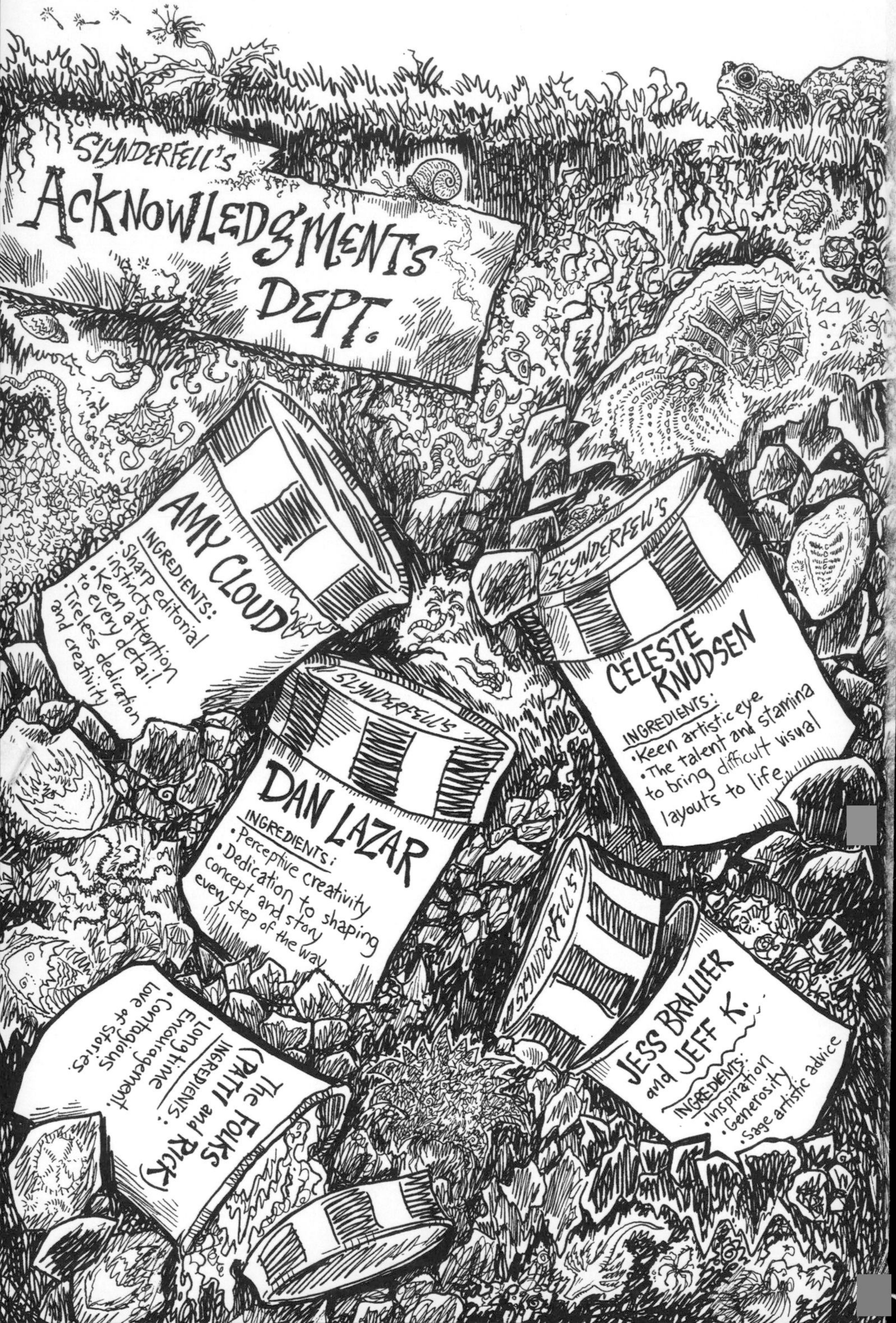
SLYNDERFELL'S
ACKNOWLEDGMENTS DEPT.
AMY CLOUD
INGREDIENTS:
• Sharp editorial instincts
• Keen attention to every detail.
• Tireless dedication and creativity
SLYNDERFELL'S
CELESTE KNUDSEN
INGREDIENTS:
• Keen artistic eye
• The talent and stamina to bring difficult visual layouts to life.
SLYNDERFELL'S
DAN LAZAR
INGREDIENTS:
• Perceptive creativity
• Dedication to shaping concept and story every step of the way
SLYNDERFELL'S
JESS BRALLIER and JEFF K.
INGREDIENTS:
• Inspiration
• Generosity
• Sage artistic advice
The FOLKS (PATTI and RICK)
INGREDIENTS:
• Longtime Encouragement.
• Contagious love of stories.